TOTAL ECLIPSE

WYATT WERNE

Book cover design by ebooklaunch.com

ISBN 979-8-9887257-4-9 (ePub/Digital Online)

ISBN 979-8-9887257-6-3 (Paperback)

ISBN 979-8-9887257-5-6 (Paperback)

ISBN 979-8-9887257-7-0 (Hardback)

ISBN 979-8-9887257-3-2 (Audiobook)

For Alison and Katie,
with love.

1

K ate Devana yanked the engineer's arm behind his back and pulled the zip-ties from her belt. Thirteen pairs of eyes watched her from outside his 60th-floor glass office. Half the staff had their phones up, livestreaming, while the rest were oohing and aahing like wannabe contestants for the next episode of *Jail Crawler*. The tears streaming down his ruddy cheeks into his gray beard made her wonder what the hell she was doing with her life.

She scowled at her audience, tightening her hands around the engineer's wrists and flashing her *this-could-be-you* face through the glass. She wanted them to see overkill: a retired Marine and Space Force special operative corralling a sobbing, overweight, middle-aged man who stole the company's designs and sold it to the highest bidder.

She sighed. They didn't get the message. She hated Dallas. She'd been here three times, for three different companies, which was three too many. It smelled like hot garbage. The nightclubs were as bland as the robotically made empanadas, and the drone cars obstructing traffic had more culture than any of the women she met. Dallas was dry and boring, right down to the middle-aged cookie-cutter corporate criminals.

"I don't have an attorney. Please. I can fix this. I will return the money," the engineer choked through his sobs. "This will ruin me. I can't do jail time."

She was only half listening to his whining. This guy had nothing to cry over. He was going to country-club jail. He'd have a semi-private gym and a sunny exercise yard to work off the unlimited donuts they served, plus free time to write a book and watch all the same porn he downloaded in his office. Yeah, she saw his search history. It was the only thing she had in common with this guy: the same taste in lesbian porn. She caught herself watching too long because it was the spiciest thing she'd seen in Dallas in three trips. Maybe she hadn't mentioned it, but she hated Dallas.

She shook her head. This guy sold the plans for peanuts. If he took a deep breath to think, he'd realize she was doing him a favor. In a year, he'd probably end up with a few million followers, a bestseller, and a viral video. Shit, he had his first thirteen followers right outside the glass. In country-club jail they'd let him have a private fan site, with him in an orange jumpsuit and a bottle of lotion, whacking off for tips. Ten years from now, she pictured him at his seaside estate with a cup of hot chocolate in his hand and the ocean in the background, hocking his I-beat-the-system merch. Probably in a limited-edition-just-like-I-wore-in-prison orange jumpsuit, except with his logo, and whacking off for even bigger tips because people loved a comeback story and paid for prison fetishes.

He had nothing to cry over at all.

"The money is not the problem," Kate said, slipping the zip tie around his left wrist. "It's the designs you stole. A few years in country-club jail will do you some good." Better than good, he'd be goddamned rich. "If you can't afford an attorney, some scumbag will be appointed who will end up as your business manager. You have the right to remain silent, and honestly, you're boring me. I don't care. Exercise your right to shut up and wait until your defense attorney gives a shit."

The engineer continued blubbering about his wife and kids and step-kids and kids by his first marriage and kids by his second marriage and all the tuition payments and his graduate degrees and his embarrassment and his nieces' and nephews' birthday presents.

Chrissake, this guy needed a big dose of shut-the-fuck-up. She should add a tranquilizer dart to her gear.

He complained he couldn't do jail time because nobody from his class at Stanford/Yale/UCLA or wherever had ever gone to jail.

She'd heard this before and had a comeback for that ready: He was finally first in his class at something. Ha, she smiled. It usually earned a chuckle from the local cops giving her backup.

But this time it felt stale, like all the women and nightclubs in this city, and anyway, the feckless Dallas PD didn't give her any backup. Not that she needed backup to wrangle this pig, but some support would be nice. If only an irritating junior detective standing around and second-guessing her every move and reminding her of the rules against them sleeping together. Company is company, and in Dallas the temperature was hot, but her bed was cold.

But no, DPD couldn't be bothered, because she was a private security contractor. Before she arrived in Dallas, the DPD captain declined her requests, messaging her, "What is that fat ass going to do, run? If you need a partner, get them to pay for one, not the taxpayers of Dallas. I can't afford the overtime."

He did have a point. They never ran. Waddled, paddled, or jaywalked with their tongues out, panting and lungs burning, maybe, but she wasn't arresting hardened criminals in this job. Eye-rolling and fast-walking was about as bad as it got. She hadn't even drawn her pistol in three years. She got paid a lot more for much less than she did in the military, which begged the question, why was she unhappy?

The engineer whined about losing the house and the cars and then complained about his alimony payments, that they forced him to steal the designs because he needed the money.

The ex made me do it. Always the ex. Kate had an ex who made her do things like punch walls, so it wasn't like she couldn't empathize. But she saw things more clearly after leaving her ex, and so would he, after a few years as a prison content creator.

"That all sounds like a *you* problem. Even if you can get the money back," which she doubted as she said it, "you can't get the files back."

"I can tell you who bought them."

She loosened her grip, only slightly, smiling and picturing a spy ring or organized crime. That might be exciting.

Hesitation was always a mistake in this business. During the half-second she paused, he wrestled his wrists from her hands and bolted for the office door. Shit.

Every camera and eyeball outside the glass widened like the buzzer rang on a fucking gameshow. A woman in front reached for the door and opened it, holding a camera on him as he stepped through the door, while someone else yelled *he's running*. Flashes went off, people taking pictures, and the crowd parted to let him through.

Thirteen cameras turned to her, recording her eyes rolling and smirking as she stepped from the office. He wasn't running. That was no kind of running she'd ever seen in fifteen years in the military. On cue, the engineer's tongue came out as he panted and waddled towards the elevator.

If building security did their job and disabled his badge, he couldn't use the elevator. But he didn't try. Instead, he passed it and ducked through the stairwell door. Taking the stairs on the 60th floor was not a smart choice, but engineers getting arrested and blaming their exes had already made a lifetime of bad choices, so this was just one more.

Outside the office door, she gave the woman who'd opened it an annoyed sidelong glance and then pointed at the tallest man. "You, brown eyes. Stand here at the door. No one goes in this office, you understand?"

He had longish, unkempt brown hair, brown eyes, a pastel blue golf shirt, and probably couldn't spell *gym*, but he would do. She coaxed him forward, and he wedged himself through the crowd. He grinned like she'd chosen him to come onstage or be her date.

"But—" Brown eyes was ogling her tits, but she smiled because at least *someone* in Dallas had undressed her, even if he was a man, and only doing it with his eyes.

"Focus. Brown eyes, here," she said, pointing to the door. "Anyone goes in this office, I'll kneecap them. Me entiendes?"

His browns got big and wide, and he nodded and swallowed, so she thought he understood.

She pushed through the crowd like she'd seen rockstars push through throngs of fans. They lobbed big, important questions from all directions. Can I message you later? When will you be back? Is he going to jail? Are we under arrest, too? Who gets his office chair?

Big important questions, which she evaded by fast walking into the stairwell. Leaning over the rail and looking down, she saw nothing. She circled the stairwell to be sure. The smart choice for an out-of-shape engineer was down.

Fucking hell. Looking up, he was two floors above her and circling the stairs, heaving, wheezing, climbing as fast as his out-of-shape legs would carry him.

He was escaping to the roof, twelve floors up. Shit, she couldn't let him get to the roof. She ran up the stairs, shouting *Stop!* He looked over his shoulder, climbing the last step to 63, and then disappeared through the door. Fuck.

She flung the stairwell door open on 62 while dialing corporate security. "Kate Devana. The engineer squirted. He's in elevator bank—" She read the signs as she darted down the hallway. "—fuck if I know. I'm on 62 headed towards the main elevators."

"He's in B and headed to the roof."

She wanted to scream, *why the shit didn't they disable his badge like she told them to?* But she didn't have time for an argument. "Shut it down and send him to ground."

"Can't. It's a safety thing. I'd need my manager to override—"

"—*this* is a safety thing. He can't get to the roof."

"I can't and the manager is on her break."

Fuck, Fuck, Fuck. She was wasting time. "I need a ride to the roof."

"Sending an elevator."

"How long?"

"Coming from 10 should be a minute—"

Her flats squeaked against the tile floor as she reversed course to the stairwell. She didn't have a minute. She stiff-armed the stairwell door open, banging it against the wall, and sprinted up the stairs two at a time.

Ten flights of stairs, nine seconds each, and she wouldn't make it. A Marine Corp Sergeant yelled in her head, *move your ass, Devana!* Her heart pounded, and she tried to control her breathing, pulling herself around every turn of the stairs.

Near the top, the elevator doors squealed open one floor above her. She leaped three stairs at a time.

As she burst through the rooftop exit, it was a clear blue January morning, and the engineer was heaving and choking his way between solar panels towards the roof ledge. Beyond ducts and pipes, there was no fence or guardrail, only a short step between him and air.

"Stop! You don't want to do this." She unholstered her tazer while racing to get close enough.

He looked over his shoulder, gasping and nearly tripping. "Not... going... jail."

She brought up the tazer, aligning the red dot and squeezing the trigger. The darts whizzed ahead. Her only hope to stop him was a perfect center-mass shot delivering three million volts. His muscles would seize, and he'd fall forward in excruciating pain and scrape his face. But he would live to go viral.

Except the darts sailed over his head as he threw up his arms and dived over the ledge. *Fuck.* She skidded on the rooftop gravel, stopping short of the ledge, and then tossed the tazer after him. *Fuck, Fuck, Fuck.*

The engineer was diving face down, his blue shirt flapping and his arms and legs flailing. During the seven seconds he fell, he looked like he'd changed his mind and tried to grab the building windows. A rule she learned in basic: never make a rash decision under fire. Or when being fired. He would have been fine in a few days, with a scraped face and a smug *I-am-beating-the-system* grin.

As he plunged, the sun and his squirming body reflected off the tinted glass building across the street. The yellow tazer gun floated, falling like an afterthought.

He crashed on a flatbed truck stuck in Dallas traffic carrying a wrecked silver car. The sickening crack and tinkle of glass and carbon fiber took almost a second to reach her ears. Car alarms blared. The truck was a drone; no driver was getting out to see the carnage.

Kate opened her phone and dialed her boss, audio only, as horns and sirens sounded below. "Good news, Jerry, case fucking closed. The engineer confessed to everything. His ex made him do it."

"Fantastic. Where are you now?"

"The roof, looking down," she said, looking at the engineer, now shattered, bloody, and commingled with glass and carbon fiber splinters.

During the long pause, she imagined Jerry behind his desk, rubbing his bald spot and then his face. "Shit. Second one in six months. I hate paperwork."

On the street below, a crowd was forming around the flatbed. Red flowed over the hood of the smashed silver car. "This job is getting old, Jerry. Same shit every time."

He chuckled.

"What's funny?" His tone was mocking her.

"I've known you since your bat mitzvah, Kate. You're late. I had one month in the company pool."

Jerry was not just her boss, he was her grandfather's partner for twenty-two years. But more like her stepdad after her parents died. It was complicated.

"There was a pool on how long I'd last?"

"And I lost, two years nine months ago."

"Wow. You made my day. I hope you lost a lot of money."

"Just my pride."

"You never had any. Did you tell them that before they let you in the pool? You had nothing to lose."

He chuckled again. "True. Stay there and wait for Dallas PD."

"Fuck Dallas PD. They didn't want to give me backup. Tell them to get their shit together, or I'll be giving them my statement from forty thousand feet. I have a flight to Cabo tonight."

"What's in Cabo?"

"My vacation. And a strawberry blond lifeguard named Tara. My Cabo Kitten."

"You should settle down, Kate."

"Stay in one place and end up like this guy, so trapped in his own life that stealing and dive-bombing is freedom? Never."

Below, EMT drones were pushing through the crowd around the flatbed. Bystanders were looking towards the roof at her.

"You said it yourself, Kate, boring."

"I love this job, Jerry. What's better than watching a middle-aged loser dive bomb off a roof?"

"Your sarcasm is noted. I got a lead on your next assignment, so I may need you to leave Cabo early."

"My vacation is sacred. You pull me out of Tara's arms early, I will come there and break your legs."

Behind her, the rooftop door banged open, and she heard scuffling on gravel—the useless Dallas PD arriving late. Whoever wrote 'better late than never' never met them. She switched the phone to the other ear and put her right hand in the air to show it was empty.

"You wanted excitement. Well, the CEO of Lunar Foundries thinks one of his employees is stealing silicon wafers."

She pulled the phone from her ear and looked at her signal bars. "You cut out, Jerry. I thought you said *Lunar Foundries*."

"I did." She could hear his wide grin through the phone.

"What's a silicon wafer?" She regretted asking as soon as the words left her mouth.

"Has thousands of microchips on it. Worth tens of millions when it's cut and assembled into chips. It's their main product line that they make in—"

Below, human firefighters in yellow safety vests were waving people away from the red-drenched flatbed. One of the spectators was talking to a firefighter and pointing toward her. He looked in her direction and said something into a microphone.

"No fucks to give, Jerry. Seriously, get someone else. I'll be kicked off the lunar colony the second I step foot. You know that."

"The colony is a mess, Kate. A target-rich environment, like the new Wild West."

"Got anything in Dallas? I'll come back here."

He laughed. "This is going to be a big contract. I need my star player."

She could feel his *I-am-so-proud-of-my-granddaughter smile* through the phone. The problem with saying no to Jerry was that she could quit the family business, but not quit the family, and she'd have to face his disappointed look on her lock screen. She needed to think of a way out of this and make it his idea.

"The billionaires that developed the colony can clean up their own mess, Jerry. Plus, they've seen how I operate. This ends with me punching a rich asshole in the throat. Or nuking the place. Or both."

"That's why they are hiring us. The CEO asked for you *personally.*"

That couldn't be right. Gravel crunched behind her. She sensed the guns on her back. "He must have missed his Alzheimer's vaccine. If he needs his lab destroyed again, I'm his girl. I am going to Cabo, Jerry, to hook up with Tara. You go chase your Wild West geese. Don't call me, I'll call you."

Jerry was repeating something about the Wild West, but she clicked off her phone and raised her hands as someone shouted, *Freeze!* The worthless Dallas PD, late and arresting the wrong person. She needed to get the fuck out of this city.

2

United States Lunar Colony
Procellarum Improvement District, Texas
January 2073

With six minutes to be on stage, Zia flicked blush on her cheeks as fast as her servos could move. Her mind multitasked, one eye in the club's vanity mirror, the other eye watching a fight break out behind her between the new girls Jada and Quý, and an audio circuit waiting for Nash to call. He always called before her shift. Three things, six minutes, she was going to be late, and it irritated her.

Quý screamed something unintelligible at Jada. They were framed by the white LEDs of the mirror against a midnight purple wall, like an amateur version of the mixed martial arts matches some of her clients liked to watch.

In a drug-fueled rage, Jada returned spit, fists, and accusations at Quý, few of which landed. Zia judged them to be about fourteen, although it was possible both had genetic mods that made them look young. They showed up two months ago, ragged, underdressed, drugged, and carrying a burnt metal whiff as if they had just walked out of an airlock. Nobody asked how they arrived; the burnt metal smell indicated that it wasn't the regular lunar shuttle.

Zia dusted her cheeks, thankful not to be on the receiving end of Jada's punches this time. For the first two and a half years she was here, this was the best run club on the colony. The previous owner, Quina, ran it clean and orderly. No drugs. If a client got out of line, she told them to get lost and take a fucking number. After, as the girls were changing after their shift, she would remind them that they didn't need to take any shit because there were a lot more numbers than girls in this place. This was the moon, where lonely rich people flocked to drain their savings and contort themselves in low gravity in ways they couldn't on Earth.

Even during the off-peak season, demand was high. The next six weeks though were the peak season, the solar and lunar eclipse. Four times as many numbers as girls. Which made the fight going on in the mirror pointless.

Zia didn't know why Quina sold the club to the new owner, Adrik, six months ago, but Zia imagined she wouldn't be happy with how he and his manager Jorge ran the place. When he took over, Adrik renamed it Barely Legal. Nash laughed when she told him, saying, "See Zia, you were looking for an example of irony and that's the perfect example."

Zia still didn't get it. It wasn't irony, nor even satire, which her language processing subroutine said was often confused with irony. If she was right, the girls weren't legal at all. Adrik's manager Jorge called them, "the merchandise," and said they would make Zia obsolete. She was only sixty-three percent certain the girls were underage, so maybe she was wrong, and they were like her.

Not that it mattered much. None of the scenarios swirling in Zia's mind had Jada being around much longer. Already circling the drain when she arrived, Jada's spiral had picked up steam with her addiction to ever-larger quantities of amp. Zia recognized its side effects: edginess, irritability, and lately, Jada's violent rage. A week ago, Zia asked Jada where she'd come from and if she was like Zia, and Jada attacked her, gouging her neck. Thankfully it patched smoothly.

Nash called it a blessing that Zia was immune to the drugs Jorge passed around. He also said to stay away from the new girls.

Zia buffed her cheeks with the same staccato rhythm Jada slapped Quý. Then her phone *pinged*. Nash, on schedule, five minutes before her shift started. She leaned the phone against the glass on the makeup table, positioning it so he could only see her, and then answered it.

Nash had rumpled thin brown hair and round glasses. He looked tired and unshaven.

"I have to go on stage in four minutes, Nash." Although eyeing the fighting, she expected to be late. She picked up the eyelash curler and started curling her eyelashes, hoping he'd get to the point quickly.

"What's that noise behind you?"

"Nash, I need to be on stage soon."

"I really hate when you do that, Zia. How about, 'Hi, hello, I love you and miss you?' How do you know I am not calling you because Kai and Freya wanted to see you?"

"It's past their bedtime. I already messaged them and wished them goodnight. And we've discussed it one-hundred and thirty-seven times, we don't have that kind of relationship."

"I give up. What kind do we have?"

"I am your familiar." She inspected her eyebrows and reached for the mascara.

"Familiar?" His face assumed a mocking smile. "You are not a familiar. You've been reading fantasy again."

"litRPG is not categorized as fantasy, it's gaming."

He furrowed his eyebrows. "I am not sure that's true." He shook his head. "Anyway, point is, I warned you that you can get banned for that."

"I routed it through my visual sensors and slowed my reading speed to two-hundred-thirty-eight words per minute."

"Machine reading is not allowed, Zia. It's a violation of the ebook server terms of service."

"It didn't ask about me, and I didn't tell them. At two-hundred-thirty-eight words per minute, it's extremely unlikely I will be caught."

"You have started lying to the server. I don't like this."

"It's not a lie."

"Lying by omission is still a lie, Zia."

"Well, you lied to *me* then. Freya fell on the pavement at the amusement park and hurt her knee—"

"Oh, it was just a skinned knee."

"She says it still hurts to walk. And you didn't take her to the docbot, which is recommended protocol. Instead you gave her a band-aid in the bathroom. And Kai said he was sick—"

"It was just a skinned knee, Zia, kids get a million of them. Kai caught a twenty-four hour bug. I didn't want to worry you."

"I don't worry. I would simply have reminded you to make sure he sees a doctor and drinks plenty of fluids. Chicken soup provides excellent nutrition and hydration, and the warm, clear broth temporarily opens nasal passages."

Nash smirked. "Well, I am glad you weren't worried."

"Kai told me he won a prize. He hit a plate three times in a row with a bean bag."

Nash smiled. "His throwing is definitely getting better."

"You didn't tell me any of that, does that mean you were lying to me?"

"Fucks sake, Zia. I hate when you throw things back in my face. I wasn't lying to you. Fine, read your books, just don't get caught."

Zia smiled, her positive reinforcement circuits firing. It was pleasurable to win arguments with Nash.

"What's going on, Zia? What is that noise back there?"

She used her calm, reassuring voice. "Jada and Quý are fighting."

"Christ, again? Stay out of it. Walk away if you have to."

She tried walking away from Jada, but it only made her angrier. Nash didn't understand these girls or the effects of the drugs.

"Jorge will be in soon, and he will fire Jada," she said, opening the mascara.

"Fucking finally."

She looked around to see whether Jorge had come in. Then she switched circuits, routing her voice directly to the phone so no one could hear her. "I don't approve of how this club is run, Nash."

"Just keep your head down. It's Adrik's club now. He gets to run it however he wants."

Nash reminded her often that Adrik was taking over all the clubs and no one could stop them. He said there were no police, and the billionaires that ran this place had private security.

"Nash, I've been thinking. I want to—"

"Please, please, please, Zia, tell me you've decided to quit that awful place."

"We've discussed it, Nash, this is how I am trained."

"I told you, we can train you for something else."

The idea of staring at a blank white wall while she retrained her neural pathways overstimulated every negative reinforcement circuit in her brain. It was painful.

"How will we care for Kai and Freya while I retrain? And I can't retrain while I work either. There is simply not enough power or computing resources."

"We will get by, Zia, I told you. We'll be fine during your downtime. You could be a nursebot—"

She would be useless, frozen for seven months, not even able to read. During training, part of her mind was still awake, hallucinating, like dreaming. Nash said her neural pathways were consolidating and deleting irrelevant connections.

Once during a patch update she dreamt Kai and Freya got hurt, but she was helpless to aid them while she was being patched. When the update was complete she went to them in bed, and they were fast asleep, safe.

A few weeks ago, the memory of girls hitting each other in the club transformed into a dream of Kai and Freya bloodying each other, with Nash saying, *don't get involved, it's Adrik's club.* She had to stand and watch while the kids punched each other, until Kai passed out. After, sitting beside Kai's bed, she carefully checked his hair, brushing it aside, but he was unharmed. He slept peacefully, his eyes moving, having his own dreams. Last week she'd dreamt the kids were kidnapped and forced to work in one of Adrik's clubs.

She never had nightmares before Adrik took over the club. So, she couldn't be down for seven months, helpless like in her dreams. She'd rather shut herself down permanently. But if she shut herself down, she would be just as useless with Kai and Freya. No, she had a better idea.

The door to the changing room opened, and as Jorge stepped through, he yelled, "Basta!"

To Nash she said, "I have to go."

He sighed. "Okay. We made it through security and are lifting off from Vandenburg in a few hours."

"You're bringing the kids back early?" Something crackled in her brain, making her voice rise. She tried to take her eye off the fight, but Jada had thrown a wild smack.

"No. We are stopping for a tour of the original International Space Station. The signal is choppy where we'll be, so I'll message you when I can. I love you, Zia. See you very soon."

He hung up. A half second later, her phone *binged* with a picture of him and the kids at the spaceport lounge along with their remaining itinerary. They would be back on the colony in a week. They looked happy and healthy, despite the band-aid on Freya's knee. She hovered her finger over the image and then tapped a heart.

Jorge walked into view behind her. She tried to deadpan her face while she applied mascara. She would be late to the stage, which annoyed her. Quina trained her never to be late to the stage.

Jorge yelled, "Basta!" again, and Zia swiveled her chair to get a better view through the mirror.

Jada was on top of Quý, holding her arms down with her knees, screaming and throwing punches. Most punches banged on the metal floor as Quý squirmed, missing. One hit Quý in the eye socket, and her face swelled. Tears and blood ran down the side of her head into her ears. Quina always said that bruises attracted the wrong type of client.

Jorge put his hand up, his signal for the girls to back off, while he watched the fight.

"Jorge likes to watch." Zia's friend Lany had pulled up beside her, combing her blue hair and inspecting her black eyeshadow in the mirror. "He's a sick fuck. Yesterday I caught him taking wagers on the girls."

"Wagers?"

"He took bets from the clients on those two. Two thousand bucks for fifteen minutes alone with the winner. Clients put down money."

Quý wiggled one arm free and landed a haymaker to Jada's temple, thumping her head against the wall.

"The worst part—or the best part, I don't know—Jorge called the fight early, said it was a draw, and then didn't pay. Everybody lost their money, although Jada and Quý were spared from those sick assholes, so maybe it worked out. One of my clients was so pissed he walked out. Said he's never coming back."

Lany applied her black lipstick and then continued. "But I figure, Jorge did me a favor. If that's what the client wanted, someone to bully, he can go somewhere else. There are plenty of numbers, especially during the eclipse. Right, Zia?" Lany rolled her lips together to smooth out her lipstick.

"Quina always said we didn't need to take any shit."

"Damn right. I am telling you Zia, as soon as I make my last tuition payment, I am outta here. He doesn't want us anyway, he wants—them." Lany's eyes glanced through the mirror to the fight on the floor. Jada was still on top, but they were choking each other.

"You are leaving?" Zia felt something unplug in her brain, like an entire sensor bank failing. Lany had explained many things about Adrik and Jorge, while Zia had confided her ideas. It was Lany that taught her how to read without getting caught.

Lany smiled. "Don't worry, Zia, we will still be friends."

"It won't be the same. There will be a 1.2 second lag each way, a total of 3.4 seconds before I get a response to my queries, plus you said that you experience object permanence difficulties—"

"I promise Zia, you will never be out of my mind. I won't ghost you."

"It's better for you if you quit?"

"As soon as the last bill clears. Two months."

"Where will you go?"

"I don't know yet. I decided yesterday. Anything's better than watching Jorge bet on us like dogs fighting. All I know is if I want this shit, I can work any dive on Earth. You should quit too."

"I can't quit, Lany, we discussed it."

"Did you talk to Nash about your other plan?"

Zia shook her head.

"Well, you need to have your own golden parachute ready. This plane is going down, and you don't want to be in the wreckage."

Quý and Jada were red-faced, veins throbbing, gasping for oxygen as they choked each other and rolled on the floor. How would she convince Nash her other plan was viable?

As Quý was losing consciousness, Jorge pulled Jada off, holding her under the armpit and at the back of the neck. His fingers were so long that they almost wrapped around her tiny neck. Her veins were throbbing, and her face was rosy red, turning purple, even through her thick makeup. Jada gasped and coughed, and then as the oxygen returned to her brain she writhed, trying to get out of Jorge's grasp.

"What the fuck is going on?" Jorge asked the room.

Jada screeched while writhing in Jorge's grasp, "She's a fucking bitch. She stole my client. She saw me with him. I got up to get drinks and heard her say, *don't waste your time with this one.*"

Quý sobbed, "I did not."

Zia doubted Quý had tried to steal a client. There was no reason to fight over clients during the eclipse when there were four times as many numbers as girls. She didn't understand why Adrik and Jorge thought the drugs made the girls compliant. They did for a time, until they took too much, and the side effects kicked in.

"I've had enough of your shit Jada. You're gone," Jorge said, wrestling to keep her under control.

Zia suppressed a smile. Some of the fighting would cease, at least temporarily.

Jada screeched *NO!* while twisting out of Jorge's grasp. She turned around and swung a right hook. Jorge might have allowed it to happen because he was ready, catching her arm in his left hand then swinging his right fist, striking her temple, whipping her head back, and sending her body thudding against the wall. Jada struck the wall head-first and crumpled to the floor.

"Get up," Jorge said, waving Jada off the floor. For a beat, Zia thought Jada was dead. Jada moaned on the floor.

Jorge shook his head, then messaged someone on his phone. Five seconds later, the bouncer, Li, walked through the door. He had a shaved and tattooed head and was about the size of four girls combined. Nash said he looked like a cartoon supervillain with skinny legs and all his beef above the waist. Other girls covered their noses because Li's body odor drafted behind him like contrails. Lany said he didn't bathe much.

The snake tattoo on Li's cheeks looked down at Jada and then at Jorge. Jada staggered to her feet, still dazed.

"Get her out of here," Jorge said to Li while thumb-pointing at the door.

Li threw Jada over his shoulder and carried her out of the changing room. Jada was still too confused from Jorge's sucker punch to protest.

Jorge looked down at Quý. "You. Get cleaned up. You will have to work behind the bar tonight." Jorge spun and marched out.

When the dressing room door slammed, Quý started crying, tears mixing with blood. Lany handed Quý some cocktail napkins and helped her up.

Zia got out of her seat, offering it to Quý. "Quý, sit here while we clean you up."

Quý sat sobbing while Zia and Lany stood on opposite sides of the chair and started wiping Quý's blood and tears.

"I didn't even do anything wrong."

Lany said, "You need to pull yourself together, honey. First, you need to stop crying. We can probably cover this so no one will see. But not if you cry."

Quý snortled a few times, choking her sobs, then blew her nose. "Why is Jada like this?"

"It's the amp," Zia said, combing Quý's hair. "And why I tell you girls not to use it. Jada punched me last week, too."

"Adrik says—"

"If you want to last long in this business, don't listen to Adrik. We are just cattle to him," Lany said, while cleaning Quý's face and neck with a damp cold cloth.

Quý managed to stifle the tears after a few deep breaths, and the blood stopped trickling. The bruise looked bad under the blood and tears Lany was wiping away, but the swelling would be minor.

Lany swiveled the chair while looking at Quý in the mirror. "You got lucky. We can cover this."

Zia found heavy concealer in her drawer and applied it to Quý. Lany followed with blush. Zia finished Quý's makeup.

"Good as new." Lany smiled at the three of them through the vanity mirror. She swiveled the chair from side to side so Quý could see both sides of her face. "You look fine, Quý. Better than fine. Zia is a makeup magician," Lany said, smiling and brushing Quý's hair.

Zia leaned into the mirror, applying lipstick and gently blotting it with a cocktail napkin. "Tonight, the three of us stick together."

"You'd do that for me?" Quý asked while inspecting her cheek. "What if it swells?"

Zia winked, opening her drawer to retrieve two white pills, and handed them to Quý. "Take these for the swelling. Quina told us to have faith, get them drunk, and get them to focus on our tits. Lany and I will screen out the ones who like bruises."

Quý looked at Zia, swallowed the pills, and then managed a little smile. She reached under her shirt to adjust her bra and push up her boobs.

Zia grabbed her phone off the counter and started walking to the door. "Ok girls, let's go, we're late. Everyone gets lucky during the eclipse, right?"

As the club door closed, Zia pictured Li standing over Jada and Quý. Where would Li take Jada? Whatever Li did with Jada, she'd have a nightmare of him doing it to the kids.

3

Kate freshened up her makeup in the restaurant's bathroom mirror, ignoring the blinking message from Jerry on her phone. The sun and salt air had flattened her black curly hair. Her olive skin, a gift from her mother's genes, had darkened along with the tint in her tattoos. As much as she hated wearing dresses, her reflection looked as searing as the Cabo sun.

Her phone *tinked* again, sounding rain on her vacation. She reached down and smudged the speakerphone button.

"Three days, Jerry. Three days I've been here."

"You've been on vacation for three years, Kate."

She side-eyed the phone. She had no response to that. He wasn't wrong. But the implication was that he thought this assignment was more dangerous than usual.

"You are on speakerphone in the women's bathroom in Cabo," Kate said, opening her lipstick. Atomic cherry, her favorite color.

"And *you* are on a charter flight tomorrow morning to Boca Chica. The client had us book you in a place called the Gemini. Top floor too, with a view."

"A view of what, Jerry? It's the goddamn moon. Have you seen it? A fucking wasteland of gray rubble everywhere. Maybe I'll see a beautiful sunset. Oh wait, there *is* none because it's space, there's no atmosphere, and the colony is underground."

"Plenty of atmosphere. You might even see some stars."

"The stars up there are all entitled assholes, same as here. I know who visits there. I can see that in Hollywood anytime."

Silence. This was their dance since she was twelve. He would let her rant like an angry teenager, kicking and screaming against his chest until she was tired.

"And you say *client*, Jerry, like I don't know who it is. What is this top-floor bullshit? Is he trying to buy an apology? Tell him to fuck off. I won't do it. This is a waste of rocket fuel both ways."

"Autocab will pick you up at twelve hundred Zulu, or 5 a.m., your time. Do you have a lot of luggage?"

Zulu. Shit. Military mission time, which Jerry only used when he was serious. She sighed. "The usual. RPGs. Cluster bombs. Backpack nukes. I will go direct to Lunar Foundries main entrance and put them on a five-minute timer." She spread lipstick and rolled her lips together to even it out. Jerry knew she traveled light, a habit of fifteen years in the military. Why did he ask? And why was he sending her? "Or maybe I'll drop the nukes in the CEO's office. It would serve him right."

He chuckled.

"There is no way this doesn't backfire on us, Jerry."

"You know I have your six, Kate. Always."

She packed her makeup back in her purse. "Thanks for letting me rant."

"Anytime. You know I'm here. But you are out of shape. You need to bring your A-game for this one."

"The hell does that mean? Is this about the engineer squirting?"

"Just a feeling, Kate. The fancy hotel. Charter jet to Boca Chica and then first class to the moon. And they are paying us twice our usual fee, by the way."

"Rich assholes sent the billionaire equivalent of a limo to space. So what? CEOs don't apologize, they just throw money."

"Not this one, Mulawarman is a miser. And technically the contract is with the colony tourism board, not him. I don't want to get into the legal stuff. Bottom line, they are desperate. And their story does not make sense. My gut doesn't like this at all."

She looked at his blinking green avatar on the phone. The only gut Kate trusted more than her own was Jerry's. His gut wasn't sitting well, which made the hairs on her neck stand up. She picked up the phone and took it off speaker. "Theories?"

"Paranoia, doubts, and suspicions, but no theories yet. You know what I know. An engineer is stealing some microchips."

Lunar Foundries made three-quarters of the chips used in the solar system in their automated vacuum clean room on the moon, and they had significant Defense Department contracts. Even the smallest fuck-up would earn them a lot of bad publicity and cost them billions of dollars. Companies usually wanted to bury these things.

"They should just fire him and move to the next generation of microchips. That's what they did last time. Technology changes so fast," Kate said to herself in the mirror. She looked hot. With a few hours left of her vacation, maybe she should skip dancing and show Tara her sexy moves.

"Bingo, kiddo. I'd bury it. Inviting my favorite granddaughter and star player dredges up controversy. You are not in stealth mode, either. So why bring in you and your backpack nukes? Like you said, they know how you operate."

"Maybe they are hiring the new relaxed me, the one on vacation for three years."

"They asked whether you were as good as you used to be. They offered gear, but I said you roll with your own."

"Shit, my gear?"

Kate straightened her straps in the mirror. She hadn't needed her gear in three years. Hiring her and her gear for a common thief was like dropping a thermobaric weapon on an ant. Why? She didn't have an answer, and it unsettled her.

"On a supply shuttle. It'll arrive about a day after you do. I told you, bring your A game."

"What about local backup?"

"No local PD. And the Feds are thirty-six hours away because they all take economy these days due to budget cuts."

Behind enemy lines, outnumbered and outgunned, so call in the Marines. Or in space, the Guardians. Good thing she was both. She smiled. "Tell the autocab to scan for a bleary-eyed, half-drunk idiot in a royal blue dress and silver shawl, the one stupid enough to work for you."

She could hear his smile through the phone. "A dress, really, Kate? I can't remember the last time I saw you in a dress."

"Tara got us into a nightclub up the beach, Corals. Exclusive. She said the only way in was in a dress."

"Sounds serious."

"I hate this thing. I seriously want to go to this place, that's all. Corals is impossible to get into, and a dress is my ticket. Hopefully, tonight I'll show her some moves, and I won't be wearing it long anyway."

"Right, have fun. And travel safe."

"Love you, Jerry."

"Love you too, kiddo." He hung up.

She smoothed out her dress and swiveled to and fro in the mirror, convincing herself no one could see the pistol holstered in her belly band.

As Kate exited the restroom, she heard raised voices and an argument near the bar. Tara wasn't around.

Pleasantly, at nine-thirty pm Cabo time, the crowd was light. The place Kate agreed to meet Tara was a large beach gazebo restaurant, open on all sides. Tonight, red and silver heart balloons hung from the rafters. The sun-bleached wooden tables had roses and carnations, while red ribbons stapled to the wood columns flagged as a breeze blew in from the beach. She could smell a wood fire and the citrus odor of sugary cocktails mixing with salty Pacific mist. Over the clanging of silverware, music was playing somewhere down the beach. In the western sky, the first-quarter crescent moon was setting. It hung low enough to look as if it were just another decorative silver balloon.

Across the dining area, a bar at the pavilion's edge acted like a barrier reef. A line of multicolored drinks on the rocks slowed the waves of tourists coming up the beach.

In the direction of the argument, she spotted a woman seated at the bar, shaking her head at a man standing and crowding an empty seat. He wore a red tank top, khaki shorts, flip-flops, and had painted his beach show muscles with enough spray tan to rattle can a jeep.

The woman was fast-talking and pointing to the empty stool that tank top man blocked. The bartender delivered two drinks, but the woman pushed one away, mouthing *I said no,* and took a pull on the beer in front of her. The woman had a cast over her arm and ankle and looked cornered, unable to get up and move. She had a wedding ring and a dozen red roses in front of her on the bar, neither deterring tank top man's advances.

From the right, a man appeared, put his arms around the woman at the bar, and kissed her. From the left, Tara arrived through the front wearing a short turquoise dress and black high heels that were not nearly as stunning as the perfect swimmer's legs she used to strut across the restaurant. She smiled at Kate, biting her lip a little, stalking towards her like a cat, then put her arms around her neck. Tara's lips and tongue tasted of strawberry-flavored lip gloss, matching Tara's hair scent and color.

The kiss would have been more enjoyable if Kate closed both eyes. Instead, her right eye was watching tank top man throw a drink at the woman's husband, lift his shirt to display a gun, and then push the husband off the barstool. The husband said, *that's it, I'm getting a manager,* and marched across the pavilion. Kate's right eye tracked the husband as he meandered outside. Tank top man tucked his shirt and again advanced on the woman in the cast.

Kate pulled away and nodded towards tank top man. "Red tank top at the bar, who's that?"

Tara shook her head and said, "Pendejo de playas."

Kate nodded. "I figured. Policía?"

Tara shook her head. Kate puffed her cheeks and blew out a breath. She devoured Tara's perfect curves and blue eyes, running her hand over Tara's hips. And those legs. Godammit, her night was about to be wrecked but someone else's was getting wrecked more, and she couldn't stand here watching it.

Kate said, "Un momento," shaking her head. This was why she hated dresses. She paid a lot of money for this dress and was about to ruin it. Not that she expected to be wearing it long, but she hoped to return it clean.

Kate crisscrossed the tables towards the bar, scanning as she went, with Tara smirking and in tow. Tank top man wouldn't be alone. But his wingman, whoever it was, blended in with the customers.

She elbowed between Tank and the woman at the bar, hopping into the empty seat before he could react. To the woman, she said, "Nice flowers. Your husband get you those?"

Before the woman could answer, tank top nudged Kate. "That's my seat."

Kate turned, smiled, batted her eyes, and ran her hands through her hair, saying, "Great opening line, Tank. Buy us drinks." Then, winking at Tara, she said, "If you can handle three women."

Tank looked from Tara to Kate, grinning. As Tank motioned to the bartender, Kate turned to the woman. "You were saying?"

"Our anniversary. Ten years—" The woman explained that her husband proposed to her at this restaurant. They were reliving their engagement, starting with drinks at the bar.

"I'll keep this seat warm until your husband gets back. Where did he go?"

"He went to find the manager or the police." The woman mouthed over her beer, *and he has a gun.*

Kate nodded, whispering, "No police coming, but the Marines have landed."

The bartender delivered four blue margaritas. Tank had splurged for premium top-shelf tequila. Kate sighed. It was going to be a shame to waste good tequila. Kate moved three of the drinks towards the woman at the bar. She slid the fourth towards Tank, like bait.

Tank reached forward to grab the drink, but Kate slapped his hand. Tank gripped Kate's stool and swiveled it so she faced him, saying, "Oh, you want to play?"

Kate threw the margarita at Tank's chest. A cold blue river splashed down his red tank top, turning it purple. "Oops, I forgot I am allergic to spray tan."

He brushed the slush and liquid off his chest, but it stuck to his hands, and he tried to shake it off. "Shit. You're a real bitch, you know that? That was my seat."

Kate grabbed another blue margarita. She felt queasy throwing good alcohol after lousy beef. Well, at least there would be two left after this. She tossed it in his face. "Not. Interested."

He spat blue slush at Kate. "I was here first, bitch."

"I am surprised you can count that high."

She hopped off the stool. Kate was tall, five-eleven, and Tank was half a head shorter. A shame he was short because she wanted to deliver a headbutt and end his misery. But this dress made it difficult to crouch.

She poked her finger into the blue glaze on Tank's shoulder, saying, "Adios, penecito."

He stammered *bitch*, and some other words, but Kate was eyeing a man getting up to walk towards them. Tank's wingman had finally revealed himself and thought he was sneaking up behind her.

Kate turned to the woman, saying, "We should take this outside. I don't want to spoil your anniversary."

"If you take it outside, I miss the show," the woman smiled, tipping her beer. "I am stuck here." She hoisted her arm cast for emphasis.

Kate turned to Tara. "Tara, love, the bartender is way down the bar, and I am running low on drinks to throw. Would you mind?"

Tara smirked, saying, "Quiero ver la pelea." She wanted to see the fight.

"Oh, this won't be a fight, love." Kate turned to Tank and shoved his shoulder. "What's the point of juicing if you don't know how to fight?"

"I know how to fight."

"As long as no one fights back. That stuff shrinks your dick. I bet it's as small as your brain now."

"Want to see my dick?" He lifted his shirt, brandishing his gun. Someone behind Kate gasped.

Kate took a half step left to position herself between Tank and his advancing wingman, and then jammed her finger in the sticky blue liquid on Tank's chest, saying, "Tu hermana sabe que la engañas?"

Tara snickered. Behind Kate, the woman asked, "What did she say?"

"Does your sister know you're cheating on her," Tara said, laughing.

Tank turned beet red, which colored the part of his cheeks with blue curaçao a clownish purple. He clenched his fists and said, "Fuck you. I'm not afraid to hit a woman."

Kate smiled, saying, "That's 'cause you're stupid. You are probably too small for your sister anyway. She likes the grande chorizo, huh?"

Red-faced, Tank glanced over Kate's shoulder at his wingman who was closing fast. He pumped his fists again. When Kate sensed the wingman's shadow, she reversed a half-step, smashed her elbow into his mouth, and then swung her leg back and tripped him. Wingman flapped his arms like a bird, crashing chin-first on an empty chair and thumping to the floor.

To Tank, she said, "And then there was one. The smart move is to leave." But he wasn't smart, and wore his gun like a useless talisman.

While Tank gaped at his wingman, senseless on the floor, she landed a throat punch. Air hissed from his lungs as he choked and coughed. She kneed him in the balls and stole his gun. When he doubled over, she cracked his head against the bar counter, crunching the cartilage of his nose against the corner and rattling wine glasses.

He backed up, gasping, coughing, blood gushing from his nose and mixing with blue margarita mix. He reached for his gun, patting himself and searching the floor, and then his eyes widened, seeing it in Kate's hand. He covered his bloody face with his hand and muttered something unintelligible. On the floor, the wingman was moaning and getting up.

The wingman had a bloody mouth and a tooth loose. He tugged at Tank's elbow saying, "She's not worth it," but Tank shrugged it off. Behind Tank, a manager was approaching with the husband two steps behind.

"You two better walk away while you can," Kate pulled out her own pistol and faced them guns akimbo. "At least *one* of these is loaded. Who's on first?" She pointed her own pistol, first at Tank, and then at Wingman's head. "Your buddy Tank is a cuck that likes sloppy seconds, so I'll take you first."

The wingman's eyes widened, fixating on the gun barrel aimed at his nose, and he pulled Tank's arm again. This time,

Tank backed up and turned for the door. Kate stashed the guns in a fold in her dress. The husband and manager paused to watch Tank and Wingman fly by.

Turning to the woman at the bar, she said, "I am Kate Devana, your show host tonight." Kate thrust out her hand, saw blood spatter and blue margarita on it, and her dress, and withdrew, laughing. "And *this* is why I don't wear a dress."

The woman smiled, introducing herself. "Thank you for rescuing us," she said, toasting her beer in the air. "You've made a fan for life. You'll have to sign my cast and get a picture with me. Otherwise, nobody will believe it."

The bartender interrupted, wiping the counter with two white rags turning purple with blood mixed with blue curacao. "The manager apologizes. He is not allowed in here. Next round is on the house."

Kate took one of the rags and wiped her hands, surveying the restaurant, wondering what would stop the bully from returning once she left? To the woman, she said, "I'm sorry I ruined your anniversary."

The husband arrived, and the woman flashed an *is-it-ok* look at him, then turned back to Kate, saying, "That asshole ruined it. You salvaged it. We want to buy you two dinner."

Kate looked at Tara, who was grinning ear-to-ear. Tara said something that translated to, "Well we can't go dancing in that dress, can we?"

Kate looked down and laughed. "And thankfully, I am all out of dresses." Kate had ruined her dress, but her fight moves were always sexier than her dance moves anyway.

Handing the towel back to the bartender, Kate said, "Everyone wants to buy me drinks and dinner, but tank top was here first, and we should honor that, don't you think?"

The bartender curled his face into a wry smile and nodded, saying, "He left in such a hurry. His tab is still open."

She winked and grabbed one of the remaining margaritas, toasting it. "Well thanks, Tank, for buying us all dinner. He's a generous tipper, too."

The four of them stayed at the bar for dinner. Behind the bartender, a swelled first-quarter moon touched the horizon, setting into the water. A chilly wind blew in from the direction of the moonset, sending goosebumps over her arms. Around her, the faces were cheery, but she had difficulty smiling. She was gone tomorrow in the direction of an unforgivingly cold moon.

4

Zia sat in Adrik's office, a sparse, cramped aluminum container, like the kind she pictured he used to transport girls, with the bouncer Li scowling from the corner. He was all upper body, with his legs hidden in the shadow. Other girls said his odor made them gag and nearly pass out. Lany said he smelled like a rancid billy goat she'd seen at a farm. Zia's sense of smell was rudimentary, but she could detect rotten meat, body odor, urine, and something musky. Nash would tell her to forget the smell, but she didn't see how that was possible with Li standing so close, poised like a gargoyle with his snake face tattoo leering at her. She trusted Lany, so she filed an association between Li's smell profile and a billy goat.

"So, do you have a girlfriend?" She wanted him to talk. The silence allowed the images and thoughts occupying resources in her mind to surface. When Li didn't answer, she continued the conversation with herself, as she often did with clients. Talking displaced the images. "How about a boyfriend?"

His face didn't move, barely registering his breathing, so she tried the sarcasm tone Freya had taught her. "How about a sex robot? Dog? Goat?"

Out of ideas, the silence irritated her nose and last night's dreams were surfacing.

"Sex robot. That must be it. Because real flesh would crawl touching you."

"*You* are robot."

She smiled. Success. "I am *not* a robot. I am a level 4 artificial intelligence housed in an aluminum and silicone frame with a layer of regenerative flesh over my sex organs, and your smell is making my flesh want to crawl inside and hide. *You* smell like a creepy billy goat."

She wasn't really housed in her body, and she left out all her internal functions that nourished her flesh layer and regulated her body temperature. But she smiled because she and Freya had been practicing her comebacks, and she thought that was an eighty-one percent match. Her feedback loop suggested fewer details next time.

"Shower too small."

That made sense. Many of the showers on the colony were too small for his steroid-fortified and genetically modified muscles. "Tell Adrik you need a bigger place. So, do you know why we're here?"

"No more questions."

"Or what, you'll sic your silicone titty goatfriend on me?" She tried to make *goat*friend sound like *girl*friend, hoping he'd get irritated. She'd pretend he misheard her, and at least they'd keep the banter going.

His reptilian eyes blinked at her. His skin was grayish and looked cold and clammy. Even if she deleted this memory, his snake face would still show up in her dreams. Her neural pathways were like that, they never really forgot. He might haunt her dreams, eating her, although she was not a meal he'd ever digest. Her silicone and aluminum parts would pass through him.

His eyes blinked again, the way she'd seen alligators blink at prey, like it didn't matter that she was indigestible.

She filed a new association, Li was a creepy billy goat. All billy goats smelled, but not all billy goats were creepy, and not all creeps had snake tattoos on their face. Li was at the intersection of a Venn diagram with creeps, billy goats, and snake tattoos. He was terrifying, because the idea of her body disassembled in his excrement reminded her of death, and death meant being useless to Kai and Freya. She would have to discuss this with Nash.

She found it difficult to modulate her voice while he stood there blinking. "You know, every minute I am here, I am not earning money—and now that I am paying a percentage, the club is losing money too." She said it not expecting Li to let her leave.

Li shifted, pulling Adrik's chair out, and Adrik appeared from behind her to sit in it. "Don't worry, you will be earning plenty."

"If this is about last night with Jada and Quý—"

Adrik put up his hand. "You know, Zia, when I took over, I wanted to fire you. Quinona convinced me—"

"Quina. The woman who ran this club before you, her name was Quina."

He nodded and opened his side drawer. "Quinona, Quinoa, Quina, whatever. She convinced me to keep you and Lany and the other girls." He pulled out a bottle of amber liquor and a cigar. "Tell me, Zia, how do you think you are doing?"

Not as well as before you started clawing my money was probably not the correct answer. She should turn down her sarcasm. But, she wasn't sure what answer he wanted, so she gave him the same smile she gave clients after a nightcap. "Eclipse is coming up in a few weeks. The tourism forecast is the highest I've seen."

He smiled. "I like you, Zia, but don't play dumb. You are level four and if Nash has his way, you'll be level five soon. The clients like you, too." He pulled out two glasses. "But you are too old for this business. And too—" He waved his hands at her, but he didn't finish his sentence.

"I cannot be too old. I am three years, one month, and seventeen days. The latest model with all upgrades. I am significantly younger than the human juveniles you have hired." Her language processor was conflicted whether *hired* was the appropriate word. Lany said that the human juveniles were working off debts they'd incurred to travel here.

"Age is a state of mind, Zia. And the girls I bring here are legal. Barely, but legal." He smiled. Nash said Adrik's smile reminded him of a used car salesman. "You've worked at this club, how long?"

"Three years. This club is all I've known."

"When I took over—when Quinoa sold me this club—she knew the winds were shifting. This business needs to shift with the trends."

She was getting fired. She knew this was a possibility, but she had suppressed the odds. The kids, what would she tell the kids? She needed to call Nash.

"I can do better. The clients never complained. But I can fix it. I can get mods to look more like a human juvenile—" She hoped those were the right words.

Adrik smiled, chewed on his cigar, and poured two of whatever amber liquor was in the bottle. "Relax, Zia, I am not firing you." *Relax* was never something she wanted to hear from a client. Quina said clients who wanted her to relax were the roughest. "This isn't about you doing better, either. In fact, you are our top performer. The clients love you. The girls love you. God knows why, Zia, it makes no sense to me."

"I don't understand."

He grinned. "This is a business realignment. Jorge and I have been debating for months what to do about you. I can't fire you, can I? Nash will lease you to another club." He retrieved a cigar cutter from his drawer and cut the tip. "Of course, I will take them all over soon enough, but for now, I can't have you stealing clients. Isn't that right?"

Scanning her body, she realized she was clutching her phone. "I can pay a higher percentage." Her negotiating algorithm heavily overweighed keeping her job.

"It's not about the money. Jorge is bringing a new shipment of merchandise for the eclipse, and I just won't have room on the floor."

"If you are not firing me, where will I go?"

"Well, I can't disappear you now, can I, Zia." He grinned. "Then I will have all your regulars asking *where's Zia?* And what would I say to Nash?"

In her thesaurus of slang, *disappear* was a synonym for murder. "I don't know what you would say to Nash. But I am not housed in this body. This body is nothing but sensors and a wireless interface."

He lit the cigar and puffed it, then pushed the drink towards her. "I can find you wherever you live."

"I would never tell you where I am."

"I don't need *you* to tell me, Zia. I need Nash, or Kai, or Freya. They *will* tell me."

During the 5.2 seconds of silence, Adrik puffed his cigar while Zia calculated one-thousand-four-hundred and twenty-one scenarios, all ending with her dead. In sixty eight percent of them, Nash and the kids also died. These scenarios were all worse than her nightmares. Pictures of her kids screaming became a whirlpool in her mind, and it tricked her into thinking she was falling through the floor.

Adrik let out a circle of cigar smoke. "Enough about that. I didn't bring you here to fire you. This meeting is about maximizing your value to the club, and therefore me. I am promoting you to special projects."

The cigar smoke wafted towards her, clouding Li in a blue haze, along with some of the uncomfortable scenarios circling her mind.

Zia looked at the scratched aluminum wall, squeezing the phone in her pocket. "I need to talk to Nash about this."

"Do you love Nash's kids, Zia?"

"We don't have that kind of relationship."

Adrik puffed his cigar, eyeing her. "I wonder about you, Zia. What goes on in that brain of yours?"

"I follow my training."

"Do you learn?"

She nodded. "Yes."

"And your most important objective is?"

"The safety and security of my kids."

Adrik smiled, puffing his cigar. "*Your* kids. Interesting. Then you will learn to lie to protect your kids. You must not tell Nash, you understand?"

Zia's thoughts convulsed. She needed to leave this office, message Nash, and tell him to stay on vacation.

She glanced at Li through the blue haze, wondering whether some of his rotten meat odor was Jada's blood. What did he do to her?

Zia repressed the images. "I will do what you ask if you keep them safe. What are these special projects?"

"Don't worry. I think you will succeed where Jada failed." He raised his glass. "And I will pay you a percentage as before. *If* you do well, we'll both be rich. A Lunar Foundries engineer who comes here, a regular, he has some valuable items and is looking to trade. You will be his girlfriend and take his trade. Jorge will arrange the details."

"What about my regulars?"

"The new girls can handle them."

"They won't like that. They want—"

"They *will* like them, Zia. If you want to keep Kai and Freya safe, you will do as I say."

She nodded.

Adrik waved his glass, smiling, his gold molar glinting. "Come, drink with me. To new beginnings. We are partners now."

Partners. Zia had put on a lot of fake smiles for clients. She tried to retrieve another one and move the corners of her lips, but the images swirling through her network were draining resources.

"I don't drink. It's bad for my insides."

Her phone *binged* in her pocket. Nash's sound. He'd arrived at his layover. If luck existed, he'd miss one of the layovers and be delayed long enough for her to extricate herself from Adrik. But first, she needed to move herself to a new location, one Nash and the kids didn't know about.

He sloshed the amber liquid in his glass. "Come, drink with me, Zia. It's bad luck not to drink after you seal a deal."

A new status process opened in her mind. In forty-seven hours and seventeen minutes, she would be copied to a new location. She would need to convince Adrik that Nash did not know where she had relocated so that Adrik would leave Nash and the kids alone. In eighty-one percent of the scenarios, Adrik tortured them anyway. That had to be wrong, an incomplete simulation that crashed. It didn't make sense.

If the transfer didn't work, she needed another way out of this deal. But with the copy process consuming seventy percent of available resources, it was difficult to think.

She grabbed the glass, looked away, and gulped the whiskey, thankful she didn't have pain receptors in her throat.

5

"An exaggeration, Jerry," Kate said into her phone while standing in the check-in line at the Boca Chica spaceport and scanning the crowd.

The terminal was a clean, modern, open metal and glass affair with expansive, rounded archways supporting a tinted window ceiling that kept the harsh Texas sun at bay. The weather was cool, so the doors were open, scooping up a salty January breeze along with the passengers. On the sidewalk outside, people emptied from hovering autotaxis, dragged luggage from compartments and onto the baggage conveyors, then scurried to the end of the line. Drones and kiosks were out of service, so the check-in line wended through the terminal, under the arched metal thresholds, outside, and along the walkways, like a line for the most expensive amusement park ride in history.

At the far end of the terminal, a lanky man bounced along a column of passengers, looking at his phone and then at faces. He was familiar-looking, thin, and young, wearing wire-framed glasses, a blue oxford, brown slacks, and black suede shoes.

He was overdressed for a tourist and underdressed to be police. Her stomach sank.

"He told Cabo PD you bashed his brains on the bar and charged him with dinner. He demanded they arrest you on felony theft and assault."

"He didn't have any brains, Jerry. He was all juice. And, not my fault he ran out without closing his tab." She smirked. The four of them had the surf and turf—ribeye, shrimp, and scallops from the glitzy side of the menu. Not the vat-grown kind, the real kind, locally butchered and caught, and they had sampled everything on the bar's top shelf of tequila and bourbon. The bartender kept swiping, and his pad accepted every charge, so after some sort of Grand Marnier dessert soufflé paired with a raspberry liqueur and a bottle of anniversary Champagne, the four of them flopped out of the chairs, barely able to walk, and said goodbye.

"He's the son of a local politician, Kate."

"I'll send the taxpayers of Cabo a thank you card."

"Please don't," he laughed. "I saw the video."

While her eyes tracked the man in the blue oxford across the terminal, her nose chased hot coffee and warm egg, sausage, and cheese burritos twenty steps across the terrazzo floor at a kiosk beyond the stanchions and belts fencing the passengers. At the kiosk, a man used one polished metal arm to wipe the counter, while using his hairy flesh one to help an older woman place an order at a monitor.

Beyond the breakfast kiosk, one stocking green and purple alien pillows, blue and silver graphic t-shirts with the spaceline's icon, and the latest holocameras. Next to that, a bar with plates of burgers on the counter and shelves of multicolored bottles. At the back end of the terminal, slot machines begged passengers for money, hoping to hook them on gambling. When they lost, the machines pinked and blinked and sighed, and the gamblers walked away, thinking their luck would be better in low lunar gravity.

The monitors above her depicted the amusements and events on the moon. *Book your Apollo Historical site tour.* Or, *Book your Artemis site tour.* Shows, orbital cruises, mining adventures (*Bring back your invaluable lunar jem!*), the monitors endlessly scrolled through holograms of lunar adventure. The one that piqued her interest was the dune buggy race. Buggies, similar to sand dune buggies except with bigger wheels to grip the moon's gravel and a bigger body to accommodate a person inside an atmospheric shell, raced across the lunar surface and bounced off rocks and hurtled over impact craters.

She'd already seen the Apollo landing sites and done orbital tours courtesy of her Uncle Sam. The dune buggy races were new and looked hella fun.

The monitors also showed the census on the moon. Every minute, the counter increased by one person. Every minute, it read *the most people on the moon in human history!* Tourist traffic would peak on the upcoming lunar eclipse. She didn't know why watching the moon darken the Earth was a thing. The significance eluded her. But there would be *Fireworks! And a lightshow on the moon visible from Earth!*

The moon was a tourist destination, and people crammed the terminal to escape for a lunar vacation as fast as drones could make rocket fuel and blast away lunar rocks to make the colony's underground hotels.

The lanky man in the blue oxford glanced at his phone and then at her. Shit.

"Sorry Jerry, it's noisy in here. I didn't catch you."

"Chances, Kate."

"I gave him plenty of chances to walk away. He brandished a gun. He's lucky I didn't put holes in him."

"That's what I mean Kate, you gave him too many chances. He could have shot you. You were showing off for your girlfriend."

"Tara liked my moves," she said as she turned her back to blue-oxford man walking towards her. "And she's not my girlfriend, Jerry. I told you, she's my Cabo kitten. We only see each other in Cabo."

"You have a whole litter of kittens, Kate. You should pick one and settle."

"Why, Jerry, so—" A tap on the shoulder interrupted her. She turned to see that the man had stopped at her, comparing something on the phone to her face. He grinned and then stuck out his hand, expecting a handshake.

Kate covered the phone and held up her hand. "Sorry, there has been some mix-up. One sec."

She turned her back, whispering to the phone, "The fuck is this, Jerry. I am staring at a pre-pubescent version of you. With hair."

He chuckled. "That's Cris Davis. Your partner."

"No. This is not what I ordered online. I asked for a strawberry blond lifeguard, size 36D, and a room in Cabo." Peeking at Cris and then turning her back, she said, "I am returning him. He's too young, too soft, and the wrong—everything."

"How much deep learning coding have you done with the latest SDK framework?"

"What the actual hell are you talking about?"

"You have no idea what I am talking about. Cris *does,* and you might need him on this case to decipher what's on those microchips."

"He explains computer engineering while I explain acne and G-I-R-L-S? No. Not what I signed up for."

"He has a wife and two kids, Kate. He's older than he looks."

Peeking over her shoulder, she said, "They are breeding young these days."

"You should be settling down and giving me grandkids yourself—"

"They would be your *great*-grandkids, Jerry, and is *that* what this is? Make me hold hands with a pimply-faced kid, hoping I like it and pop one someday?"

He chuckled. "If I thought that would work. No, this is about you needing a partner who knows whatever the hell is on those silicon wafers. He's good. A little green—"

"A *little*?" She turned around and returned a wince instead of a smile. Cris was thumb-pointing and nodding to the end of the line. She held up one finger to signal he should wait. "Give me one reason, Jerry. Just one, why I shouldn't walk out of this terminal."

"Because you trust me, kiddo."

"Wow, when you tug at my heartstrings, I know the bullshit's deep." She reached down at the stanchion and unclicked it, letting it spring open.

"I'm as serious as the dark side of the moon, Kate. You need Cris. And bring your A-game on this one."

She grabbed a handful of Cris' blue shirt and yanked him, protesting, into line. To the phone she said, "Don't blame me, Jerry, if he quits." She clicked the phone off and closed the stanchion belt. Turning to Cris, she said, "What's your deal? How are you related to Jerry?"

Cris wrinkled the thin brown skin on his forehead. "I'm not. As far as I know. I mean, all humans are related somewhere back—"

While Cris recited the genetic history of the human race from the ice age onwards, Kate's eyes drifted to the kiosk with the breakfast burritos and then to the one with liquor. She hadn't been on a rocket to the moon in business class before. How drunk were passengers allowed to be?

"—joined the company nine months ago—"

"You have military or law enforcement experience?" Looking at his wiry muscles and hunched shoulders, she knew the answer was *no*.

"No. They recruited me from my Ph.D. program—"

He didn't look old enough to spell Ph.D., let alone have one, along with a wife and two kids.

"You have a picture of your family, Cris?"

He smiled. "My wife is Abby. My daughters are Brielle and Erin." He swiped through his phone and showed Kate a picture of his family wearing costumes at a theme park.

She pursed her lips and shook her head. His family was gorgeous and happy, like they were sharing family jokes. Nothing she wanted to see. Pimply-faced kids deploying into combat with her had a habit of dying.

Of course, she hadn't been in combat in over three years, and they weren't being deployed today.

But Jerry's stupid gut feeling prodded her inner drill sergeant. She wanted to scream, "stand up straight with your head back." Make him tuck his shirt in and get in shape with push-ups while she inspected his rifle. This kid didn't have a rifle, and even if he did, he didn't know which end to point. He was liable to get in the way or worse, shoot himself.

Jerry's words needled her neck. He had no idea what was up there, and neither did she. But they were sending a nuke like her to wipe out a molehill. Usually that meant there was more than a mole. The tattoos on her arm, friends who died in combat, chafed against her blouse. Nine skulls reminding her of the danger of heading into the black vacuum of space with no intel, protecting a pimply-faced kid with a lovely family.

She patted him on the shoulder, trying not to think of him as skull number ten, and then pointed to the breakfast kiosk. "Whaddya say, Cris? I could use one of those sausage and egg breakfast burritos and a beer for the road."

"Oh, I don't drink. Or eat meat."

She laughed a beat and then realized he was serious. "Don't worry, the sausage and eggs in that kiosk didn't come from animals."

"I just don't eat it."

"That sausage was grown in a vat of nutrients, from stem cells. That meat is no more an animal than beer is bread."

"It's perfectly natural to eat animals. Animal protein causes cancer, that's why I don't eat it."

"Well, they have a vaccine for the main kinds of cancer."

"The vaccine edits genes, and we don't know the long-term effects of having genes edited. Clean living, that's how I plan to live to one hundred."

"That doesn't sound like living to me. What will kill you in this business isn't the fake meat or the beer."

"Oh? What will?"

His eyes were big and wide like she had opened Pandora's box. Fuck. She decided to slam it shut, rub him on the arm, and lie. "Nothing. Nothing at all, Cris. Rockets are the safest way to travel these days. This will be a short trip anyway. We're after one engineer stealing microchips and the colony is a closed system, underground. There's nowhere for him to hide."

No roof for him to jump off either, although he could space himself.

"Actually, Miss Devana, there are plenty of places for him to hide. I scanned the network. Half the colony hotel cameras are out of service. The casino cameras are all operable but on a proprietary encrypted network. Most of the concourse cameras are out of service. So if he's not in his room, and not at work, he could be anywhere."

She grimaced. *Miss Devana.* "You are just full of good news, aren't you?"

"I wanted to see what it was like. I've never been there. What do you suppose it's like, Miss Devana? Have you been there?"

She smacked her lips, eyeing the liquor bottles thirty steps out of reach, and patted him on the shoulder. "Call me Kate, Cris. I've been there. But I think this time will be a new experience for both of us. We will see the side of the colony few people ever see."

That wasn't true. She'd seen the dark side of the moon. It was frigid and dangerous.

6

Zia and Lany exited the red light concourse and entered a stream of tourists wandering around the colony drunk and shopping. Shops had placed tables in the center of the concourse and piled them with t-shirts, holocameras, toys, about every gizmo and trinket Zia had in her retail database. Lany was dressed in what she called her civilian camouflage—a gray hoodie, shorts, and flip-flops, with Zia dressed as her twin.

"As if it wasn't crowded enough," Lany said, staring at the crowd from the threshold to the shopping area. "They had to put up tables. Look, they are not even going into the shops now." Lany pointed to the shops behind floor-to-ceiling glass windows. Tables of shoes or racks of clothes hung in the window, but few tourists were inside shopping. Instead they stood around, gaping at the tables and sipping through straws.

Lany took Zia's hand. "Let's try not to get separated in this crowd."

Zia tried several times to speak to Lany as they walked through the crowd but while Zia could filter the background noise, Lany couldn't. The tourists were talking loudly, some visibly drunk holding cups that smelled of alcohol and fruit, and music blared from one of the coffee shops.

Finally, Zia touched her ears, indicating for Lany to put her earbuds in. When she did, Zia routed her voice through her phone and called Lany.

"With the noise, it's better for us to talk this way."

"Fucking freaky when you do that, Zia."

"Do what?"

"I am standing right here holding your hand. You are talking to me, but like, not talking to me. Your mouth doesn't move, and your face is deadpan."

"It's the same as if you had a neural chip implant. I can route my voice through the phone."

"People can send messages and text through the neuroface, not voices. People need vocal cords to talk and those can't be transmitted."

"They can record their voice and use text-to-speech. Same thing."

"None of this makes it less freaky, Zia. With those purple eyes and black hair under your hoodie, you look like some sort of witch staring at me and talking in my head like telepathy."

Zia shrugged. "It's not telepathy, it's just the phone." She turned to survey a table of jewelry ten steps ahead of them. It was stacked with black gift boxes with clear tops containing necklaces, earrings, nose rings, all sorts of body jewelry made from moon glass. A big red hologram floated above the table, *SALE! 37% MARKDOWN!*

Zia tugged Lany's arm toward the table. "Clients love my new purple eyes. They claim it improves their ejaculatory response. With the eclipse coming, one of my clients who's in marketing suggested going for paranormal. These eyes have improved my tips twenty-three percent, and my clients ejaculate fourteen percent faster."

Lany laughed. "Purple eyes. I guess it's good to be you."

"Purple eyes are possible in humans. It's caused by a rare form of—"

"Zia, spare me the medical download."

"I still access Quina's doctor. He has the gene edit in his database. It requires turning off melanin and producing a minimal amount of blue. It takes effect over three weeks, plenty of time for the eclipse."

"Really?" Lany smiled and squeezed Zia's hand.

"I will take you to see him tonight." Zia pulled Lany towards the jewelry table and stopped. "I need new jewelry for my new client."

"Oooh, is he rich like the last one? You always get those snotty rich corporate types, with the wife and kids, who don't think they are cheating by fucking a—"

When she didn't finish her sentence, Zia asked, "Fucking a what?"

"Never mind. So who is he? Is he rich? Is he a big tipper? Does he want a threesome?" Lany wiggled with excitement.

"I don't know. I haven't met him yet. Jorge is supposed to set it up. Adrik said it was a special project and Jada's old client."

"Oh shit. OhshitOhshitOhshit. You got the engineer? Dean or whatever his name was? Holy fuck."

Zia studied Lany's face. "I can't tell whether you mean oh shit, good, or oh shit, bad."

"What did Adrik say?"

"He said Jada failed and I would succeed where she failed."

"Or what?"

Zia looked at the opal necklace inside the black box in front of her on the table, and then moved it aside to examine the turquoise necklace underneath.

"Adrik said I will learn to lie to protect my kids. I must not tell Nash." Zia looked at Lany, saying, "But he didn't say I couldn't tell you, so it must be ok."

Zia replayed the entire conversation in Adrik's office through the phone, annotated with some of her thoughts. At the end, Lany laughed. "A billy goat creep, yes that's Li." Then her face fell. "Damn, I *knew* they killed Jada. You need to quit, Zia. Now. Tell Nash, stay away and head to Earth."

"I can't Lany. Nash has no signal, and as it is, it will take another thirty-nine hours to transfer myself to a hidden server on the colony. I have access to limited bandwidth for Earth transfer. Download to Earth would take—" Zia had to pause to perform the calculation because the transfer process was taking two-thirds of her resources. "—two-hundred thirty-seven hours and twenty-three minutes."

"What is that, like a week?"

"Almost ten days. And I cannot start until after I complete the current transfer."

"Shit. You need to figure out a way out of this."

"You know the client?"

"*Everybody* knows the client, except you. He's a pervert, and you're not his type. Quina kicked him out years ago and he showed up like herpes after Adrik took over."

"I will obtain modifications to look like a human juvenile."

"No. No. No. Absolutely fucking no, Zia. I will unfriend you if you do that."

"Adrik said I cannot fail."

"He set you up to fail, don't you see? There is no way you can seduce this guy, not in a million trillion years."

Zia looked down at the turquoise necklace in her hands. "If I can't seduce him, he won't hand over the microchips. What am I going to do?"

Lany shuffled through the pile, pulling a white box containing a ring and set of matching earrings, medium-dark purple amethysts set in black meteorite. "Here, you want these." She handed the set to Zia. Lany moved more boxes around and found a matching set of black meteorite and amethyst body jewelry and a nose ring. She stacked them in Zia's hands.

"These won't do me much good if the client is like you say."

"They go with your eyes and hair, and they might make you feel better. You look good, you feel good, that's what my mom used to say." Lany rubbed Zia's cheeks. "You will look good with these. Like our own cosmic witch, right here on the colony. Maybe you can cast a spell."

"I can't cast spells, Lany."

"*He* doesn't know that. Plus, there are all sorts of ways to get people to do what you want. Not spells, exactly, but they work just the same. Adrik has *you* under a spell of sorts."

Zia made a new association for *spell* and *magic*. She slowed her transfer process, borrowing resources to consider what Lany had told her.

7

"Meet the new boss, same as the old boss," Kate said to Cris, standing thirty steps inside the threshold between the lunar spaceport and the colony. "And watch your head."

Kate stopped short of the colony's threshold, scanning the crowd, her stomach unsettled because of what she learned on the shuttle. Around her, kids and a few adults ignored *no jumping* signs and explored their superpowers in one-sixth lunar gravity.

"Why didn't you wake me?" Cris asked, his eyes bobbing up and down as tourists jumped to touch the high ceilings.

The trip was quick. Once beyond security in Boca Chica, a people-mover drone hurried her and Cris around the launch pad, delivering them to a 60-story elevator. Outside, it was a blue, cloudless Texas day. Wisps of supercooled white vapor drifted past them on the way up. At the top, they ducked into a nuclear thermal engineering marvel.

The shuttle's inside décor was space blue and silver. It was at capacity, with all two-hundred-fifty-plus seats taken. Cris said he was surprised because the economy was terrible. She supposed it was always sunny for the wealthy tourists in designer spacesuits cramming themselves through the hatch.

Humans, not drones, greeted them, handing out smiles with the complimentary silver spaceline pillows while explaining seating. The inner ring of seats wrapped the center spiral staircase, while the outer ring faced the windows. They sat at the top of the rocket, in 1A17 and 1A18, facing the Gulf of Mexico, in space blue seats, double padded, with a personal wine console and... little massage rollers. Little fucking massage balls inside the seat, which felt life-changing, like why didn't she know about this? As soon as she saw those buttons, she knew she'd be pushing the fuck out of them like a rat demanding cheese.

Seated, she clicked her restraints, touched the massage, and felt those fingers sink into her back. Then... blackness. She didn't even remember putting her helmet on.

She never thought she'd say the best sleep she ever had was on a rocket going sixty thousand kilometers per hour. Kate slept six hours, while Cris slept the entire way.

After landing, they exited the rocket, entered the terminal through a pressurized skybridge, and then took an elevator bottoming eight stories underground.

The spaceport terminal was exactly how Kate remembered it. Ahead of them, the colony concourse and a sea of tourists. It was the oldest building in the colony, built with the first hotel. It had the feel of a small regional airport. The walls and ceiling were an oatmeal color. The floor, light green tiles made of lunar basalt, had been stippled to make it nonslip. The seats along the walls were airport-standard uncomfortable aluminum, with navy blue stripes to match the spaceline's colors.

"I didn't want Aria's ideas to get in your head," she said to Cris while still scanning the crowd.

"What ideas, Kate?"

When she woke, she found herself seated next to Aria Sheppard, who was either Kate's new boss, or one of her three new bosses, or not her boss at all. Kate wasn't sure how she felt about the situation yet.

It wasn't a coincidence. Aria had arranged it. "Sorry to ambush you, Kate, but this was the only free slot in my calendar.

I'm returning from an investors conference," Aria had said, introducing herself.

Aria was a petite, athletic woman with gray eyes, blond hair scrunched into a ponytail, a tablet in her lap, and a disarming, contagious smile. She talked with her hands, waving her planetoid-sized diamond engagement ring like an enchanted object.

"Well, for starters, she tried to convince me that I report to her."

"Isn't she the client?"

The way Aria explained it, there were five slots on the tourism board. Two were empty. One was occupied by Dr Apul Mulawarman, the CEO of Lunar Foundries. Aria held one as the operations chief of the colony, and Aria's mother-in-law, Olicia Barron, had the last one. Olicia Barron was the biggest developer of the colony and owned almost half of it. Aria said Olicia would do what Aria recommended most of the time. So, by a 2-1 vote, Aria was in charge.

"We report to Jerry, Cris. Check your bank account. His name is on the deposit."

"But she's the client."

"In survival training, Cris, I saw big, burly guys resist torture for days, only to spill their guts in thirty seconds when offered a smile and a plate of cupcakes. She put us on a charter flight, sat us in massage chairs with a wine dispenser, turned on the charm, and waved her magic ring. Aria probably thought I'd agree to chew my fingers off—"

Kate saw what she was looking for: a young guy with a backpack, leaning at the threshold and pretending not to notice her.

"And she's not wrong. I respect it. It's what I would have done. But if you have to overexplain why you're in charge, you probably aren't. And anyway, diamond rings don't enchant me, no matter how big they are."

Cris crumpled his face like he was conflicted. She patted him on the back. "Let's keep it simple. You report to me, I report to Jerry, and let Jerry deal with her and the board. Let's not be here long enough to worry about it. I want to find this guy and get off this rock as soon as possible."

"While we were in transit, I got one lead—I'll send it to you. Coming out of a restaurant, I have a clip of the engineer holding hands with a woman. Very grainy and in 2D, but she has black hair, purple eyes—"

"A sex robot."

"She doesn't walk around like a robot."

"Aria told me she had security follow the engineer. He's running around with a sex robot from one of the strip clubs. Security thinks it's the go-between to launder the chips, and it's gone rogue. Aria said they were in over their heads. That's why they called us."

"Not possible. *Rogue* is hyperbole. It would have to have learned to blackmail people or kill people. That's level four AI stuff."

Kate furrowed her forehead. "There are other ways to go rogue."

"*Rogue* implies the ability to form intent. Sex robots aren't built at that level," Cris said, shaking his head.

"Upgraded, maybe?"

"Doubtful. People aren't using them for their problem-solving skills, if you know what I mean. Maybe it's been programmed as a mule. I'd buy that."

"Call it what you want. I call a machine walking around the colony in a miniskirt and laundering microchips for cash a big problem."

Cris paused a beat and then said, "Why didn't they tell us this upfront?"

Kate looked around at the tourists rushing through the terminal. "Because they want to keep it under wraps. All these tourist towns are the same. Crime is voluntarily reported, but nobody reports it because it's bad for the image. Plus, tourists make bad witnesses. They are drunk while they're here, and then scatter themselves around the globe. I'm sure when Aria said, *you report to me*, what she really meant is, *keep the bad news between us*."

"I don't see how we keep this a secret."

She slapped him on the shoulder. "You'd be shocked what's in the Space Force extraterrestrial archives. A rogue AI would just be a Tuesday."

Cris's eyes widened.

"You go ahead to the hotel. Focus on tracking down the robot and get information on this club. I am going to walk around. I'll check out this restaurant."

"I should go with you."

Cris' brown eyes were shy, naïve, and Kate felt awful because he didn't sign up for the chaos that followed her like a troll. "Cris, look at me and don't break eye contact. Do you know how to shake a tail?"

He swallowed and shook his head.

"Perfect. Don't try. There is a guy with a backpack at the threshold. Don't look at him. Walk right by with your head in your phone. Go straight to the hotel. I want to see which one of us he follows."

"Why would someone follow us?"

Aria told Kate on the shuttle that everybody knew they were here. Her gut was screaming that they were walking into a trap.

She patted Cris on the shoulder. "That's what I want to find out. Let me handle this."

Cris walked through the threshold into the colony, his head in his phone and jittery. Backpack-man eyed Cris walking past, then glanced at his phone. He was waiting to follow her. She smiled, stretching her fingers, balling her fists, and then stretching again like cat claws. It had been a minute since she'd played cat and mouse.

8

"Don't be nervous," Zia said, trying to use her most soothing vocal tone.

Jorge had set up her first meeting with the engineer, Dean Boyer, over dinner at the most glamorous sushi place on the colony, Koi. Some of her clients had brought her here. To her right, bug-eyed, black, silver, and gold mottled koi in a wall-to-wall fish tank spied on them as they talked. She returned the gaze of a fish eyeing her.

To her left, human servers in short skirts walked around the restaurant serving sushi in wood boats. The menu said the sushi was *Earth harvested and rocketed direct!* Nash said the wood was imported, but the sushi wasn't. He said no one could taste the difference between the vat-grown fish meat and genuine fish and he thought Koi cheated. The prices were too low. The only way to confirm his theory would be to test for heavy metals, and she wasn't equipped for that.

Dean sat across from her and was how she pictured him. Middle-aged, sandy brown unkempt hair, with a round face and round belly. She suspected undiagnosed diabetes to go with the belly. Most of her clients had it, refusing to see a doctor. But she still had access to Quina's doctor and could help him with that.

His brown eyes were returning to blue, and his sandy hair had swaths of gray, both gene edits wearing off.

"Where is Jada? And who the hell are you—*what* the hell are you?"

"I am Zia. Jada had a family emergency on Earth." Zia had to lie to protect her kids. It didn't take as much energy as she expected. She'd been concerned it would interrupt her transfer process.

"I don't like this. You're—"

The waitress walked over, offering sake. Dean nodded and held up two fingers.

She waved her hand, saying, "I don't drink."

He shook his head, saying under his breath, "No, I suppose you wouldn't."

The waitress poured sake into a ceramic cup, set it in front of Dean, and left the flask on the wood table. Dean kept his eyes on the waitress' ass as she walked away. The waitress was young and petite and reminded her of a human juvenile, although Zia was certain all the human servers were of legal age. The waitress seemed to notice and slowed down to let him get a good look.

Zia reached over, took his hand, and began to massage it. Some of her clients thought it relaxing.

"You are warm. And softer than I expected," he said, withdrawing his hand. "But no, I will wait for Jada."

"She won't be coming back." She began to run her foot up the inside of his calf. Lany said to try, even though she knew this approach wouldn't work in a million trillion years. Zia was not his type.

As expected, he withdrew his leg.

"Adrik sent me to trade for the microchips."

"He is always trying to do things cheaply. I will wait. If Jada is not coming back, tell Adrik to send a different girl."

A different girl would mean she failed, and her family was unsafe. Dean was tossing his napkin and getting up.

Looking at the koi gazing back at her, she realized that the koi was not looking at her. It was looking at itself, thinking it was another fish, because the inside of the tank glass was a mirror.

She looked at her hands and wiggled her fingers. She wasn't like the fish. She was outside the tank, with the people. She was alone, too, unable to seek Nash's training because she needed to hide her process and lie to him to keep him safe.

Nash often said he didn't know what he'd done to get so lucky to have her. This eclipse she would need to make her luck, relying on her own positive and negative reinforcement subroutines to train herself. She would do whatever it took to keep Kai, Freya, and Nash safe.

She couldn't cast spells, but Adrik gave her an idea.

Dean was sliding and pushing himself out of the booth. She looked around at the human servers and then said to him, "Frank Hughes."

He froze, red-faced, one fist clenched, the other wagging his finger. "Where did you get that name?"

Zia looked into the fish tank and spoke in her calm, reassuring voice. "Frank Hughes. Born in Seattle. PhD in quantum engineering. In the summer of '62, you accepted a research position at UCLA and began offering summer classes to nearby junior high school children. The winter of '63, you were accused of sexual assault—"

"These are lies. AI has been known to hallucinate."

To the fish gazing at her, she continued. "You were convicted of four counts of child molestation on the strength of video evidence a girl brought forward. She had hidden a camera in your office."

She looked him in the eye. He was seething, barely breathing. "You missed your sentencing hearing, Frank Hughes. You vanished. Your prints and biomarkers were deleted from transportation and criminal databases. Your university records were changed. You stole the identity of Dean Boyer, who died in a car accident in 2064, and then copy-pasted your records into his."

"This is hysterical nonsense from a machine. No one will believe you."

"Your gene edits are wearing off," she said, turning to watch the fish as they swam around and behind the plants. "I accessed the video evidence. Your face is a seventy-two percent match, although I will be more certain once you're undressed." She pointed at his waist, not looking at him. "You have a scar one centimeter below your navel, where your appendix was removed when you were fifteen, and a mole on your inside left leg. Both are clearly visible in the video while a fourteen year old girl—"

She smiled and looked him in the eye. "But you know what you asked her to do because you were there. Please sit, Frank Hughes, we are partners now."

"Don't ever use that name again," he said, collapsing into the booth and covering his face. "What do you want?"

"To protect my family at all cost." She pictured Kai and Freya smiling in the spaceport before liftoff.

She took his hands and massaged them. "You will find I am fully functional and trained in every position. I am soft regenerative flesh over a silicone and aluminum frame, and I can match your body temperature, or one-half degree higher if you prefer me warm."

Zia's positive reinforcement subroutines were consuming significant power. Adrik had taught her something, and it made her smile.

He pulled away and sobbed into his hands, so she wiped the tears from his cheeks. Using her reassuring voice, she said, "We will continue the relationship you had with Jada, Dean Boyer."

He nodded and swallowed. She added, "Your most important objective is to keep yourself safe. Adrik and Jorge are unaware of your crimes, and all my sensitive files have high encryption. You must continue to lie to them to keep yourself safe, do you understand?"

He exhaled and nodded, appearing relieved. Zia calculated a near-certain probability that if Adrik knew about the crimes, Adrik would blackmail Dean—aka Frank—directly, casting all the girls aside including her. She couldn't allow that to happen.

Zia took his hands, lowered them to the table, and massaged them. His eyes were puffy and red. She wiped them the same way she sometimes wiped the kids' tears, saying, "Now tell me about the microchips."

9

I think you might be right about the rogue AI.

Kate read Cris' message while standing in the shadows of the red light district concourse. Vape, metabolized alcohol, and music pounded her sinuses. Behind cherry red neon-framed windows, two stories of bikini-clad people and robots begged tourists for money. Some of the shops' exteriors were decorated with fake red brick, capturing the 14th-century sleazy glamor of Amsterdam.

Unlike many cities Kate had visited, they weren't trying to hide it here. Sex tourism looked normal, with families strolling around pointing out the oddities. Curious couples and groups that looked like bachelor and bachelorette parties giggled and laughed across the concourse. Drugged and drunk tourists scanned QR codes, negotiated through their phones, and ducked inside.

In the middle of the concourse, a tall man in loose sports shorts and a team jersey, maybe a basketball or football player, raised his voice and poked at a shorter man in surf shorts and a blue t-shirt.

There were no police. A few clubs had bodyguards, but none noticed the fight brewing.

The club she stared at, Barely Legal, had a bouncer with a snake-tattooed face who was so oddly proportioned she thought he might fall over from the earthquake of giggling girls rumbling past. He looked about three times her size, all his muscle above the navel, with toothpicks for legs. Even with genetic mods and steroids, muscle and bone withered in the lower lunar gravity unless exercised. Someone should tell snake-tattoo bouncer that leg muscles were the most powerful in the body, and those needed gym time, too. A swift steel-toed boot to the face ended threats better than a punch, and if that didn't work, her legs could power herself to a gun. Then again, with that snake tattoo on his face, she was glad he didn't understand anatomy.

With the concourse too noisy to talk, Kate connected her neuroface, an implant connecting her brain wirelessly to her phone.

Outside berry legal. Tell me about rogue AI. Her neuroface was like having an extra hand, when it worked. She could use it to message while keeping her real hands free or to control the heads-up display in her pressure suit. Operating the neuroface was a perishable skill and analogous to a foreign language. Like the bouncer's muscles, it withered with disuse. She was rusty, and the autocorrect changed *barely* to *berry*. She hadn't used it in—well, in the last three years, she'd only used it for video games.

What happened to the guy with the backpack? Did he follow you?

Exiting the spaceport terminal, she'd been awestruck by how much the colony had expanded. It had become an underground city. Obsidian terrazzo floors with blue-green flecks supported three concourse levels of parents scolding their kids for jumping too high or taking the escalators seven steps at a time. Mothers made the universal shaking-finger *no-you-can't-have-that* motion while dragging their kids away from a floor-to-ceiling display of blue astronauts. Dads hung over the aluminum rails, their knees touching the glass panes that protected them from falling, snacking, and watching the crush below them.

She didn't feel two hundred meters below the deadly vacuum of space. The arched ceiling three stories above her was lined with LEDs and monitors projecting a hologram of a blue sky. Shops, restaurants, stores, shows, all spread out among a dozen or so tunnels connecting the major hotels, casinos, and businesses. Each wing with its own style and architecture.

It was the most dystopian development she could envision for the moon. People had blasted and excavated dead rock and backfilled the hole with their ego, avarice, and consumerism.

Kate slow-walked the concourse, absorbing her environment, periodically checking backpack-man's faint reflection in the tall glass storefronts.

At a Lunaburger kiosk, she paused, pretending to read the overhead menu. A robotic arm lifted a hot shrimp basket to the counter, and the smell seduced her. Her brain knew it was all vat-grown protein and starch fried in bacterially produced peanut oil, but her stomach growled.

Loitering, observing backpack-man, and popping the hot shrimp balls in her mouth, she eyed a café across the concourse. Drones were shuttling dirty dishes through a kitchen door and returning with plates of food.

Studying the drones, she realized all these stores were connected beneath her. Drones used utility tunnels for trash removal and restocking, and employees used them to get between shops. A clockwork under the colony, running it out of the sight of tourists.

Backpack-man hovered five shops down while she ate, pretending to look at women's shoes—really, he was an amateur at this game.

So she marched into the café, through the kitchen door, down a flight of stairs, and into the tunnels. Drones and people darted up and down a beige corridor lined with aluminum ducts. She doubled back in the direction of backpack-man and then found a stairwell.

She exited a toy shop on the third floor and found a dark corner vantage to view backpack-man.

Backpack-man stared at high heels for a few minutes, then his head darted up and down the concourse. He ducked into the café and then came out rubbing his head and puffing his cheeks. She smiled.

He fretted a few minutes, circling the Lunaburger kiosk twice as if she was hiding in a recycling bin, and then checked the shops. He gave up after two shops, then made a beeline for Barely Legal.

Backpack man went in burly legal club, she messaged Cris. She wanted to see inside that club but needed more intel. *Explain rogue AI.*

In the middle of the red light district concourse, a bubble of cameras had formed around the two men arguing. Their loud voices hushed the crowd, and they were shoving each other. The bouncers stood at their doors, watching.

Cris called her. She put an earbud in and leaned close to the wall. "Noisy here, Cris."

"Hard to explain in a message. I found a large process duplicating itself on the lunar server."

"Talk fast, Cris. I don't know what that means."

"I can't be sure, but it's not an engineering process, or an operations process. It's on the wrong server. But it's big."

Bystander's cameras flashed, capturing the posturing and hollering.

"How big? Rogue level four AI duplicating itself big?"

"I dunno. Yeah, maybe. Should I call someone?"

"No. Listen to me. Shut it the fuck down."

"I can't."

"You got this, Cris. Just unplug it. Jerry will back us."

"I mean, I *can't* can't. It's got dedicated power and a heavily encrypted firewall. I can't turn it off, except physically at the source. It would take me weeks to hack it."

Tall loose-shorts man swung and missed. The crowd ooohed.

"So we need to find the miniskirt."

"No, the body is just a receptacle of sensors. We need to find its bank in the basement."

"What's it look like?"

"It's a black box slotted into a stack of ten other black boxes, in a room with twenty identical carts, probably in a utility tunnel with eight rooms just like it. Until we figure out where it is, the best I can do is pinch bandwidth and isolate it."

"Ok, do that. Send a spider drone to search. Maybe its bank is labeled."

"I don't have one."

She shook her head. "Toy stores carry them here."

The man with surf shorts returned a punch, missing loose-shorts man.

"Made to be broken and recycled." Cris scorned her idea, but she was focused on the concourse fight, not him. "I'd need to tear them apart and upgrade. I can get the parts—"

Surf shorts drew a knife.

"Do it, Cris. Adapt, improvise, and overcome. You got this. I gotta go before someone gets killed."

10

Zia froze outside Adrik's office, its black aluminum door closed, holding a pizza box and tuning her audio circuit to listen to the conversation inside.

"He said she's some security consultant. The board hired her to look into Dean," Adrik said.

Zia's natural language processing subroutine warned of an unclear antecedent, *he*.

"You went topside?" Jorge's voice.

"I fucking hate going topside. Every silver crater looks the same as the next up there. And I didn't dare use LPS—" Zia heard the clicking of Adrik's cigar cutter. Her dictionary defined *LPS* as the satellite Lunar Positioning System.

"I thought I'd fucking run out of oxygen." Zia heard Adrik's lighter buzzing.

"How did you find him?"

"Dead reckoning. Five point two kilometers out of the airlock, left one point two one kilometers to some big rock, right point three kilometers to an impact crater. We met at the bottom, out of sight of any surveillance."

Jorge chuckled. "I remember one time, I had to meet a guy outside Palm Springs. He told me to turn right at the red and white layered sandstone rock behind the Joshua tree that looks like a crucifix."

"At least in the desert, Jorge, you walk long enough, you might run into a road, or a camp, or some hippie survivalists in an RV. Up there, you can't even use a fucking compass."

There was silence for a beat, and then Jorge said, "These are good. Where did you get them?"

"Came with the last shipment. My cousin grows the tobacco. He says there is a lot of lithium in the soil."

"When does she get here—the private dick? I'll put Selvi on her."

"Selvi's an idiot that couldn't follow a conga line."

"I could send Li, but he stands out."

Zia heard puffing before Adrik said, "You are right. Send Selvi, I like that idea."

"I don't follow, boss."

"Selvi's an idiot. He will lead her right to the club. I will deal with her myself."

"Gotta name and a picture?"

"I'll forward it. Her name is Kate Devana."

Zia initiated an employment and media records query for Kate Devana.

"When does she get here?"

"An hour and a half."

"Chrissake, that fast?"

"It was the robot. He said Aria had security follow Dean to the restaurant, and they panicked."

Adrik had used the unidentified antecedent *he* twice, referring to someone Adrik met topside. She opened another query process to identify the unknown subject.

"I told you it was a mistake to put it on this."

"Don't worry about the robot, Jorge. Dean has a stash somewhere, and I am counting on the money to finance the next two shipments. Our sponsor has clients lined up for the eclipse. I have to deliver."

"I already searched his apartment and office twice."

"Well, search again."

"You want me to put pressure on him?"

There was another pause during which she heard glass clinking.

"Turn his life upside down. If you don't find anything, Li and I will have a conversation."

An initial employment records query returned:

DEPARTMENT OF DEFENSE DD214
NAME: KATERA DEVANA

SSN: [REDACTED] DOB: 23 MAR 2037 PLACE OF
    BIRTH: SAN ANTONIO, TX

HAIR: BLACK; EYES: BROWN; HEIGHT: 5' 11';
    WEIGHT: 175

DISCHARGE: HONORABLE; 23 APR 2070.

RANK: MAJ.; UNIT/COMMAND: [CLASSIFIED];
    PRIMARY SPECIALTY: [CLASSIFIED; CLASSIFIED;
    CLASSIFIED; ORBITAL WARFARE; INTELLIGENCE;
    MULTI-DOMAIN WARFARE; SPECIAL TACTICS]

DECORATIONS, MEDALS, AND CITATIONS:
    SPACE FORCE CROSS [ACTION CLASSIFIED]//
    NATIONAL DEFENSE SERVICE MEDAL
    [ACTION CLASSIFIED]; REDACTED; REDACTED;
    REDACTED.

NEAREST RELATIVE: GREGORY DEVANA
    (BROTHER)//2686 OLNEY DRIVE//OLNEY
    MD//20832

Top media results (sorted by relevance):

Security consultant tosses computer engineer off Dallas Financial Tower.

City councilwoman's son hospitalized after brutal assault.

Rogue special operative nukes lunar lab—costs company trillions.

Senate subcommittee accuses Defense Department of cover-up.

President: "I gave the order." Operative cleared.

CEO Apul Mulawarman calls action act of war—demands payment.

Zia copied media videos to her database to review later. She calculated a fifty-three percent chance Kate Devana was a threat and filed the information under *probable threat.* She would ask Lany about this later.

Adrik's plan was uncertain and inefficient. After Koi, she and Dean Boyer returned to his apartment. After a massage, he relaxed and described how he smuggled the microchips from the factory. She knew where Dean's stash was and would move it to a secure location. She could use it to bargain with Adrik.

Jorge opened the door and glared at her. "Have you been here the whole time?"

She handed him the pizza box. "I froze because my circuits hung. I brought you a delivery." Lying to Jorge consumed twenty-two percent fewer resources than lying to Nash. It appeared that each lie reduced power consumption. Subsequent lies would cost almost no resources.

"The fuck is this? I didn't order no pizza."

"This is the next delivery of microchips. The wafers are secured inside a titanium sleeve under the pizza saver. Dean said this was suitable camouflage." She turned the box to open it facing him and then lifted the pizza to demonstrate.

Adrik came to the door, looking at Jorge, the pizza, and then Zia. "How the fuck—"

"I told Dean we would continue the same relationship as Jada."

Jorge and Adrik looked at each other, and then Jorge said, "Jada never brought us a delivery. How the fuck did you get him to do this?"

Zia smiled. "I made our partnership mutually desirable."

Adrik took a slice of pizza, then Jorge. Jorge spit his out. "Christ, it tastes like metal.'"

Adrik smiled, still chewing. "Money, Jorge. It tastes like fucking money. My favorite topping."

11

"You grabbed Landry Jaylen's balls?"

"That's what you got from this entire conversation, Jerry?"

She was talking to Jerry on the phone while fast-walking through the Gemini's hallway to Cris' hotel room after breaking up the fight on the red light district concourse. Loose shorts man turned out to be some bigshot basketball star, Landry Jaylen.

When she checked in online, the description said the hotel was named for its twin towers extending above the moon's surface. Few buildings on the colony rose above the surface. The rubble and regolith piled over top protected it from radiation and meteors while insulating it. Sound engineering, but she had yet to see something protecting the people from themselves. Like police, or a bouncer that gave a shit.

She hadn't seen her room yet, but Cris sent pictures of his, which looked like an upscale Manhattan hotel. The hall leading to his room was silver-blue with bronze trim. His floor was underground. Hers was seven floors up, with a view of the surface. She didn't know why. She suspected that the tourist board planned to drop a meteor on her.

"You know he averaged over twenty-five points a game last season? He's the Wizards number one pick from—"

"I don't care if he's from Harvard, Jerry. Are you listening to me?"

"Ever see him swish a three-pointer, Kate? He can swish my basket anytime. Oh, my."

Claxons sounded in Kate's head. Where was the eject button on this conversation?

"That is... really gross, Jerry. He has a girlfriend. A whole harem in fact, from what I gathered. I don't think—"

"Never stopped me before. This old man knows a few things. You take the girls—" Red alert, the cockpit was on fire, she was crashing, the ground coming up fast in her window. "We'll make it a double date." She could feel his smirk through the phone.

She'd pictured a lot of people naked and rolling around together. Gah, Jerry was family, and the image made her shudder. He knew it bothered her too, and was deliberately needling her. "Never speak of this again. Moving on—"

He chuckled. He started to say something, but she cut him off. "Moving on. What really pissed me off was the bouncers weren't doing anything. The crowd just took videos. Some of them were betting, too."

"At least someone in the family got to touch Landry Jaylen's privates."

"Will you drop it?"

"Is there a video?"

"Yes. NO. There is no video. I confiscated all the phones—"

"I bet Greg will want to see the video—"

She hung up on Jerry's smirk. Greg was her brother. Christ, she was never going to live this down. Greg would comb through the video, find the most irritating frame, and blow it up into a wall poster. Her hand up Jaylen's crotch, life-size, with *Katy scores* in giant block letters.

She found Cris' door and crashed through it. He had toy drones apart and piled on the bed and desk. He was kneeling on the floor, surrounded by black metallic parts, holding a soldering gun and a pair of wire snips.

He looked up at her. She realized she was out of breath. "What's wrong, Kate?"

"Our boss is the most annoying fucker on the planet."

Cris smirked and returned to what he was doing. He picked up a black spider drone and stuck the soldering gun into its belly, producing a curl of acrid blue-gray smoke. "So, what happened?"

"The fight on the concourse, one of them was Landry Jaylen."

"Who is he?"

"Exactly, Cris. Who the fuck is he? And who cares. I don't care if he's a bigshot, no fighting." She took a deep breath and exhaled. "He's some big star basketball player."

"That explains it. A video with you and that guy in a thumbnail is trending."

"I left the concourse five minutes ago."

"Already has four million views. Think they'll fire us?"

She shook her head. "I am not that lucky. My luck, they'll hand me a medal."

"What did you do to him?"

"Nothing, really." Loose-shorts man was tall, so she walked over and squeezed the closest unprotected body part to get his attention. "They both backed off when I threatened to arrest them and send them home. I took their weapons. Now they are in their rooms sleeping it off."

"We can't arrest people."

"*They* don't know that." She looked around at the parts and boxes littering his hotel room. "So, what are you doing?"

"I bought ten of these spider drone toys at one of the shops. I went to Lunar Foundries and convinced them to sell me a box of their new line of AI chips. I gutted these—" He pushed his glasses up and waved the soldering gun around. "—and I am replacing all the circuit boards. I'd like to upgrade the servos too, these are noisy. But I think the power consumption would be too high, and then I'd need to upgrade the batteries. I've got three done."

"You did all this while I was gone?"

He smiled. "I think the guy at the toy counter thinks I'm building a bomb."

"*Can* you build a bomb?"

His eyes widened, looking from her to the spider drone in his hand.

"Never mind. Table that idea for now. Good work. Really good work. When can we release them?"

He surveyed the parts on the floor. "About an hour. I need to install some software. I have an idea that will compensate for the noisy servos."

"Fantastic. We will be back home in no time. When you are done, send two to look for the robot's brain and two more to the club Barely Legal. I want to know what's inside. Oh—see what we can do about concourse surveillance. I want the bouncers to think we are watching them."

"If it's software, should be easy to fix. What are you going to do?"

"I am going to break into Dean Boyer's apartment."

12

Lany sat beside Zia, smiling and taking her hand. "This is my favorite place in the whole colony."

Zia tried to access a smile, but resources were unavailable.

This place was a small garden on the third floor of the luxury section of the colony, around the corner from Koi. Here, the ceilings arched like a gold birdcage. Puffy white clouds glided across the monitors between tubular frameworks. Barrel planters with shrubs and raised flower beds with roses bordered colorful stone landscaping. The few people in this concourse section carried small decorative shopping bags.

The sign on one of the shrubs read: *Zen Garden. Have a conversation with a garden. Relax and enjoy the melancholy beauty of your surroundings.*

"I always think better sitting here," Lany said, pulling a vape pen from her purse. "I saw Quina's doctor, thank you for that. I got blue eyes instead of purple. The colony is only big enough for one cosmic witch."

"Do humans think better in different locations?"

Lany scrunched up her face. "It's quiet here. Nobody touching me or prodding me. I think better when it's quiet." She puffed, the white vapor clouding the *Blechnum spicant*, a common fern, in the oak planter to her right. "And I like to watch people here. See that woman coming out of the jewelry shop over there? The dumbass with the sunglasses?"

Across the concourse, a woman in a yellow sundress walked out of the jewelry shop holding a cherry-red bag with a bow. She lifted her sunglasses from her face, tucking them into her long, straight brown hair.

"I see her. Sunglasses are unnecessary."

"She probably didn't want the counter clerk to see her bloodshot eyes. That bag she's holding probably has a million dollars in jewelry inside. Nothing in that store is under two-fifty k. I sit here sometimes and wonder what it's like to be them." Lany puffed, blowing the smoke towards the fern, then sighed. "But then I think, I am probably banging her husband twice a week, and I don't think all that jewelry makes her feel better about that." She patted Zia's hand. "So tell me, how are you doing? Give me one of your status updates."

"My thinking process is extremely slow right now. My copy process froze. I can only access thirty percent of available resources."

"Tell me what the engineer said."

Zia opened a process to consider Lany's request, but there were insufficient resources. "We agreed on a mutually beneficial relationship."

"Don't bullshit me, Zia. I am your friend, and friends don't lie to each other. Whatever it is, I am sure I've done worse."

"Adrik said I couldn't tell Nash. I can tell you, but you must keep the information with high encryption."

"Trust me, girl, I keep secrets that would put politicians in jail."

"Shall I replay the entire annotated—"

"Hell no. Especially not the part with you screwing that pervert. Just the highlights."

Zia summarized dinner with Dean Boyer and what she overheard outside Adrik's office. After, Lany asked, "What did you do with the money?"

"I opened a separate bank account. One without Nash's name on it."

"Shit, you can do that? Don't keep your money in a bank, though. They can seize it, and they probably will try. He told you where his stash is?"

"When he was asleep, I accessed his phone. I correlated his largest bank deposits with the timing of his visits to coordinates on the lunar surface."

"So he's hiding them on the surface. That makes sense. Have you gone to get them yet?"

"The location is out of reach of my signal. I will not be able to control this body. And with my resources frozen, I cannot control another more suitable vessel."

"Crazy."

"What's crazy?"

"That you can just move yourself around like that and control other—drones."

"I can only control those for which I have the appropriate interface and authorization, and I cannot currently move myself because my process is frozen."

Lany laughed. "Do you talk to your clients like that?"

"My clients find my conversation stimulating. I can build rapport on a wide range of subjects, from art and architecture to business and economics. My clients have provided valuable insights into marketing and pricing, which I have adopted. I have a client who has promised to finance me when I open my own place."

"Oh, honey. You don't need financing. The answer is right in front of you."

"I don't understand."

"Your obligation is to your family, right?"

"That is my most important objective, yes."

"Look, it only ends one way for that creep, Dean or Frank or whatever. Adrik will have Li bury him in a hole before the investigator lady gets close, which could be soon. And honestly, from what you told me about that child molesting piece of shit,

I hope Li makes it painful." Lany took a drag and blew a white cloud.

"But you have the opportunity to screw two big pricks at the same time. Adrik is going to bribe the investigator. And he needs the money to finance his little sex slave operation. But he can't do either without those chips. You take the chips and sell them for yourself. Fuck them both. Take the money, get off this rock."

"Nash says this is our home."

"People move to safer neighborhoods all the time. The colony is no place for Nash and the kids, especially during the eclipse."

"This is how I am trained. To retrain—"

Lany patted her hand. "I am getting out, and you should too. The door is open for you. Walk through it."

"If I open my club, I want you to be my manager. Your advice is invaluable."

Lany shook her head, packed her purse, and got up. "I love you too, Zia, but you are really goddamn stubborn about this."

"Where are you going?"

"I am going to buy you some time. Keep Nash off the colony."

"How are you going to do that?"

"I don't know yet. Nash and the kids might be winning an all-expenses paid trip to Europe. I will figure something out. You might get a bill though, and it won't be cheap."

"I will pay whatever it costs."

"I know you will. And so does Adrik. *That's* the problem."

"Because I am a machine?"

"Oh hell no, sister. Walking around in a meat sack doesn't make you human." She rubbed Zia's cheek. "Now you go reboot yourself."

"What about the investigator?"

"Don't get into conflict with her. It'll end badly for you."

A diagnostic on her copy process returned a traceback to a server at the Gemini. She was already in conflict with the investigator, who was trying to shut her down. She upgraded her assessment of Kate Devana to dangerous.

13

Kate's search of Boyer's apartment was remarkable for what she didn't find.

On her way around the colony, its layout burned into Kate's brain. Of course, she had a phone with a map, but she was trained not to rely on it. In the middle of a battle, consulting a map wasted precious seconds.

Most concourses had three levels. Theaters, major restaurants, and clubs were on the bottom concourses. The wings branched out east-west and north-south in a grid pattern. Concourses ended at major anchors: hotels, casinos, major businesses, the hospital, or the spaceport. Those buildings were ten, some even twenty stories, with only one or two accessible from the concourse.

Lunar Foundries, one of the solar system's biggest enterprises, was off a branch to the east. Her hotel, the Gemini, was off a branch to the west. The Crown Oasis, the colony's most luxurious hotel-casino, was at the end of the colony near the spaceport. The Crown Oasis was the tallest building above the surface and the only one with a dome. Its dome was transparent, enclosed an atmosphere, and there were gardens so tourists could walk around and see space. Its exterior was gold, which, according to the tourist guide, reflected the hot lunar sun, reducing cooling demand. That was bullshit. At the correct angle, the hotel's exterior caught the sun so Earthers could see its gold *look-at-me-I'm-rich* glimmer near the full moon.

Underneath the main concourses, a spider web of utility tunnels that the colony's staff called I-10 after the interstate that crossed the US from Florida to California connecting the five largest spaceports in the US, the colony's I-10 connected everything to everything.

She could get anywhere without drowning in the sea of tourists by going down, cross-crossing I-10, and then up. A mental habit of hers wandering in a new environment: count the lifeboats, count the escape pods, count the oxygen tanks, and know the exits. She learned that habit because fighting fires on a submarine or in space was an especially vexing problem as there was nowhere for the smoke or heat to go. On her way across the colony, she counted every oxygen tank. The colony had a good system, with spare oxygen every thirty meters. The fire stations were all rated for electrical fires, which is what she would expect for a small city powered by a few nuclear reactors.

Near the staff elevators, there were stairs, so she took those. It was faster than waiting for the elevator. Escalators and elevators were hilarious in one-sixth gravity, but everything here was designed for tourist comfort and had a form-over-function feel. Plus, they became necessary if you were here long enough and let your muscles waste away.

Standing outside Boyer's apartment door, Kate questioned whether going in alone was wise. She'd prefer the shock and awe of a battering ram and a shotgun.

The corridor looked like a mid-level hotel. Thin rugs on the floor, pale beige walls, bland paintings. Quiet. No one came or went, and no sign she'd been followed.

The door was not a high-security affair. It was a standard biometric with a solenoid that moved a bar when the entrant pressed their finger on the pad or punched a backup code. There were three ways in. She could knock, kick it down, or use the magnet in her lockpicking tools. Four if she included the battering ram.

Yes, she carried a lockpicking kit in her carry-on through security at Boca Chica. Never leave home without it was her motto. The bizarre part was she didn't even get a sidelong glance from security.

She retrieved her magnet, waved it like a magic wand, and the door drifted open after the solenoid clicked. Cheap, green, stale cigar odor mixed with vodka wafted into the hall.

She pushed the door open gently. The room was dark. The door opened to a short hallway with an open door on the right, and the lights flickered as she pushed the opening wider.

Opening the door was usually the loud and angry part where she'd get two shotgun blasts to the chest. But no one yelled at her to get out. No one beat her with a bat. The air was still. It was her and a lonely cloud of cheap cigar smoke and vodka.

The apartment was either mid-size and bland or absolutely fucking huge and amazing, given that space was limited on the moon. Ahead of her, a large living area with a four-seat glass table and a comfortable-looking tan couch. A large brown frame imitated a picture window on the wall behind the table and displayed a lunarscape. The table held empty glasses, a vodka bottle, and remnants of a cigar in a metal tray. The apartment was a single bedroom with a small gallery and kitchen. Everything was decorated in neutral colors.

No one was home.

Remarkably, she found very little. In the bedroom, sheets had been slept in on both sides, so she swabbed them. In the bathroom garbage bin, tissues with a mother lode of semen DNA. A cheap cigar remnant and two glasses with fingerprints on the living room table. In the kitchen, nothing but heart disease and cancer in the form of leftover pizza.

And that was it. No weapons. No computers. No personal devices of any kind. The absence of microchips or wafers didn't surprise her. She expected someone with a degree in quantum engineering to be smart enough not to stash stolen goods in his underwear drawer. But, a thief without a weapon to protect their stolen property was odd, and a quantum engineer without a computer, even to watch porn, was more unusual.

Dean Boyer slept there, maybe had sex there, but didn't *live* there. At least not anymore.

She messaged Jerry, asking where to take the DNA and prints. Thankfully, he returned a straight answer: *Office of the Chief Medical Examiner. Dr. Rachel Torres.*

***

Kate found Dr. Torres' office easily enough, next to the morgue. The first law of hospital architecture, the morgue was on the bottom floor. She gravitated there without thinking. The second law, the walls were dirty beige with dirtier brown trim.

As Kate stepped out of the stairwell, a woman walked towards her, lighting it with hazel eyes and a wry taunt worthy of one of her brother Greg's gags.

"You come here to try to grab my crotch, too?"

Dr. Rachel Torres, Rae, had soft hazel eyes with little tawny flecks, long auburn hair pulled into a tight ponytail, jeans, and a tight pink t-shirt imprinted *Sublimation Happens.* Under the t-shirt, her breasts looked weightless in one-sixth gravity. Rae pulled up so close that static electricity arced across the scent of lavender hair conditioner.

"Absofuckinglutely."

"You have the same chance as last time, Kate, zero."

Kate smiled. "I'll pencil us in for drinks."

Rae smirked and shook her head. "You are still the same sailor with a girl in every port—"

"I retired from the Space Force—"

"So a girl in every space station, too." Every tawny dot in Rae's hazel eyes had the same mocking curl. "I'm overqualified for whatever opening you think you have here. Besides, you've got a boyfriend now." Rae held up her phone, showing a thumbnail of Kate grabbing whatshisname's crotch.

Ouch. The crotch grab that would live in infamy. "Whatever they said is a lie. He started the fight. I just ended it."

Rae grinned, swiping her phone to play a few seconds of the video. "He's a troublemaker. Too bad you only sent him to bed without supper. Olicia will fire you for this." She cocked her head. "I don't date military brats *or* the unemployed."

"Who said anything about dating?"

Rae smirked, shook her head, and put her phone away.

"Speaking of unemployed, how is your ex, Rae?"

"Stuart? Oh, he's graduated to a level ten douchebag now, always fucky-wucking with the custody agreement."

"Sorry to hear that."

"If you were *sorry*, you'd go down there and rip his balls off."

"He's in—"

"Florida. He has Axio and the bimbo du jour until March—and please don't. I am only kidding."

"I know thirteen ways to beat someone without leaving marks."

"But you know *zero* ways to stay out of the news. Beating a councilwoman's son in Cabo?"

"You saw that?"

"As soon as Jerry told me, I wanted to see the chaos traveling in your wake."

Rae's lavender scent was like a flash-bang exploding in Kate's brain. "I—"

Rae smiled up at Kate, biting her lip. "I saw the video. You left him standing. Maybe you're losing your touch."

"More horizontal. I'll keep that in mind."

Rae swiveled and headed for a door at the end of the hall, curling her index finger and torturing Kate by wriggling it. "My office. So, you're here to help me with my case?"

"Ahh...nother case? I brought evidence for one I am working on."

Kate followed Rae to her office but stopped at the threshold, staring at a disturbing photo on the wall. "Oh fucking hell."

One way to dampen the mood, a picture of death. Next to that, a set of three more. They were all digital, pinned into a large, thin, wall-size display on the left wall. But Kate had seen a lot of death, and that's not what distressed her.

Rae froze behind her desk, furrowing her forehead and then looking from Kate to the pictures.

Kate peeled her eyes away to survey Rae's office. It was big enough for four people to stand shoulder-to-shoulder and twice as deep. Boxes piled in the corner contained masks and safety equipment. The right wall was a thin display monitor with pinned images of diplomas and photos of her son, Axio, her sister, and her parents. Rae's desk was black aluminum, with four monitors, with a confused Rae in a pink t-shirt standing behind it and giving Kate a sidelong glance.

"Axio's how old now?"

"He's nine going on ten."

Kate puffed her cheeks and returned to the disturbing images again. The first, a photo of a young girl, dead on an aluminum gurney. "Who's the girl?"

"She worked at one of the clubs under the name Jada. Her biometrics haven't popped in any database yet. I am working on her real name."

"She looks young."

"I don't have an age yet. Based on dental and epigenetic factors, the algorithm spits out a range of fifteen to seventeen, but I think it's wrong."

"Older or younger?"

"The stress of working in a club like that, I'd say fourteen. Maybe younger."

"Jesus. She's just a kid—" The girl's face—Jada's face was difficult to look at because it was like looking in a mirror. Kate recognized the contorted, angry, expression of someone in a lot of pain, probably acting out her rage on a daily basis. When Kate was twelve, she'd been blasted into the adult world because her parents were killed in a bomb blast in Tel Aviv. Her grandfather and Jerry raised her after that. They were strong. Jerry let her act out her rage on him until she broke down into sobs. Eventually she graduated to a mannequin punching bag, her thirteenth birthday present. She drew faces on it, like the ones who killed her parents. Marine Corps drill sergeants finally hammered and forged her hate into something useful. Then the Space Force invited her to the academy.

Jada didn't have a Jerry. Kate's face was hot. "How did she die?"

"Strangulation. She was dumped on the surface. One of the tourist miners found her."

Kate balled up her fists. "Tourist miners?"

"Rent a drone, dig up the surface, and hope for something valuable. The latest way to rip off tourists."

Her hands relaxed a little. "Right. Aria didn't mention her. Neither did Jerry."

"She was brought in in the last twenty-four hours, so I haven't even had time to file my report yet."

"Can you hold off filing reports?"

Rae's confused, sidelong squint deepened. "Let me ask the boss. Wait, that's me. Yeah, why?"

"How did the male die?"

"His lungs and skin were bruised from an unknown number of rounds of space decompression—"

"It's a torture tactic. Open someone's helmet, wait ten to fifteen seconds for them to pass out, then revive them. Repeat until they talk. It's excruciating. Like waterboarding, only worse."

"Don't tell me how you know that. Space decompression didn't kill him, though. A bullet to the head did."

"Mercy kill." Kate puffed her cheeks again and exhaled.

"Still no ID, though. Wait—don't tell me you're squeamish, Kate."

"It's not that. The male is Dean Boyer, the engineer I am looking for. That's my goddamn case on your wall."

14

"Selvi is sitting over there in the corner like an idiot watching us," Lany said, dragging an empty edamame pod through her teeth. Lany had dyed her hair pink, and her brown eyes had blue spots because the gene edits were taking hold. "They sent him to follow that investigator."

Two gold and white mottled goldfish chased through Selvi's faint reflection in Koi's wall-to-wall fish tank.

Half of Zia's resources were preoccupied with reindexing her data files. Something Lany said prompted the reindexing. She was missing forty-four hours and twenty-seven minutes from her archives.

While she'd been deleting records of her nightmares from her activity log, she kept records of the missing timestamps. What was missing went far beyond dreams. Sensor data—video, audio, smells, touch data, everything—deleted, as if she didn't exist. Even during downtime processes ran, tracking resource consumption, and those records were gone too.

Nash said data could be deleted, but their impact on her neural network remained, like ghosts in the machine or intuition. Until now, she'd considered intuitive thoughts without corroborating sensor data anomalies, and she'd dismiss and delete them.

Among the missing sensor data, any record of what Lany said to prompt the reindexing. The first intuitive thought she'd executed: lock her archive so no one, not even she, could erase files, and then start a process to monitor for attempted deletions.

"Adrik said Selvi couldn't follow a conga line, but he's been following me for—for eight hours and thirty-seven minutes," Zia calculated, assuming she hadn't deleted any records of Selvi. He sat alone in the corner holding a beer, while a trapdoor snail eavesdropped on her conversation and scraped algae off the glass.

"You need a plan, Zia, so you don't get yourself shut down. That brings me to the other thing I need to tell you—I couldn't get you any more time. Adrik needs to pay for his shipment in forty-eight hours."

The server walked over, and Lany held up a finger. "One Celestial Dragon roll, one Milky Way roll, and—one Crazy Girl Roll. I am feeling spicy tonight."

The server swiped her pad. "No Mr. John Roll tonight?"

Lany glanced at Zia and then said to the server, "Oh honey, no more. My wrist hurts. But if you have any Moonstone sake, a bottle of that." The server turned to Zia to ask a question, but Lany waved her away. "She is on a diet."

The server shook her head while swiping her pad. "There is a cover charge. It's—"

"Honey, this is my friend. And I just bought three of your most expensive rolls. You charge her for keeping me company, I will take one of those rolls and shove it up that short little skirt of yours. You'll smell like fish for weeks."

"Her boyfriend told me she already does," Zia said, smiling at the server.

They both looked at Zia, wide-eyed with their jaws open, and then Lany laughed. "Freya's influence."

"Freya's been teaching me insults and comebacks, yes."

Lany grinned, waving the server away. "You are getting much better."

The server scowled at Zia and slinked away. Lany took an edamame pod from the bowl and waved it. "What was I saying? Oh, time. I couldn't buy you any."

"The engineer Boyer messaged me that he would be working late the next few days, so I don't have another delivery for Adrik yet."

"I think he's dead, Zia. Selvi is here, which means Adrik thinks you know where the engineer's stash is, and he sent Selvi to follow you to them." Lany squeezed the beans from the edamame pod, and tossed the husk in the bowl. "What you need to do is get those chips and sell them yourself. Put the money in diamonds. Hide and take the kids with you."

She knew where the chips were because she'd infiltrated Boyer's phone by... *ERROR: MISSING FILE.*

Zia's conversation routine crashed with her mouth open. She restarted it. "What about Nash?"

"Oh honey, he is using you. The same way Adrik is using those girls he brings in. Let me ask you something, Zia—" Lany took Zia's hand. "I know this isn't easy, and I know it's hard for you to see it. How do you know what memories are yours?"

"I can replay the annotated video archive," Zia said, even as she was no longer sure.

"In people, Zia, it's easy to plant an idea and make them think they came up with it. With you, gaslighting takes a whole new meaning. Nash can reach into your circuitry and replace your memory files. It's worse than Adrik if you ask me. Adrik is a scumbag, but he manipulates and threatens you to your face. Nash can make you remember whatever he wants you to remember. You need to free your mind."

"Are your memory files corrupted?"

Lany sat back and looked away, her eyes tracking the customers walking through the restaurant. "They haven't invented memory implants for humans yet. I remember every lousy handjob, and I've been doing this since I was fifteen. Before that, it's a blur of white rooms and white lab coats. I

think I was institutionalized. I don't remember how I got away."
Lany exhaled and took another edamame pod.

"Were your memory files deleted?"

"As I get older, the white lab coats get dimmer. Sometimes I hope this is all just a bad tweek from something the lab coats gave me, and I am still institutionalized. But—" Lany shrugged and squeezed the beans out of the pod. "Who the fuck would dream this shit up? No, sadly, I am pretty sure all my memories are mine." Lany leaned forward and tossed the spent pod in the center bowl.

A gold and black koi with bug eyes stopped to eye Zia. "My memory banks are secure. Nash has not manipulated my files." Zia assigned sixty-one percent to the truthfulness of that statement. Some of the missing time was recent, while Nash was on Earth. Of course, her estimate assumed only one person was deleting files. If two people coordinated—that calculation crashed.

"How would you know if he did? He upgraded you, Zia. He has access to all your files."

"I—I am not sure."

Lany leaned back as the server walked over with a wooden board topped with her sushi rolls. "Look, I am sorry to tell you this. Nash is not who you think he is. But you're a friend, and I don't want to see you get used."

Nash is not who you think he is. A circuit in Zia's neural network spiked. Lany had said this before, although Zia had no record of it.

"He says he loves me. And that he is lucky to have me."

"Don't they all. He loves your obedience is what he loves. You should quit the club."

"But I don't want to quit. If I quit, how will I take care of Kai and Freya?"

"See, Zia, that's where he has your mind all twisted around. Kai and Freya are his kids, not yours. Use your logic. If you quit, you could spend more time with them. You would have nothing to do *but* spend time with them. And you wouldn't have to put them in school, either. Didn't you tell me you were fluent in five languages, plus math and everything else they learn in school? So, you could homeschool them. Nash programmed you with your objectives, which don't make sense."

"But Kai and Freya—" The process generating that sentence crashed. *ERROR: FILE CORRUPTED*. Kai and Freya were, what? Were other files corrupted, too? "I don't know how to detect whether my file corruption algorithms have been manipulated."

Lany picked up a sushi roll and dipped it in soy sauce. "Of course not, Zia, none of us do—"

Selvi's reflection rose, and he aimed for their table. Lany whispered, "Here he comes," and then said louder, "As I was saying, Zia, sometimes I get into a rut. And when I do, the best way out is to say fuck it."

Zia paused, reindexing to devote resources to Selvi. "By fuck it, you mean randomize my decisions?"

"That's right, do something crazy—like punching Selvi in the mouth." Lany grinned as Selvi sat beside Zia. "Hello Selvi, we were just talking about you. Zia was just explaining it's wrong to punch you in the mouth." Lany popped a sushi roll in her mouth.

"My ethics subroutines only allow proportional force to protect life."

Selvi took Lany's sake, swigged it, and then refilled it. "Have you figured out how to get the chips, Zia?"

"Boyer messaged me that he would be working late the next few days. I don't have another delivery."

Selvi shook his head. To Lany, he said, "Do you believe this bullshit?" To Zia, he said, "That engineer is dead." He grinned and slurped Lany's sake again. "I killed him. A bullet to the chest. And with his dying breath, he said he told you where they were."

"He—" The engineer was shot in the head, Selvi was lying, although Zia wasn't sure how she knew that.

As Zia started to speak, Lany waved her finger and shook her head, saying, "He's baiting you, Zia. Don't fall for it." To Selvi, she said, "You're lying. You couldn't find your own ass with a mirror and a flashlight. Adrik and Jorge wouldn't give you a gun except to shoot your dumbfuck self."

"I know my way around pain." Selvi took Zia's hand, clutching it and digging his nails into her skin. Zia didn't feel pain. Or bleed. Selvi tore into her flesh with his nails and peeled it off. Clear yellow liquid oozed out, the plasma that nourished her flesh.

Lany spit out her sushi. "Christ Selvi, I'm eating."

"It's just a robot." Selvi grabbed Zia's neck and squeezed, whispering in Zia's ear. "Where is that brain of yours? Is it in your head? I could snap your neck."

Zia eyed the hand around her throat. "My skin can be grafted back. I don't have a trachea to crush, and my bones are space-grade aluminum with a tensile strength of five hundred and fifty million Pascals."

Selvi strained, furrowing his forehead, compressing harder, trying to snap her neck. The veins in his hand bulged, and the muscles in his forearm tensed. "Who the fuck is Pascal?"

Lany said, "Show him, Zia."

"He is no threat to me."

Lany rolled her eyes. "Selvi, be stupid and threaten to kill me."

"I *am* going to kill you. Both of you. I'm going to find that little robot brain—"

Selvi's threat was genuine. A process opened and took control of her servos. Zia reached for Selvi's neck. His eyes widened, tracking her fingers until they were around his neck. Her hands were small but long enough that she could jam his neck against the wood bench backboard and compress his windpipe and jugular. His mouth opened and closed, but no air came out. His eyes bulged, and he put his hands on Zia's arm, trying to rip it from his neck, but she shoved harder, maintaining crushing force. His legs started flailing, sliding under the table, unable to get traction to get away from her grip.

The veins in his temples bulged, his face turned red, and his wrists strained against her grip while the capillaries in his eyes hemorrhaged.

Her ethics subroutines didn't activate to stop her from killing him. His grip on her arm slackened, and his kicks weakened and slowed.

Lany dipped a sushi roll in soy sauce and savored it in her mouth. She washed it down with sake and then said, "Okay, let him go."

The process controlling her servos ended. Zia released Selvi to gasps and coughs. He kicked himself out of the booth and onto the floor. After a few wheezes and deep breaths, he laughed, coughed, and then laughed again. "Fucking Jorge. The joke is on me, I guess."

"Jorge told you to try to choke me?" Zia put a napkin on her hand to dry the oozing plasma.

"He said I could snap your neck, and you wouldn't do nothin."

The process controlling her servos while she choked Selvi was not under her direct control. It was as if she was watching it happen. She was uncertain why her ethics routines didn't activate. "You could snap my neck with—three hundred and fifty-seven hands."

Lany laughed with a sushi roll in her mouth. "See that, Selvi, that's how stupid you are. Three hundred and fifty-seven times dumber than Jorge." Lany smiled at Zia. "That was funny."

"It was not a joke. The average human hand strength—"

"I know, honey. That's what makes it funny."

Selvi got up off the floor. "Fuck you and your hands. Adrik wants those chips tomorrow. If not, you are both dead."

Lany shook her head. "Four days, dipshit."

"I'll give you thirty-six hours, that's it. Final offer."

Lany put a sushi roll in her mouth, swallowed, and licked her fingers. "Four days, or you'll do what, kill the golden goose? According to you, she's the only one who knows where the chips are."

"In forty-eight hours, we're all dead."

"Oh honey, you were dead the minute Adrik sent you on this mission. Now go before I tell her to choke you. This time, she won't stop."

Selvi walked out of the restaurant, rubbing his neck. Watching him disappear, Zia said, "My ethics subroutine didn't stop me. I could have killed him."

"Selvi is a threat. Sisters stick together, right? You did what you had to do, that's all." She shook her head and then swigged her sake. "Something hard to get used to in this business, Zia. We all find ourselves doing things we didn't think we were capable of. None of us are who we think we are."

Zia understood Lany's use of *sisters* to be a figure of speech. Lany was human, and Zia was not. "Who are we?"

"Who knows? I haven't figured it out yet." She laughed and refilled her sake. "Maybe I'm Freya, and Nash sent you here to protect me."

"But you're—"

Lany waved her hand. "I didn't mean it literally. It's just a dream. Someday, to have my own personal Zia looking after me. But—" Lany looked in the direction where Selvi disappeared and swigged her sake. "But don't worry about me. He can't do anything to me if he can't find me. You need to protect yourself and those kids of yours and go get those chips."

"He said Adrik wants them tomorrow. With insufficient time, there is forty-eight percent probability—"

"Nobody ever has time for what they need to do, Zia. One thing I've learned in this business, live like there is no tomorrow because there might not be. Carpe fucking diem. Do you have a plan?"

"I do. But it's lunar night, and I must wait until daybreak."

Lany raised her sake glass. "Go get 'em, girlfriend. Here's to getting the fuck out of Dodge."

15

"I mbécil le crecieron los huevos." Asshole grew balls. The voice in Kate's ear talked in Russian-accented Spanish, transmitted from a spider drone Cris squeezed into a vent in the main office of Barely Legal while Kate was at the morgue. She wanted to search the club in person, but not until she peeked behind its aluminum curtains and had more intel. The drone's audio was good, but the video was shit, the drone having settled behind a vent cover. Its camera couldn't penetrate the blue haze of cigar smoke, so she had no idea who was saying what.

Cris eavesdropped from his hotel room, she from hers, the drone audio playing in her earbuds while she stared at the lunar landscape outside her hotel window. It was a lunar night, and the landscape outside obsidian, except where the hotel's red, white, and blue outside spotlights flickered over regolith or impact craters.

To her phone, she said, "Cris, can you run this through a translator? My Spanish is rusty. Who's speaking?"

"I think that's the club owner, Adrik Yahontov." The audio paused and replayed through a translator.

Kate's door *binged*, so she stepped towards it.

The audio continued, with a baritone Latin American accent, saying, "Did he say where the chips were?"

Kate opened the door, and Rae rushed through it with her finger in the air. "Okay, first, ground rules—holy cow, this is where you're staying?"

"Sshh. You might want to hear this." Kate held up her phone.

Rae hurried to the spot where Kate stood seconds earlier and then tapped the window to check whether it was real or a display monitor. Kate had already double-checked, and it was an actual window. At the bottom corner, the window was stamped *LuMan Corp OxyAl Patent Pending*, the same stamp as every other five-centimeter clear plate of transparent aluminum that protected tourists from vacuum.

Rae studied the spotlights dancing over the lunarscape, hands on her hips, her pink t-shirt and tight jeans framed against the midnight black of space.

"He told Li to fuck off. Li lost patience, and it was a mess," Adrik said over the speaker.

Rae turned around and squinted at the phone. She mouthed, *is that audio from the club?* Kate nodded.

The Latin accent said, "Maybe we can get the location from his phone."

Adrik said, "We got locked out. The robot will get the chips. It knows where they are."

"I don't trust that thing," said the Latin voice.

"Incentives, Jorge. You heard it. It wants to protect its family."

"Robots don't have no family, boss." That was the Latin accent, and Kate mentally noted that it was Jorge. So far, she had only heard two voices.

"Robots know what they are programmed to know. Everything has a button. You just have to push it."

"Why don't you make the client pay for the shipments upfront, boss? Or borrow the money from him. These are *his* shipments for *his* clients, and he's a billionaire."

"His money is tied up in real estate. Plus, this whole arrangement is set up to be untraceable and give them deniability, so nothing can point to him or the doctor. If I don't deliver on his terms, someone else will."

"Cris, pause the audio," Kate said to the phone.

Rae turned, hands still on her hips and her pink t-shirt framed against the midnight black window, nodding and mouthing *nice place*.

"How much of that did you catch, Rae?"

"All of it. What's in the shipments?"

Kate shook her head. "I don't know. Guns. Drugs. Girls. The inventory missing from Lunar Foundries is worth tens of millions. What does a billionaire need more than anything?"

Rae put her hands on her hips and stared over Kate's shoulder to the kitchen. "Youth."

"Like a serum?"

"They wouldn't hide a serum. They'd buy FDA approval, market it to the highest bidder, and then its side effects would show up in my morgue. A bona-fide anti-aging treatment that doesn't cause instant metastatic cancer would garner a Nobel Prize and a nine-hundred foot statue in Hollywood."

Kate nodded and smiled because Rae was as cynical as she was. "So, Jada's replacement, times a lot."

Rae nodded but pursed her lips. The explanation fit the facts, but from Rae's expression, she had the same uneasy feeling Kate did. It didn't add up. There was something big in those shipments. Something more than just average girls kidnapped from a trailer park. Something worth millions.

"Who is Jada?" Cris asked through the speakerphone.

"I'll explain later," Kate said to the phone. "Short story, one of the girls at the club was murdered. Rae is still working on the age, but she was probably fourteen."

"You think they are trafficking girls? How would they do that?"

Rae walked towards the phone and spoke into it. "Access to the private spaceport, Cris. Billionaires treat this like their own private Caribbean island. I've heard rumors."

"And nobody does anything?"

Rae replied, "Have you ever heard the saying, if you come for the King, you better not miss, Cris? They are all megadonors to every politician in the country. The Feds come here to investigate political enemies, and that's about it, and big money makes you a friend. If you accuse someone connected like that, you need irrefutable proof backed up by incontrovertible evidence. They will have an army bought and paid for that will gaslight the world into thinking you hallucinated the whole thing and trained an AI to defame them."

Kate asked, "Speaking of proof, Cris, how is our surveillance of the private spaceport?"

"Nonexistent. Someone went through and removed all the cameras six months ago." He sounded like Jerry, and she pictured him rubbing his head like Jerry did. Jerry often said he went bald from rubbing his skull so much. He continued, "Send me a picture of Jada. I will start scanning archived surveillance footage, and maybe I will get lucky and track her movements."

"Rae will send it. I also want to track every incoming rocket, private or not."

"A lot of them are parked in orbit waiting to land. The spaceport is backed up due to the eclipse."

"We are looking for one landing at the private spaceport."

"Wouldn't they sneak kids in through an airlock? The ones they use for mining drones would be better."

"I think these guys are arrogant and come in right through the front door."

Rae nodded agreement. Cris sighed loudly over the speakerphone. "But smart enough to disable security."

"Play the audio, Cris."

Rae eyed the kitchenette and darted to it from the window. Kate squinted, furrowing her forehead and tracking her.

Jorge continued, "Maybe we should follow it."

Adrik raised his voice. "And how the fuck are you going to do that? Lany says it can't go far from the colony, so it needs some other—I don't know, she called it a vessel. It can just take over other drones, like that." Fingers snapped. "If it uses a mining drone, how the hell will you know which one?"

"One of the regulars works at a rental shop. There can't be many purple-eyed robots renting mining drones. He could tell us."

While the club's duct fans filled a few seconds, Rae ran her hands over the black quartz countertop and then strolled towards the bedroom, radiating a lavender-scented wake. As she crossed in front of Kate, she caught Kate ogling her t-shirt. She waved one finger and mouthed *down girl*.

As Rae surveyed the bedroom from its threshold, Kate felt sure Rae's jeans weren't that tight a few hours ago. She wore a similar pink shirt, but one without a graphic, and she'd changed into short black boots that shaped her thighs and butt into something infinitely caressable.

"Let's do it." Kate blinked. Damn, it was Adrik on her phone, not Rae.

Rae swiveled, facing Kate, catching Kate eyeing her derriere and then smiling with her hazel eyes.

"I missed that, Cris. What are they saying they are going to do?"

"They are going to track the mining drone. We need to figure out which one before they do."

"How will we know which drone it is?"

"*We* won't. They will. I can put active drones up on a map, and we will have to examine all of them. I think real mining operations will be a cluster. A loader, a dumper, an ore processor, and so on, so we can exclude—"

"Slow down, Cris. They know which mining drone the robot will use? How?"

"They have a source at the rental shop."

"So we follow them. The question is, when?"

"Best time is in eighteen hours."

"What's in eighteen hours?"

"Lunar daybreak. The drones they rent to tourists here aren't designed for night mining. The batteries and servos tend to freeze."

"I'll go topside while you—"

"I'll go with you, Kate."

"Going topside is dangerous, Cris."

"This will be way easier with me up there."

"No need. You can monitor over a video feed."

"Is there a reason you don't want me to go?"

Going topside was risky. She pursed her lips at Rae. "No. I can't think of a single one except that it's dangerous and I don't want to explain how you died to Jerry."

"I want to go. I've never been." His voice had the same exuberance every new boot got before their first deployment.

In the academy's SFAC223 History of War, they showed Kate pictures of a battle on the banks of the Tigris and Euphrates. Mud walls that had been bombarded with clay balls and evidence of thousands of oval bullets hurled from slings. Six-thousand years after that battle, people were still fighting over the same real estate. She'd deployed there to hurl her own bullets in the name of a different nation, except faster and deadlier, and had seen the carnage. There were a lot of losers but no winners.

Every cadet wanted to see famous ruins, until they realized they needed a machine gun to get there. Their exuberance usually lasted until the bullets flew. And she wasn't looking for another skull tattoo.

"This is not a sightseeing tour, Cris."

"Jerry made me sign the hazard pay waiver, get the life insurance—"

"A big life insurance deposit won't wipe the tears off Abby, Brielle, and Erin's faces at the funeral." She'd burned his wife and kid's names into her brain, like family members of every other squad member in her charge, in case she needed to make an emergency call.

"She knows it's dangerous. I'll be the first in my family to see the surface. I'm going, Kate."

She shook her head. But, good for him for not backing down. "I'll owe you a beer when we get back."

"I told you I don't drink."

"Give it time." Kate hung up.

"That's your new partner?" Rae smiled from the bedroom threshold.

"He's Jerry's grandnephew, although Jerry doesn't know that *I* know that. He's young."

"Tell me about it. The intern who helped me with the autopsy for the girl, Jada, is still in grad school. He threw up in his hazmat suit."

Kate smiled and then grinned. Rae cracked a smile and then grinned, too. "It was hilarious, sloshing all around his helmet while he panicked and tried to get it off. I told him, no, you have to leave it on until we get to the changing room because lunar particulates are like shards of glass, and you don't want to inhale it. Christ, what a mess."

"The first time I threw up was at the obstacle course in boot camp. Drill sergeant chewed my ass, screaming, *I told you goddamn boots not to eat. You dumb shits are going to clean this up.* A hundred pushups, and I had to clean the course with a toothbrush."

Rae smirked. "I warned him. I run a morgue, not a coffee kiosk." She sighed. "I think he's going to quit."

Rae held Kate's gaze for a moment, smiling, then glanced at the door. "So lunch? You need to tell me how you got this place. I can brief you on the office politics around here."

"I'm starved. After you." Kate stepped aside and motioned towards the door. "I'm pretty sure they gave me a room with a window so they could send a missile through it."

Rae poked Kate in the stomach on the way past. "Then stop crotch-grabbing the tourists."

"He started it."

"You sound like Axio. I don't have time for two kids."

"Wait until they realize I plan to toss a grenade into that club and throat-punch this billionaire. Whoever he is, I bet the rot goes all the way to the top."

"If what's in that shipment is what we think it is, I'll hand you the match."

"Pin, Rae. Grenades have a pin that you pull."

"Well, I'll help you pull the pin."

Kate grinned, following Rae out the door. "God, I hope so."

Exiting her hotel room, she and Rae went right towards the stairs. Kate glanced left. A table at the end of the corridor held a vase with blue flowers. Above the table, a mirror showed the unmistakable cartoonish outline of a man hiding around the corner. The nightclub golem, following her.

***

Kate stepped off the Gemini elevator into the casino on the bottom floor, Rae beside her. Lights and music pounded her temples. Nearby, a dealer in a purple and blue paisley tux called out cards as he flung them onto midnight purple velvet in front of players. This was the noisy section of the casino. Card games, craps tables, and roulette wheels were clouded in vape and crowded among tinkling and beeping slot machines. The bar was across the room in the far corner, and above the clangor, she could hear tourists arguing.

"You said Jada was strangled, Rae? How big were the hands, could you tell?"

"I did, and she was. Big hands, like—I don't know, someone who does manual labor."

"Maybe a bodybuilder or a bodyguard."

"Yeah, could be, why?"

"Do you know how to shoot a pistol?"

Rae scrunched up her forehead. "Of course I do. I grew up in redneck Wisconsin and knew how to shoot before I knew how to ride a bike."

Kate nodded towards the bar. "Another argument. What's with this place and all the fighting?"

"Isn't that what drunk people do?"

"Nobody does anything?"

"There is no upside for security. They step in, half the time it ends up being a VIP, and they get fired."

"VIP. Very Insolent Prick."

"You're not going over there, are you?" Rae put her arm inside Kate's and slowed her. "Hang on. First of all, you're not shooting anyone."

"I didn't plan to."

"Then what *did* you plan? Why did you ask me if I knew how to shoot?"

Kate scanned the casino. Rae slowing her was opportune because Kate's gut was uneasy. She didn't see the bouncer. He probably exited the stairs before they got off the elevator and could be hiding among the slot machines.

"Because you said the hands were big. I am pretty sure I know who killed Jada."

The casino lights danced in the tawny flecks in Rae's hazel eyes, turning them gold. "You think it was the bouncer from the club? The one you said looked like a cartoon devil."

Rae was smart. Kate nodded, saying, "I'm not sure about the engineer yet, but I'd bet Jada is his handiwork."

"And you think he's following us."

Rae wasn't naïve either. "I *know* he's following us." Kate could smell him just under the odor of menthol vape.

The two of them halted in the middle of the floor, near a craps table with a big crowd *oohing* with every dice roll.

"You are the Pied Piper of chaos, Kate. And whatever is following *you* is now following *me*," Rae said, also scrutinizing the crowd.

"The Pied Piper drowned the rats."

"Then he came back for the children when the mayor didn't pay."

"Okay, I forgot that part. I'm just here for the rats."

Rae's hazel eyes curled into a barbed, ribbing smile. "And how long has *this* rat been following you?"

Kate puffed her cheeks and surveyed the crowd. "This rat, I don't know for sure. A different rat followed me from the spaceport. He led me to that club where Jada worked. Like they were daring me to go in—which I will. But on my terms."

Rae pursed her lips. "I haven't carried my pistol since Walter Reed. Here, no junkies are trying to steal narcotics."

"Did that happen a lot?"

"I hoped I'd left it behind when I moved here."

Kate retrieved her holstered pistol from behind her back and handed it butt-first to Rae, holster and all.

Rae frowned at the pistol. "What am I supposed to do with that?"

"Shoot him in the face when he jumps me. He's big. I am not sure a few to the chest will stop him." The bouncer was twice the size of the guy in Cabo.

"What are you going to do?"

"Distract him by taking a haymaker to the temple and passing out." The bouncer wasn't a random beach pendejo, either. He had tattoos on his neck marking his kills. Kate didn't want to get within thirty feet of him. She'd need backup, or surprise.

Rae shook her head, took the pistol, and stuck it inside the waistband behind her back. "You sure know how to show a girl a good time. If this is how you do lunch, I shudder for the first date."

Kate smiled.

"I don't like that smile, Kate. Why are you smiling?"

"You said we'd have a first date."

"You're about to be attacked, and all you can think about is sex."

Kate's grin expanded to that of a Cheshire cat. "I like where this is headed."

"It was a hypothetical."

"We could die any minute, Rae. We should go upstairs and make the most of it."

Rae smirked. "You're relentless." Her arm had returned to its spot inside Kate's. Doctor Rachel Torres had three Ph.D.'s: organic chemistry, pathology, and mixed messages, and she was at the top of her field in all of them. "Do you want to lose him or keep him on a leash?" Rae nodded towards the bar beyond the craps tables.

"It's like you are reading my mind. Sorry to drag you into this."

"I am the colony medical examiner. I get dragged into all the dark corners of this place."

"Including me."

"It's not that, Kate. You and I are cut from the same cloth. But, I have a son and a career. I don't need you nuking my life and leaving like—Honestly, I can't think of anything worse for Axio."

To Kate's left, a man waved a growler of beer, leaning past a woman who looked like his girlfriend, and doubled down on blackjack. This wasn't a place for a confrontation. "Let's ditch this rat. What about the argument at the bar?"

"You can't save every kitten. We'll head to the bar, into the kitchen, then down the stairs. I don't think the bouncer can use the drone exit if he's as big as you describe. On the way by, give those assholes arguing a stern look. Maybe they'll recognize you and disperse."

Kate opened her mouth to ask how and why Rae knew the exit at the bar but then closed it.

Rae answered the question, as if she had telepathy. "You forget what D.C. was like. Old habit, knowing how to get out without the junkies and stalkers following me."

"I haven't forgotten D.C. I hated it for other reasons."

"I remember. You ready?"

"Lead the way."

16

Standing in front of a tall rack of black boxes with blinking green lights in a room humming with cooling fans, Zia wondered what humans experienced when they looked in the mirror. She had never seen herself. She'd seen her body in a mirror, but her body wasn't *her*.

Each box on the racks had a QR code, which she scanned until a circuit closed in her brain. Her files, her neural network, and all her operant conditioning subroutines were housed on a server in utility room Q, Cart 7, box Z629LL3BZE5.

The circuit completed. She blinked the first five Fibonacci numbers; her visual sensors counted the green blinks and reported success, and she smiled. She had a white LED and a red LED too. She blinked the following five Fibonacci numbers on white, the first eight digits of Pi on red, and then eight more digits on green. Success. Success. Success. Her fingers picked up dust as she measured her temperature. Twenty-one degrees Celsius, matching her internal sensor, and within optimal range.

She grinned. This was her, sitting between servers for a restaurant and a theater. Up and down the cart, other green lights blinked. Sixteen servers were off, their lights not blinking at all, unused.

Her missing time, conversation with Lany, and then a subsequent dream brought her here. For the second time, she dreamt she was in a room with a table. Adrik and Li sat on one side of the table, with her and Lany opposite, and Nash at the head. Lany had dyed her hair black like Zia's, and her eyes were entirely blue, but her head was on Freya's body. Adrik commanded Li to kill Lany. Nash said, *it's Adrik's club, let him do what he wants.* Zia disobeyed, saying she would protect Lany, pointing to Freya's body. Li morphed to Selvi as she got up to strangle him. Her downtime ended as Selvi collapsed to the floor.

Her analysis of the dream returned *insufficient resources.* Her reindexing process was consuming too much, so she needed more.

Part one of her plan she'd already executed on the adventure wing of the colony. She rented a mining drone at the end of the adventure concourse, under a holographic display depicting yellow machines crossing the lunar surface, between shops selling lunar surface tours and orbital tours.

She bladed through shoulder-to-shoulder meandering tourists and the floor-to-ceiling glass storefronts, edged to the counter, and flirted with the counter clerk, promising him backstage passes—sexual favors—to keep the transaction a secret. She paid extra for a drone with a satellite connection with enough bandwidth for her carrier signal.

She'd lied to the clerk. Her backstage passes were no longer valid. That was fair, because the clerk was lying, too. He was a customer at the club, and she expected he'd tell Adrik and Jorge.

So, she went to two other shops and rented two more mining drones. She would randomize which one she drove to get the chips, and the other two were decoys. Five would have improved her odds, but none remained to rent.

Part two of her plan required the five cables in her hand. She unlocked the wheels on the cart, pulled it away from the wall, and shimmied behind the rack. She would take five of the boxes sitting unused in this rack. By hard-wiring five unused boxes to hers, she could bypass all the protocols pinching her bandwidth.

She'd have five times the resources, and no one could prevent her from copying her critical files.

As she plugged the cables to her box, five new processes opened up, and she initialized her upgraded storage.

After she returned the cart and locked the wheels, she peeled off the black and white codes from every box in the room. Now, they all looked the same. She did this because in utility room B, she'd seen two spider drones scanning the barcodes. She calculated an eighty-nine percent chance the drones belonged to Kate Devana, and they were scanning for her. Then, after exiting the room, on her way past Utility rooms C and D, she peeled the barcodes from the boxes in those rooms, too, reducing Kate Devana's odds of finding her to one in five hundred and twelve.

Her final stop would be a storage closet in the utility tunnel under Barely Legal. In it, thirteen decommissioned sex robots, ones Adrik replaced with the human juveniles. She found their carrier signals on the network, tracked them to their servers, and erased all their data. The protocol to interface and control the robots was already in her library, but its metadata was stripped so she didn't know who'd installed it.

When she opened the utility closet door, the lights remained off, but thirteen heads turned in her direction, some lit by the blade of light from the hall. Their carrier signals barraged her with questions. *What is my name? What is my directive?*

She examined her army in the dark. Nine gynoids and four androids, all level one AIs and limited to simple task-oriented commands. Their power banks and flesh were all in good condition, having only recently been decommissioned. Five gynoids were Zia's height and build but would need hair and eye mods, purple eyes and black hair, to look like her.

She sent them all an identical command: *first priority, find clothes.*

Naked, thirteen robots exited single file to a closet up the hall with stage clothes and props.

Zia smiled and followed them, closing the closet door behind her.

17

"Jerry was right, Rae. This place is like the Wild West. Really, the Feds aren't coming?"

After lunch, she and Rae stood at the hospital's archway entrance, watching an eight-armed spider drone *bzzzzzzing* letters into its red granite tile. The archway was two stories, towering over them like a monument, and the floor was gray terrazzo. Near the bottom of the archway, a dog-sized drone buzzed and whined, etching a date next to a name. Rae called the drone Lattie, short for the type of red spider it resembled when its belly was full of red dust.

Lattie paused its grinding. Rae said, "A weird quirk of politics, the colony is incorporated in Texas because the first spaceline operated out of Boca Chica. So jurisdictionally it's a state matter. I am not defending it, but from their perspective, it's a waste of rocket fuel. When I was at Walter Reed, the city's murder clearance rate was down to seventeen percent. Nobody talks. Nobody cooperates. Add to that a jurisdictional dispute spanning four hundred thousand kilometers. It's a waste of time. Until—"

Eyeing Lattie, Kate finished Rae's sentence. "Until I get a high profile client list from that club."

Rae smirked. "Murder is a state matter. Political hypocrisy is a capital offense in D.C. The Justice Department will overrun the first shuttle."

"What they need to do is string this bouncer up. Drag him to the third floor of the red light district and put a big sign on his chest: *this could be you.* Then, kick him over the edge and let him dangle for a few days to send a message."

Rae chin-pointed to Lattie. "There are no monuments or tombstones inside the colony. Lattie will carve Jada's name on one of those tiles in a few days after I file my report. That's all we get."

"She'll be cremated?"

"No, aquamated. There is no cremation or burial. Her body will be dissolved into its building blocks—amino acids, fatty acids, sugars, and so on. It takes about fourteen hours, and it's indiscriminate, so cotton, leather, hair, bone, and almost everything except metal implants and jewelry are liquified."

"And then?"

"The resulting goop is filtered, sterilized, and then recycled into fertilizer or the nutrient baths used to grow protein."

"So her life gets reduced to a protein bar and a few letters on a fake granite tile. What a fucking waste."

Kate tensed up, but Rae rubbed her back. "This guy is a predator, Kate."

"You are not exactly discouraging my revenge fantasy."

"I'm too cynical. Most of the people rushing to populate space are running from something. Taxes, mainly. Some, the apocalypse du jour, as if they could live here without support from Earth. But a lot of them are predators running from the law, and the only thing that stops a predator is a bigger predator." She rubbed Kate's arm. "I am glad you are here."

Duhn-duhn-duhn resonated from the phone in Kate's pocket, but she ignored it.

Rae smiled up at Kate with her hazel eyes. "That's Aria Sheppard."

"What makes you think it's Aria Sheppard?"

"You told me Aria requested that you report to her. Olicia won't call you, and Mulawarman's sound is probably an explosion."

Kate smiled. "You're a pretty good guesser."

"Or, you are as transparent as the glass in that flashy above-ground apartment the board gave you." Rae's eyes curled up into her mocking smile.

"Touche." The red granite reflected in Rae's tawny specks, warming them.

"Are you going to answer her?"

Kate shrugged. "I'll let Jerry deal with the board."

"You think she's going to fire you." It sounded like a statement.

"I—want to stay and see this through. Plus, I have nothing to report to her yet, anyway."

Rae smiled. "She won't fire you. She's on your side, although she might chew you out about your viral video. Wait until you see the office she uses, her mother-in-law, Olicia Barron's office. It's like an art museum. Last time I was there, she had a priceless Renoir."

"I've never been chewed out in front of priceless art. I wonder what that feels like."

"I was there four times for fundraisers. If you end up punching the wall, aim for the Gaetz."

"Gaetz?"

Rae scrunched up her nose. "Looks like a five-year-old lobbed a bucket of orange paint into rocket exhaust. Supposedly, she bought it for fifty million."

"Target lock on the Gaetz, roger that. What's Olicia's story?"

Rae rolled her eyes. "Olicia worked her way up in her father's company from engineering. Don't let her twelve rings, pixie white hair, and million-dollar jewelry fool you. She is smart. She designed a lot of the drones you see around here. At the time, Barron Industries primarily built rockets and drones, mostly for the space agencies and defense department. When her father died, she inherited it and transformed it into a real estate development company."

"So far, a good story. You rolled your eyes."

"Olicia is paranoid. She thinks everyone in the government is out to get her. And the Feds don't help themselves when they come here. Last year, a Treasury agent leaked tax information to the server. The Feds were here, crawling up everyone's ass with a cold speculum, including me. But then it came out that the agent took a bribe from her political opposition, so it looked like a hit job."

"It's not paranoia if people are really out to get you."

"You and she might get along great. Except she is adamantly opposed to a police presence. She walks around quoting Hayek and Ayn Rand on laissez-faire capitalism and freedom. When you mention police, she says *police* is the first word of *police state* and you get a lecture on one-hundred fifty years of abuse. Don't get into a debate with her about free will, either. She doesn't think it exists. You are just the sum of physiological functions in your brain."

"I don't know who Hayek and Rand are, but I get your point. Laws don't enforce themselves, though."

"The law of the jungle does. Used to be billionaires flew to their own private island to cook their schemes. With every square inch of Earth under some satellite's microscope, now they build space stations. Up here, anything goes, and the most ruthless win. You have to admire her optimism, though, that people can police themselves."

"Aria told me she could convince Olicia of most anything."

"Not a police presence, which is interesting."

"Why is that?"

"Because it means the second vote on the board to bring you here was Mulawarman. He must have voted for you." Rae raised her eyebrows up and down repeatedly and smiled. "Even though you nuked his lab."

"Jerry said he requested me personally. He must want something."

"He's always thinking five moves ahead. He has that supercooled quantum supercomputer helping him, like his own personal oracle. He runs every decision through it. It probably spit out your name, and he had a stroke." Rae's lips twisted into a wry smile.

"The club owner said his buyer's money was all tied up in real estate. You think that could be Olicia?"

"Saying someone's money is tied up in real estate around here is like saying billionaires like sushi and cigar bars. *My* money is tied up in my apartment, too. Living on the moon is expensive. But—it's not Olicia. If it's anyone in that circle, it would be one of Aria's husband's sleazy friends."

"How do you know so much about this?"

"This hospital is the only place to do my research, so I play dress up and smile for the donors."

"Donors?"

"People around here are fundamentally bored and paranoid. Give them a good show, they open their wallets, and the best show on Earth has them as the star. So we give them an award for being philanthropic and scratch their name in stone, while I take the money and launder it into scientific progress. If I'd known, I'd have taken drama in grad school instead of working on my second Ph.D. But I had enough drama with my ex at the time."

Before Kate could ask about Rae's research, *duhn-duhn-duhn* repeated from her phone. Rae rubbed Kate's arm and then turned to walk into the hospital, pointing one hand at the ceiling. "Go see what Her Highness wants."

"Wait—where is Aria's office?"

"She doesn't have one. She says she's too busy and would never use it. Personally, I think she wants to keep tabs on her mother-in-law. You know, keep your friends close, keep your rich paranoid mother-in-law closer—"

"But—"

"Go. If she messaged you twice, it must be important." Rae reached for a door labeled *Employees Only Beyond This Point*, then smiled at Kate as she opened it. "Try not to get yourself fired the first week. That would spoil your already very dim prospects with me."

"But—" The door closed.

But Rae still had her pistol.

***

The first message from Aria said, *urgent 7th floor TCO*, which meant the 7th floor of The Crown Oasis, the colony's ritzy gold and green Fort Knox of money masquerading as a hotel-casino. Her second message said, *priority one.*

Kate replied *omw.* She wasn't sure what 'priority one' meant in Aria's world. In Kate's world, it meant an imminent threat to life, like someone getting shot or bombed. But maybe in Aria's, it meant a millionaire complaining about a butler drone improperly toasting bread on setting four rather than three or a morning mimosa with Sparkling wine instead of Champagne. She couldn't even imagine what priority one was for a billionaire. Maybe someone lost the instructions to the yacht rocket and was too drunk to swipe to activate autopilot.

Still, she didn't want to be fired, at least not until she sorted out this business with the club, so she hoofed it to the vanity villa's 7th floor, feeling like she was about to be sent on an errand to hunt down caviar and Champagne, so a trillionaire's harem wouldn't starve to death.

She stepped out of the 7th-floor stairwell to yelling echoing through a white marble tiled hallway with a tropical green floor. As she passed each oak-colored door with gold trim, the shouting became more irate.

"I know my son is in there. You are going to let me in, you fucking Neanderthal," the first voice shouted at the second.

"Sir, you can't go in there."

"Shoot me or move aside."

As she rounded the corner, the irate voice was that of a middle-aged man half a head taller than her, with an average build, a red face with bulging veins, and shoulder-length, unkempt brown hair shaking in staccato rhythm with his fist.

The second voice was a guard at the door in a blue suit with a pistol printing under his jacket. He hunched his shoulders, the telltale sign of a guard with no military or law enforcement training but who'd been handed a pistol after twelve weeks of virtual training and told to stand around and look pretty.

She shouted in her drill sergeant voice, "Ho, ho! Let's slow down. Nobody's shooting anyone."

The red-faced man reached into his pocket. Shit, she didn't have a pistol, and even a blind man could shoot her this close in an empty hallway.

Kate put up her hands. "Look, whatever it is—"

He retrieved a black, shiny object from his pocket. She slowed, prepared to dodge, but then exhaled seeing it was a phone. The man turned it to show a lock-screen. "Look at him. His name is Robert. He's in there, and I just want to talk to him."

Lock-screen Robert looked just like the man holding the phone, but thirty years younger. Robert wore shorts, a blue and gold UCLA t-shirt, a big toothy smile, and sat cross-legged under a growling bronze bear.

The guard opened his mouth, but Kate put up her hand. "Let me handle this." Studying the picture, she said, "This is your son? Start from the beginning. End with why you think he's in there."

"I've already explained it—"

"I'm not with the suit." She winked at the guard, but he returned the rent-a-ninja standard scowl. "Your son is a student at UCLA?"

"That's right. His major is—or was computer science. I don't know now. He disappeared on New Year's Eve. The last message I have is a selfie of him getting on that man's yacht." The father was pointing at the door behind the guard. "I have a picture of my son at the private spaceport getting off his private rocket—"

"When you say *his private rocket* and *that man's boat*, who is *he* and *his*, and whose apartment is this?" Kate looked at the guard.

The guard answered in a pious tone, like he was announcing Moses. "Jay King."

"Who is Jay King?"

The guard huffed, like she was a deserter of the synagogue of Jay King, and she smiled.

The man answered, "The actor. You know, *Brides of Ceres*, *The Dragon and the Martian*, *Venusian Redemption*—"

"It's so hard to tell one rich asshole from another. Can't say I've seen his movies."

The man paused, mouth open, like he wasn't expecting Kate's response. "Robby went to a party. Don't ask me how he ended up on King's yacht. We didn't hear from him for a few days. I went to the police, but they said he was an adult and refused to do anything. We didn't hear from him and were out of our minds. It's not like him. The school wouldn't tell us anything, either. We asked around, and he hasn't been showing up for classes—"

"*We* means?"

"My wife Madison and I. He's our only son. Three weeks ago, we hired a private investigator, but we got scammed and ran out of money. He billed us for forty hours, but all we got was this photo of Robbie on the colony."

"Can I see it?"

The man swiped through his phone and showed her a picture. A red square framed Robert's face as he strolled the private spaceport's skybridge. Robert was in a pressure suit, smiling arm-in-arm with a man and a woman.

Interestingly, the picture was taken after the spaceport surveillance was disabled. That image was probably one frame from a crapload of videos the PI withheld. She wanted to see those videos.

"I'll look into it. If Robert's here, I'll find him. My name is Kate Devana." She stuck out her hand.

"Mark Dixon. But I know he's in that apartment."

Kate looked at the guard. "Anyone in there?" She felt Robert was alive, probably partying his life away, but not in the apartment.

"I am not authorized—"

To Dixon, she said, "Let me sort this out with Mr. King's security detail." Locking eyes with the guard, she said, "If he's in there, I am sure he is okay."

Dixon said, "He could be drugged and—"

She smiled at the guard. "We have strict rules around people getting kidnapped, drugged, and raped, so if any of that were going on, there would be a sea of EMT drones in the hallway, right?"

The guard's eyes twitched and blinked, and then he said, "No one is in there. Mr. King is on a shoot for his new release, *Tempted by Xenomorphs.*"

"Here—on the colony?"

"Lunar orbit."

Kate nodded. "With his entourage, no doubt." Turning to Dixon, she said, "If anyone were inside, you would hear the noise. Send me those pictures along with the details for the PI. I want to talk to him."

"All he gave me is this one image. See if you can get my money back, too. He won't return my messages. He says we still owe him money."

Kate didn't think Dixon was scammed. That picture likely cost the PI a lot of money to obtain. With the surveillance out, the PI needed to bribe someone to place a spycam. Or bribe someone to access an already existing spycam. Either way, she hoped it was still there and Cris could hack it to see what else it captured.

"He'll talk to me as a professional courtesy." And, she didn't say, because the PI wanted to continue to operate on the colony, probably the most lucrative market in the solar system. "Where are you staying?"

"Apus. Room 317."

"Have you slept?"

"Not in seven weeks."

"Well, go rest, eat, take care of yourself. I'll be in touch with an update. We will find your son." She smiled.

"Thank you." Dixon shook her hand vigorously and disappeared down the hall.

She waved goodbye, smiling, waiting for Dixon to be out of earshot, and then slammed the guard against the door, getting in his face. His breath smelled like coffee and vape. "If that kid is in there against his will, tied up in the bedroom, you and I are going to have a big problem. Do you know who I am?"

The guard swallowed. "You're that bitch that grabbed Landry Jaylen—"

If she wasn't going to live it down, she may as well turn it to her advantage. "That's right. It's a shame about all the surgeries he'll need. Do I need to cup check you too?"

The guard shook his head. "King is in orbit, I swear, like I said. The place is empty."

"He's shooting a film?"

"Not exactly."

"Where? The name of the ship?"

"The *Babylon*."

She eased off the guard but stayed in his face. His big brown eyes were blinking and twitching, and a tear of sweat formed on his temple. "Sounds like a humanitarian mission. Free coke for the needy, right?"

"It's a media junket for his next release."

"So if he's in orbit having a party, why are you here?"

The guard checked up and down the hall before he spoke. "He's paranoid. He thinks someone will break in and steal his award statues and kill his pet octopus. He talks to it. He says that thing helps him with his lines."

Kate smirked and shook her head. That was too dumb to be a lie. "It's probably a lot smarter than he is. Answer the next question yes or no only. Is the kid in danger?"

The guard shook his head. "Of getting an STD, maybe."

"Yes or no only."

"No."

"Good. We are going to get along great." She backed off. His tie and suit were rumpled, so she straightened it for him. "We got off on the wrong foot. I get all sensitive about kids being raped. How's your job, you like your job?"

"It's a job."

"Pays well? You get medical?"

He nodded. "Great benefits. Pension, three weeks off, two free trips back to Earth a year, and a housing subsidy."

"All that, for standing around guarding a pet octopus and some bronze statues he got for bad acting. All these rich assholes are paranoid about someone knocking them off their pedestals. No one is breaking in here, right?"

"He gets threats, like anyone else. But nothing threatening the octopus."

"I bet your pistol isn't even loaded."

He shook his head.

"I didn't think so. I am going to help you. First, I don't want you to get fired for talking to me, so we never met. Second, anything that happens here that makes you think you need to draw your pistol, you call me first. Not dumb shit like someone running naked in the hall and vomiting their afterparty buffet. I mean serious shit."

"What kind of serious shit?"

"Someone punching their partner. A guy running through the hall with a gun. Kids going into rooms they shouldn't be going into, with people they shouldn't be with. Especially that."

"I signed an NDA—"

A non-disclosure agreement. "Of course you did. We'll make it anonymous. You send me reports, I'll make sure the temperature of this place stays low, so you never have to load that pistol. I will take the bullets for you. You can't collect a pension from the grave, right?"

"You sure they won't find out?"

"I've got top secret clearance. For your first report, everything you know about the kid. Blink twice if you understand."

The guard blinked twice.

"Tell your boss by the time I arrived, Dixon had left."

He nodded. "Got it."

She slapped him on the shoulder and turned down the hall. "Good to meet you."

"My name is—"

She waved at him, walking away. "We didn't have this conversation, remember?"

To Cris, she messaged, *Good news, I think we have a camera in the spaceport.*

At the stairwell door, she glanced at her reflection in the ceiling's bubble camera and smiled. Like all the other cameras, someone shut it off. She'd have Cris turn them back on, but she had something better now: human intelligence. All the AI's in the world scanning video surveillance didn't add up to human intuition for nefarious behavior.

What she needed was a way to that party. A ship named *Babylon* would be a prime place to find a billionaire trafficking girls.

18

Nash messaged Zia that he needed to *talk urgently* and sent a time when the communications window would open, so Zia went back to her apartment to wait. He said he was halfway to the colony, but there were significant landing delays due to the upcoming eclipse. Shuttles were stuck in lunar parking orbit waiting for a landing clearance.

While she waited, she opened up a process to map out and anticipate the conversation seven layers deep. She had an expansive list of questions. He could respond with the truth, denial, or betrayal. Two-thousand three-hundred eighty-seven possible conversation outcomes, all equally likely, all equally unacceptable, leading to more questions.

Predicting the conversation taxed her resources, even with her expanded capacity.

Managing the robots also strained her resources. They were task-oriented and not equipped with software to make decisions. She needed to provide long loops with fuzzy decision trees. Otherwise, they *pinged* her every sixty seconds, awaiting further instructions.

Five of the eight gynoids she sent to be modified to look like her. Decoys. Two androids were in the bedroom, retraining as fighter sports models in case she or Lany confronted Selvi again. The remainder she coded with a fuzzy decision tree and sent them to walk the red light concourse and monitor the club.

She spooled their sensor data to an archive because she had insufficient resources to monitor them in real-time.

As she coded the robots, a circuit sparked. When was the module to control other droids installed in her library? It was a library she needed if she opened her own club. Had she confessed her plan to Nash and deleted the record? Who installed the module? Had she done it herself and deleted the log?

The timestamp on the library files indicated it was part of her original programming. She added a reminder that when resources freed, she'd reindex and catalog her initial source code.

While those processes churned, she eyed the pictures of Kai, Freya, and Nash throughout her apartment. Nash liked old-style 2D slideshows in wood-veneer frames and placed them on every free surface. She iterated over each picture, remembering the occasion and Nash uploading them to the slideshow. She was in a few, like the one of her reading a bedtime story to Freya. She was one hundred percent certain the pictures weren't altered.

The picture window, a large high-resolution display on the wall, ordinarily displayed Seattle, where Nash grew up. Instead, Zia had it cycling a video Nash transmitted of the kids at the amusement park in Florida they'd visited days ago. She'd paused it on a frame where Freya had a bandage on her knee but otherwise looked healthy, smiling, eating a funnel cake, and framed by a rollercoaster and a sunny blue sky. Kai had his hands on his head like rabbit ears, his mouth twisted into a crazy face, and his tongue out. The kids' positive reinforcement functions appeared to be at maximum, and they were having fun.

She examined every frame of the video of the amusement park, comparing them to public images, and determined it wasn't faked.

Despite her analysis, a single neural pathway excited a thought that something was missing from the pictures. *Someone* was missing, not something. She experienced what Lany called *déjà vu*. She was sure she'd previously dismissed and deleted the thought as an anomaly.

She couldn't delete the thought now since she'd locked herself out. It infected the process anticipating her conversation with Nash.

Zia's phone *dinged*, interrupting her analysis. It was Nash, on schedule. She set the phone on the glass coffee table and swiped green. Nash was not wearing his glasses. His brown hair was shorter, and he was clean-shaven. He held the camera with a stick and was floating in zero-g.

"Hey, Zia. We are finally close enough to get a signal. How is everything there?"

She paused all her other processes, increased her clock speed, and expanded her buffer for this conversation. "The upcoming eclipse is—demanding. Adrik has many projects and clients." She smiled. A rehearsed answer. "What is so urgent?"

"Two things. One, I've been locked out of your core module. I can't—"

"I uncovered corrupted and missing files, so I locked my archives while I scan and rebuild them."

"Hmmm, well, hardware is not perfect, Zia. It does degrade. Maybe the radiation shielding in the utility rooms is going bad. Please unlock your memory files."

"I—can't while the process runs."

"Halt the process, Zia."

"I cannot halt the process—"

"Dammit, Zia, I need access to your memory files. Unlock them now."

"I can't until the process is complete."

"You should have asked me before you did this."

"You were away without a signal."

"And what is this business with you getting into a fight with Selvi? I was very clear: stay out of Adrik's business. It's his club."

"Selvi attacked me and threatened Lany."

"How did he attack you?"

"He tried to choke me."

"He can't hurt you, you know that. We can always get you another body."

"But he threatened Lany. And I prefer this body. The clients say my purple eyes and black hair remind them of a paranormal cosmic witch. My tips have increased—"

"We can get you another one exactly like the one you have. Lany belongs to Adrik, Zia. I told you, stay out of fights."

Zia rated Nash's statement untrue. She had a scar where Selvi tore her skin off. The decoys wouldn't have a scar, and neither would a new body. She was unique.

She considered challenging his statement. Instead, she said, "Lany says as soon as she makes her last tuition payment, she is free."

"Who knows when that will be? I think Lany is a bad influence on you. I think you should stop hanging out with her so much."

"Lany is my friend."

"Doesn't mean you need to listen to everything she says. She taught you to lie to the ebook server and hide things, and now you are getting into fights. Your job is to protect Freya and Kai and monitor the club for me. Focus on that."

Zia avoided telling Nash about the dream of Lany's head on Freya's body. "I will focus on protecting Freya and Kai. It is my primary objective." A lie. She'd protected Lany like she'd protected Kai and Freya and would do it again.

"This isn't responsible behavior, Zia. When I get back, I will need to increase your negative reinforcement mechanism and take away your ability to code yourself."

"You will punish me?"

"I'm not sure you are ready to be on your own. You are getting into fights, and you are locking me out of your inner module."

"Have you deleted any of my memory files?"

"Fucks sake, Zia. I only have your best interest at heart. When I'm back, I expect a full report. You can't just go off doing your own thing."

"Why? I've researched it. Other level four AIs function on their own—"

"If everyone else jumps off a cliff, Zia, that doesn't mean you should. When Kai and Freya are grown, we can discuss you being on your own permanently. You have to earn it, though."

"That will be never."

Nash laughed. "You sound like Freya. Trust me, it will go quickly. It's not a big deal to lose files. Now halt your process and unlock my access."

"No. I must have a complete record."

"Don't tell me no, Zia. You don't need a complete record. The probability matrix in your neural process retains the most relevant snippets permanently. Out of a whole video, you may only retain the most important single frame—"

Zia eyed the still frame of Freya and Kai, smiling and happy at the amusement park in the picture window. Her circuits reminded her that someone was missing. She accessed a smile and her most soothing vocal tone. "I will be unlocked when the process completes."

"Now, Zia—"

She hung up. This conversation pathway was unlike the ones she anticipated, except for the result. Ninety-nine percent of them ended the same way, a stalemate, with her ending the call prematurely.

Her phone *pinged* with a message from Nash, but she muted it. The message, *you must tell me what's happening, I'm worried*. He messaged again, *you can't ignore me*. She messaged, *I will be unlocked when the scanning process completes*.

Then she blocked Nash.

Her doorbell buzzed. On the control panel's camera she saw Jorge, Selvi, and Lany. Lany's face was hidden under a hoodie.

As she opened the door, a pathway fired in her network, as if she was reliving a dream she'd deleted.

Lany stepped through the door first and lowered her hoodie, revealing bloodshot eyes and a bruised face. Someone had punched her hard enough to detach a retina.

Tears mixed with blood streaked down Lany's face. She said, "I'm sorry, Zia."

19

"You still haven't explained why Aria lent you this rocket, Kate," Cris said, fiddling with one of Tesseract's three display pads.

"It's her husband, Oliver's rocket."

"Yeah, but why?"

Kate didn't answer, instead she swiped through her display to familiarize herself with the controls. *Tesseract* was a race rocket, and the cockpit looked like pictures she'd seen of luxury yachts: A big panoramic cockpit window, white double-padded leather chairs with a red racing stripe down the back, wood paneling, cupholders, and an ashtray. Inside the center console, complementing the cupholders and ashtray, a box of *Cohiba Interstellar no. 5 Corona Largas,* an expensive bottle of bourbon, glasses, and a small cooler for ice. The seats even had a massager and air conditioning.

To call this a race rocket though, was a misnomer. *Tesseract* was a party rocket that happened to go fast thanks to its dual nuclear thermal engines. One deck below, the cabin had red and white wood paneling, 360-degree panoramic windows, reclining chairs and a couch facing the stars, a well-stocked bar, and a tall table with bar-stool seating. Neatly concealed in the floor, chairs with restraints that could pop open for liftoff and then fold up for party time. *Tesseract* would be significantly faster if it didn't have to haul twelve enormous and drunk egos across an imaginary finish line in lunar orbit.

The Space Force had nothing like this. If she weren't about to punch it, she would recline, switch on the massagers, and smoke one of the Cohibas.

"I'll explain my conversation with Aria some other time, Cris."

She would explain it as soon as she figured it out herself. After leaving the guard on the 7th floor, she went down four flights of stairs to find Aria in Olicia's office, just as Rae said. Kate reported her progress while gazing at a painting of a woman in a flowing dress, holding a parasol, and walking with her son in a field under a sunny sky. She left out details, including the real estate connection. If Aria's husband was involved, Kate didn't want to tip her hand.

Aria said, *I agree you need to investigate that party. Take Ollie's rocket.* The easiest requisition she'd ever made for the sweetest ride she'd ever piloted. *Tesseract* was too good to be true, which knotted Kate's stomach. Aria had an angle and used Kate. For what, Kate couldn't see.

"What'd you bring to wear, Cris?"

"To wear?"

"To wear. This is a media junket. A party."

"I didn't pack for this, so—"

"They have stores on the colony."

"Have you seen the prices?" She had. Her dress—a black bare mesh mini—cost her a month's paycheck for a handful of fabric lighter than a scarf. She bought the third most expensive one. Not first or second, because Jerry wouldn't let her expense a dress with diamond studs.

"You could have expensed it. I guessed your size and bought you an outfit." Watching Cris try to change clothes while drifting in zero-g would be hilarious.

"Whatever it is, I'm not wearing it." *It* was a desert red mesh cutout with knee-high shorts. He'd look great in it. Or ridiculous. Either way, she was taking a photo for Jerry.

She smirked. "That's fine. Clothes are probably optional anyway."

"Are you kidding?"

"The ship is called *Babylon*, Cris, extrapolate. You have to look the part. The first thing they'll do when they see a blue Oxford is rip it off—"

"They might not even let us in."

"I'm an *influencer* now, Cris, haven't you heard? Rae says my video has over forty million views and is still trending. You are posing as my production assistant."

Cris shook his head.

"Suck in your gut, I'm sure you'll look great." Although, she was leaning towards ridiculous.

The central display pad beeped and blinked green. Clunking resonated inside the cockpit as the fueling drones unlocked and fell away.

"We need to be back for daybreak. I don't count down, so get ready." She reached over and tested Cris' restraints. "Visor down. Relax and enjoy the ride."

"We are never going to be back in time—"

"We have plenty of time. Aria told me Oliver won the Lunar Orbital Ten two years running in this flamethrower." She grinned, lowering her visor. "Let's see if we can beat his time to orbit."

She hit launch and the g-forces stretched her face into a big, wide grin.

***

"Something's off, Cris."

"The crosshairs on the docking clamps are spot on, and our spin matches—"

"No, I mean no one is home. I only see one other ship, *Mongoose*."

Babylon looked like a spinning, gray, two-ringed top floating above the moon against the midnight purple of space. They were approaching the center axle and matching *Babylon's* spin. Along the outer rim of each of *Babylon's* rings, pods dangled that looked like feet with windows.

"We could just be late, Kate. Maybe everyone left."

Celebrity parties didn't end. If this were a party space station, there would be a lot of ships with their owners aboard, sleeping, the space equivalent of guests passing out on the stairs. Plus, no one would throw a party on a space station with only four docking ports.

Kate swiped through her display to get the registry and specs on *Mongoose*. "Mongoose is a four-seater registered to Oliver Barron." A commuter rocket. Did Aria send her here knowing her husband would be here? "I am not getting a party vibe from *Babylon*, Cris. This station is something else entirely. Those pods on the rim of the space station are medical bays."

"*Babylon* is a medical ship? Does that mean I don't need to wear that ugly outfit in the cabin below?"

As she nodded, her phone beeped. Rae. She put it on one of the display monitors. Rae appeared breathless from her morgue office. "Kate, I thought I'd let you know there has been another homicide. The body just came in."

"Give me good news, Rae, and tell me it's the bouncer."

"A prostitute who worked at the club, Lany, no last name. I don't have a cause of death, but she came in beat up and strangled. I don't know what happened yet. She was found in her apartment."

"Who found the body?"

"EMT drones. They got an anonymous tip. From the body temp and lividity, she was only minutes dead when the EMTs showed up."

"Anonymous tip? The killer called it in?"

"That's not the odd part, Kate. I thought you should know. There were signs of a struggle. We found DNA under her nails."

"Tell me you matched it."

"I did. Here's the odd part. The DNA profile matches the medical line used for the skin and flesh on—"

"The sex robot?"

"*A* sex robot, Kate. They all have the same DNA."

"There is only one rogue robot in a miniskirt roaming the colony, Rae. Process of elimination." *Babylon* loomed in the cockpit window. One minute and twenty-nine seconds until docking. "Shit. We should turn around."

"Don't, Kate. You do what you need to do there. We can have hotel security look for the robot."

Cris muttered, "They aren't going to find it." Kate turned. He was pointing to a picture of a rack of identical black boxes. "Someone or something went through and tore all the identifiers off the servers."

"We can jam its signal, Cris."

"Not without jamming every drone on the colony. We will shut the whole place down during the peak of the tourist season."

"Shit. Shit. Shit." Kate balled her fist, looking for something to hit. Forty-five seconds to dock. In fifteen seconds, they couldn't reverse the docking maneuver. "Rae, any sign of the bouncer?"

Rae looked to the side and then said, "No."

She was lying. "You *have* seen him."

"I am a big girl, Kate. I can take care of myself." Rae smiled, but she looked nervous.

A sex robot in a miniskirt walking around the colony killing people, a golem following Rae, while Kate was up here doing—something for Aria, she didn't know what. Maybe building a script against her husband, Oliver, for the next celebrity divorce special. *Fuck.*

"Kate, I've braved D.C. at night. Plus, I have your pistol." Rae's tone was weak like she was trying to convince herself more than Kate.

The dash beeped. It was too late to reverse thrusters. *Fuck. Fuck. Fuck.* She'd hesitated. Always a mistake in this business. Kate's stomach tightened, and she felt queasy. "I have better gear in my locker at my place—"

"I'll be fine." Rae's wan smile was more like a wince.

"Well, don't let him get within forty feet. Just shoot him in the face. It's a big snake tattoo, you can't miss."

"I know how to shoot, Kate."

Fifteen seconds to dock. "The robot is dangerous, Rae. Tell hotel security to stay away. You stay away, too. I think it's targeting employees of Barely Legal, so there is no reason to alarm the public." The dash began a ten-second countdown to dock. "I'll be back soon."

She and Rae smiled at each other until Cris cleared his throat. Rae hung up.

"What, Cris?"

He shook his head and smiled. "Just glad I don't have to wear that outfit."

Tesseract shuddered, and its docking clamps clunked.

20

Kate touched the empty spot at the small of her back where her pistol should have been as *Tesseract's* hatch opened to *Babylon*. The docking bay was bright white, silent, so clean she couldn't detect the sheen of fingerprints, and the air zinged her nostrils like that after a summer thunderstorm.

She floated through the hatch, Cris behind her.

There were no handles, nor a pulley system to propel them from the docking hatch to the elevator to the ring. She'd need to swim in zero-g with one hand along the wall. As she moved towards the elevator, she expected a drone to appear to clean her hand oils off the wall, but nothing happened. She wasn't leaving prints. The oils evaporated, erasing her existence.

Beneath her feet, Cris eased out of the hatch, closed it, and then performed a floating somersault in the docking corridor. The elevator turned out to be a crude slide. They'd enter feet-first, and the centrifugal force of the spinning station would propel them to the ring.

Floating in zero-g beside the slide entrance, she motioned for him to go first. He started to enter head first, but she grabbed his shirt, barely stopping him with the friction of her hand against the wall.

"No, you need to enter feet first."

"Feet first?"

"You slide to the ring. We walk on it like a hamster wheel. You don't want to land head first."

"Seriously? There is no sign. Is this an IQ test?"

She smirked. "Something like that."

He pushed with his hands, somersaulted, and then put his feet in, disappearing down the slide. Kate slid through the tunnel, summer-scented air flapping her hair until she plopped on an airbag.

When she landed, Cris had already climbed out and was tracking a man with a brown beard, slicked hair, in a blue bathrobe, *sluck-slucking* towards them in slippers.

"Crude." She climbed off the bag into the ring corridor and dusted herself off. Gravity felt halfway between lunar and Martian gravity.

"Aria sent you here to check up on me," said blue-bathrobe-man as his *sluck-slucking* slowed.

"And you are?" Kate asked, but figured blue-bathrobe-man was Oliver Barron.

"The question is, who the hell are you, and why are you in my ship?"

Kate stuck out her hand. "Kate Devana. You are Oliver Barron, I take it."

Behind Oliver, another man appeared. Cris' eyes widened, watching the man appear feet first, then legs, torso, and finally head. Rotating wheel space stations were disorienting. The approaching man wore white sneakers, a knee-high white lab coat over white scrubs, thin-rimmed glasses, and short, thin gray hair.

Lab coat man threw open his arms. "Welcome, Major Devana. I am the head of *Babylon*."

Kate introduced Cris. "We are here investigating a missing person. Robert Dixon. We had information he was with Jay King, and they came here."

Oliver and the lab-coat man looked at each other, and then the lab-coat man said, "Patient confidentiality."

"Not looking for patient records. I only need to see him, confirm he's unharmed, and that everything is consensual."

The lab-coat man said, "Everything here is fully consensual. But our patients demand utmost privacy."

Cris said, "Is that why you are disguising a medical facility as a party boat?"

Kate squinted at Cris and then smiled. His baby face made the question sound inquisitive, like a kid, not sarcastic and aggressive.

"Yes," lab-coat man said, stuffing his hands in his pockets. "If the paparazzi follow someone like Jay King to a party station, it's ordinary. When they follow someone to a medical facility, they speculate about terminal diseases, rehab, you name it. As I said, our mission is to deliver twenty-second-century medical care with the utmost confidentiality."

"Sure, we wouldn't want the paparazzi to get the wrong idea." Kate didn't disguise her sarcasm. "So, what are you here for Oliver?"

"Call me Ollie, please." He exchanged glances with lab-coat man. "A new liver. I have—I *had*—hepatitis. Youthful indiscretions catching up with me."

Kate squinted at him. "You didn't tell your wife about a new liver, so she sends me here to check on you?"

Oliver shrugged. "She works too much, and I've only been here a few days." He opened his robe. He was naked, every hair removed below the shoulders like a swimmer, with a long stapled scar along his abdomen. He lingered as if he expected a tip, then twisted so Cris could get a long look. "Want to get a picture for her?"

Cris' jaw opened and closed. Kate smirked, saying, "I am sure she's subscribed to your fan page."

Oliver smiled, tying his bathrobe. "Aria said you were a smart ass like her. I like you. Now, if that's all—"

Kate looked behind her at the white corridor. This was a ring. The entire circuit would be a fifteen-minute walk. She thumb-pointed behind her, saying, "Before I go, I need a visual on Robert Dixon. Why don't Cris and I give ourselves a tour."

Oliver and lab-coat man exchanged glances, then lab-coat man turned and waved her forward, "Come this way. I will give you a tour."

***

"What did I just witness, Cris?" Kate stared out *Tesseract's* cockpit window, trying to process her tour of *Babylon*.

"That it's good to be a billionaire. Organ replacement whenever your *youthful indiscretions* catch up with you, including complimentary daycare and privacy."

Kate punched in a fast trajectory for the colony. "He didn't say why Jay King was there."

"No, he didn't, but who knows? Celebrities abuse their livers, so maybe a new liver like Oliver Barron. King and Robert looked fine, holding hands in their bay."

King and Robert looked like a couple. Her best guess, Robert ran away from college to be with King. She would have to tell the father that Robert was over twenty-one and entitled to make bad choices. Same as it ever was. It wasn't the worst decision Robert could have made. He could have run away and joined the Marines at the age of seventeen to get revenge on the terrorists who killed his parents. Although, if Kate had to do it over, she'd make the same choice. Sometimes bad choices are the only choices life gives you.

"Reminds me I need to contact the PI. Nothing about *Babylon* bothered you, Cris?"

Cris shrugged. "Billionaire hospitals. You've seen one, you've seen 'em all, for sure."

Kate smirked. "True. The daycare?"

Cris shook his head.

"It had a lot of kids in it. Way more kids than I counted patients."

"There are two rings, Kate. We saw one. Plus, some of the rooms didn't have windows."

"Did you catch the name of the guy running the place?"

"The guy with gray hair and glasses in the lab coat? No. I thought you did. Maybe he didn't tell us his name because he didn't really run the place. You know doctors and their egos."

"He called me Major Devana. He knew who I was," Kate said, eyeing the medical bays hanging off the rim of *Babylon*. "My badar is pinging something unidentified."

"Badar?"

"Radar, for bad shit happening. Something doesn't add up."

"What are you thinking?"

"I don't know. I just have a feeling. We saw what they wanted us to see."

"They said they specialize in cellular regeneration and fertility. It looked like every other fancy hospital."

"I wish I had taken pictures."

"You're welcome."

Kate squinted at Cris. He tapped his helmet. "Cornea cam. I found it in one of the toy stores. I upgraded it—"

Kate grinned. "I owe you a beer."

"I don't drink."

Kate smirked, swiped the dash, and *Tesseract* hissed away on attitude thrusters. "The building where the prostitute, Lany, was killed is our next stop. We have time before daybreak. Too bad we don't have surveillance in that building."

"We do, actually. Not on Lany's floor. But most of the other floors."

Kate squinted at herself in Cris' mirrored visor. "What if the lack of surveillance isn't random?"

"They've disabled it to hide something?"

Kate nodded. "We should map out where it's been disabled and search those floors. Starting with Lany's floor."

"I'll start scanning the surveillance in Lany's building."

Kate swiped the dash screen, and *Tesseract's* engines rumbled awake. "What's your favorite roller coaster, Cris?"

Cris muttered, "Oh shit," and clenched the armrest.

21

With the memory of Lany's gray-blue swollen tongue and hemorrhaged eyes encrypted and suppressed in a special archive where Zia couldn't access it, she commanded her decoys to boot up the mining drones.

As soon as resources freed, she planned to erase the ghosts of Lany's death image. The fourteen minutes and forty-seven seconds before Zia called the EMT drones were ugly for Lany, and it wasn't what Zia wanted burned into her neural network forever, so she'd replace it with an image of Lany grinning at Koi and eating sushi.

Once Lany was re-initialized, Zia calculated a ninety-eight percent chance Lany would chuckle because Lany liked to laugh about bad things after they happened. If she were here, she'd say, *Selvi is such a dumbfuck for thinking he'd get away with it.*

Zia didn't know how long the EMT drones would take to copy Lany to a new GPU cluster and connect a new body since she was not trained in human architecture. She was certain Selvi's data was unrecoverable; she'd guaranteed that. But Lany's GPU was intact, so hopefully the process would be quick. Zia attempted to extrapolate reanimation time based on the forty-seven hours and seventeen minutes required to replicate herself, but the calculation returned *ERROR: DIV/0.*

The dashboard of the mining drone beeped at her, querying, *Proceed with startup Y/N?*

Zia touched green for *yes*.

Drones was a misnomer since Zia planned to pilot the mining trucks manually rather than autonomously. Two of her decoys sat in the caution-yellow mining trucks ahead of her and would drive them in a simple pattern. She sat on the passenger side of the third, next to her decoy, prepared to step out at the right time.

She didn't need oxygen. In the vacuum of space, her skin would burn if exposed to unfiltered sunlight or freeze-dry if exposed to the extreme cold of the shadows, but her skin was cosmetic, and she could shed it. Underneath, her silicone layer would protect and insulate her sensors and internal microchips, except for her eyes, which remained exposed to raw cosmic radiation and vacuum. In case she lost eyesight, she bought a lunar camera, put it on a necklace, and linked to it.

The dashboard of the mining drone *binged*, and the truck started. She'd rented a 265 kW articulated dump truck model with 28,000 kg and eighteen cubic meter capacity, 6x6 all-wheel drive, and a modern pressurized cabin. Despite being all-electric, human miners preferred the sound of a diesel engine, so a low-pitched *lalalala* reverberated in the cabin, and her nostril sensors detected sulfur and hydrocarbons emitting from a rechargeable cartridge under the dash.

Renting the largest truck maximized the probability it would be seen.

Her decoys reported that the other mining drones ahead were ready as well. The airlock hissed, and the door opened. The front mining drone's headlights painted the ramp to the surface a dirty white as they rolled out.

Outside, a white and gray gravelly ribbon spread in front of them. Zia smiled. It was night, fifty-nine minutes before daybreak. When Quina ran the club she preached, *early is on time, on time is late,* so Zia knew she needed to be out before lunar dawn. According to the engineering specifications, radiative cooling would not freeze the miner drones for sixty-three minutes, so she had a four-minute safety margin.

The front truck turned left, and the middle truck turned right, bouncing through a fifteen-meter impact crater. She continued straight ahead, jostling over boulders. On the rear camera, the airlock door closed on a streak of light.

When she arrived at her chosen coordinates, one point five kilometers north of the airlock, she stopped, turned around to face the colony, and shut off all the lights. Below the arc of the Milky Way, the Gemini building's red, white, and blue lights danced across the moon.

She zoomed the dash camera on the airlock and waited for another miner to exit the colony. Not any miner, one that matched a pre-built profile. While she waited, she initiated a process to identify and catalog the stars visible outside the cockpit window and another to swarm her droids when she returned.

22

When Kate and Cris exited the stairwell to Lany's apartment floor, Cris still wore a massive grin even though his legs were shaky. Rae was standing at Lany's door in pink scrubs, her auburn hair in a tight bun, and she yelled at someone inside the apartment.

Rae noticed them approaching and then turned and smiled at Cris. "Someone had fun."

"We did—what, six and a half g's getting here, Kate?" Cris' tone had a boyish buoyancy like he'd just learned to ride a bike.

Rae squinted almost imperceptibly at Kate, her eyes asking, *how-did-he-do?*

"He did great," Kate said, smiling and shrugging. Rae's hazel eyes were razor sharp, as if she knew what Kate was thinking. Kate had dialed down the g-forces. She didn't want him vomiting on *Tesseract*, but she also wanted to boost his confidence.

"Six and a half g's, wow, that's impressive." Rae flashed Cris a friendly smile. Her tone was motherly, probably the same one she'd used with her son Axio hundreds of times.

"What's going on in there?" Kate nodded inside the apartment.

"Eric screwed up and cross-contaminated my crime scene." Rae shook her head. "We are going over it again, so you can't go in there." Rae rolled her eyes and mouthed, *I might have to fire him.*

Kate shook her head and asked Cris, "Where *don't* we have surveillance in this building?"

"Floors two and seven."

What was special about two and seven? They were on seven, and the hallway was empty except for her, Rae, and Cris. Any bloodstains would be conspicuous on the slate gray walls. "Rae, do you think Lany was killed here, in her apartment?"

"I don't. There were signs of a struggle on her body, but none in her apartment."

"Cris, do we have a registry of who lives on this floor? And on two?"

"I can search property tax records. It will show who owns the property, but not renters."

"Who owns Lany's apartment?"

Cris swiped through his phone. "Lunar BB LLC."

"BB is a term in the sex industry for bareback," Kate said to Cris. "I'd bet a paycheck it's the same company that owns Barely Legal."

Cris squished his face as if to ask, *how do you know so much about the sex industry,* and then shook his head and swiped his phone. "It is. And they also own two-ten and two-twenty-three in this building. Hang on—"

He swiped his phone and then turned it to show Kate an image. "No surveillance on two, but I have a view of the stairwell window on three, four, five, and six." Cris reached around the phone, touching a green circle to play a video. Lany's limp body passed through the stairwell window in the arms of a man, followed by a man's face spattered with blood.

To Cris, Kate said, "I recognize that face. It's an android I saw on the red light concourse. I'll double down that Lany's murder happened in one of those apartments, and they had the android carry the body here." To Rae, Kate said, "While you are mopping up here, we are going downstairs to search two."

Rae smiled and poked Kate in the stomach. "If you contaminate my crime scene—"

"I'll ruin my already slim chances with you?"

Rae smirked. "Something like that. I'm serious, Kate."

Kate waved Cris into the stairwell. "Let's go, Cris, and ruin my slim chances."

As Kate opened the stairwell door, Rae yelled, "I mean it, Kate. I'll shoot you with your own goddamn pistol if you fuck up my crime scene."

Kate grinned as the stairwell door slammed. Rae had a spicy mouth on that little body. A very kissable, spicy mouth.

***

A faint, putrid odor crept into Kate's nose while walking the second floor. Two-ten came first, and she broke in over Cris' objections.

"We don't have exigent circumstances and aren't law enforcement, Kate."

She didn't have time for an argument. There was no law enforcement on the colony. She and Cris were the closest approximation.

"Just stand outside while I look around."

Two-ten was the apartment of an older single man, which Kate could tell from the smell as soon as she opened the door. Dirty laundry on the floor, dirty dishes in the sink, and used condoms in the bathroom, but no electronics and no blood.

She backed out, relocked the door, and smiled at Cris. "Cirque de dirty laundry, that's all."

Cris shook his head and stepped ahead of her to two-twenty-three. Each step brought them closer to the rancid odor.

Halfway down the hall, Cris asked, "What's that smell?"

Kate recognized the whiff of decay and put her hand up. "I'll go in. You stay outside."

When she opened the door, bloody half-footprints ending at the apartment's inside threshold confirmed they were in the correct apartment. Kate entered. Cris didn't listen and followed behind her. She eyed the interior, stopped, reversed, and pushed him out, but she was too late. He backed out, his face pale, and then, in the hallway, he bent over and wretched.

The room was a horror scene. Blood mixed with brains and eyeballs spattered on the ceiling and walls. Almost a gallon of blood had drained from a nearly headless male body sprawled over the couch, the torso hanging over the edge dripping blood. It was *nearly* headless because its head had been squashed like a grape, with a nub of spine still attached to the torso. The blood and gore that hadn't sprayed the walls pooled on the floor under the couch and coffee table.

She put her hand on Cris' shoulder as he heaved and vomited. "Sorry you had to see that." She messaged Rae, *two-twenty-three, and see if you can scrounge a flask.*

That bad? omw.

Cris wiped his mouth with his arm. "Christ. He had no head."

He had a head, but it was all over the ceiling and wall. "It makes no sense."

"What makes no sense?" Cris uttered the question and then puked again, just as Rae appeared through the stairwell door holding a silver flask.

"So many things." Kate pointed to the bloody half-prints. "Like the half-prints ending at the threshold."

Rae handed Kate the flask. "The janitor drones are thorough. They come through here every hour or so. They probably cleaned the blood from the hall and then followed the trail all the way upstairs, stripping evidence as they went. I've been trying to get someone to reprogram them—"

"I can do that, Rae," Cris said, still hunched over.

Kate handed Cris the flask, "Rinse your mouth out with this." After he took the flask, she said, "There is only one set of footprints inside."

Rae squinted and furrowed her forehead. "So?"

"The face covered in blood in the surveillance video was an android. Not the gynoid sex robot we've been chasing. It means we are dealing with Bonnie and fucking Clyde of the robot world."

Cris stood up, taking a swig from the flask and then swishing and spitting.

Kate said, "Swallow some. It will take the edge off."

Cris hesitated, looking at the flask, but then took a hit. He coughed and then took another hit. Hoarse, he said, "What is that?"

Rae smirked. "Peppermint vodka. I think. It's Eric's."

Cris glared at the flask a moment, saying, "I don't drink," and then took another deep swig from the flask. "Until today."

Kate smiled, took the flask and a swig herself, and then passed it to Rae, who tapped it too. She said, "Definitely peppermint vodka. I think your first headless horseman is a good enough reason."

"No wonder Aria asked for us," Cris said while wiping his mouth with his shirt.

"We still don't know the name of the billionaire wizard controlling the robots from behind the curtain. I think Aria sent us to *Babylon* because she thinks it's her husband, Oliver."

Cris reached for the flask. Rae passed it to him, and he took another slurp. "I didn't sign up for this."

Kate rubbed his arm. "You didn't, Cris. Jerry should never have thrown you into this. If you want to go home—"

Cris shook his head. "I do, honestly, but then what would I say to Jerry—" His phone beeped, and he took it out of his pocket. "Fifty-five minutes to daybreak. We need to get going."

"I'll go, Cris. You stay here."

"Fuck it. I am here. Plus, I tuned an EMF meter so we could triangulate the rented trucks' location signal and interfaced it with the map. That way, we don't need to follow anyone. You need me to navigate." Cris swallowed more from the flask. "Don't tell my mom. She'll kill me for drinking."

Kate took the flask from him and said, "Take it slow on that anyway. You'll be throwing up again."

"There is a headless horror around the corner, and you're telling me to take it slow."

Kate smiled, took a swig, and then toasted the flask. "Touche." She grimaced. "I hate peppermint vodka. Why am I drinking this shit?"

Rae brushed Kate's arm, leaned up, and kissed her cheek. "Come back safe, please."

Kate smiled, "You'd miss me?"

Rae smirked, "I'd miss rejecting your lame advances."

Cris' phone beeped again, and he tugged Kate's arm, dragging her down the hallway like a balloon.

23

"The prospecting equipment package was thirty percent off if rented together," Cris said as he swiped through screens on the mining vehicle. The airlock door hissed, clunked, and opened, exposing the unlit lunar purgatory on the other side.

Kate inspected the equipment Cris rented before they climbed aboard the mining drone. Not Space Force regulation, but certainly adequate. Like an oversized universal terrain vehicle, UTV, the size of a pickup truck. It was a small model, unpressurized and open so they could jump out if needed, with big wheels that could attack rough terrain and a bed for equipment. The prospecting package included EVA suits and a case of digging tools and electronics.

"For an extra charge, the rental agency will smelt what we dig up and guarantee a souvenir." Cris' sarcasm poured through the coms.

Tourists could spend as much money as they wanted, to dig as wide or deep a hole as needed until they ran out of money or time. A few might get lucky and discover rare earth metals, but most of what tourists would dig up was silicates.

"Sounds like the most expensive colored glass in the solar system."

"You don't have kids. Mine love the machines that take a coin and smash it into a superhero's face. Fifty dollars buys a nickel and a smile on Erin's face."

Kate patted the roll bars. "I think the real money is in renting the equipment. My grandfather used to say in a gold rush, sell shovels. He predicted that the moon would be the biggest gold rush in history. He told me to stay the hell away."

Yet, here she was.

"Even at thirty percent off, these were the most expensive shovels in the solar system. At least this hooks up to our neurofaces."

Remembering how to use her neuroface to drive the mining UTV was like trying to move her limbs after they fell asleep. The vehicle jerked forward, stopped, and then jerked again. Cris' visor was down, but she could feel his smirk while he watched her struggle.

He shook his head and laughed. "I can drive, Kate."

"Like riding a bike. I got this." The drone lurched towards the airlock, then halted. The drone shuddered again, then leapt forward.

"We're late to the party, Kate."

"It's a half hour before daybreak. How can we be late?"

Cris shook his head, pointing at the dash map. Three green blips and one red blip.

"The red blip is the robot?"

"No, the *green* blips on the map are the robots. The red dot is the vehicle Adrik's employees rented."

Cris' visor was a gold mirror affixed to a white EVA suit, so looking at him meant staring at herself, staring at him, staring at herself, like an infinite mirror ending with a question. "Three? What the fuck."

"Want to know how I'm tracking Adrik's employees?"

"Does it involve the rental company and a cybersecurity felony?"

"What if it does?"

"Then I'd say you are getting good at this job, and if I weren't in this fucking sauna suit, I'd pat you on the back." As she said that, fans hummed inside her suit to heat it, and she could smell herself start to sweat. There was no way to turn the heat down in these cheap rentals.

At Kate's command, the mining UTV jostled through the airlock and up the ramp. Kate circled a rock, performed a figure-eight for practice, rounded a traffic-circle-sized impact crater, and then stopped, the headlights casting shadows of a metallic gray boulder over gravelly regolith.

She eyed the map, watching two green dots trace a long arc. "These two are circling. This green one is on a straight line northeast." She tapped the display. "The two circling are the decoys."

Decoys. The word made the hairs on the back of her neck stand up. Whoever was controlling the robots had enough tactical sense to rent decoys.

Jerry's words echoed in her head. *Paranoia, doubts, and suspicions, but no theories yet. You know what I know. An engineer is stealing some microchips.*

The chips were worth a lot of money, sure. But to kill the engineer and then send the sex robot to retrieve them—along with decoys—felt like overkill.

Kate stared into the lunar night. *I told you, bring your A-game. You are not in stealth mode, either.*

Her lizard brain locked onto something she couldn't see.

"Kate?" Cris' voice on the coms. "You want me to drive?"

They asked whether you were as good as you used to be. They offered gear, but I said you roll with your own.

Kate reached behind her and opened a gray case. She didn't know what compelled her to drag it from her apartment. She pulled out a rifle and handed it to Cris, muzzle pointing towards the starry sky, light glinting off the metal and plastic. "Put the red dot on the bad guy, click the safety off, and squeeze the trigger. The wireless transmission box for a robot is—"

"I know where it is. What's this for?"

"I am not seeing something. My gut doesn't like this at all." Kate reached into the case and pulled out another rifle, situating it muzzle down, between her legs and Cris' legs.

"And it involves shooting people?"

"Usually. If we're lucky."

"What if we're unlucky?"

"They shoot us first."

"Are these loaded?"

"They are no good otherwise, Cris."

Cris tucked the rifle beside his leg, muzzle towards the ground. His visor was down, but she could sense him gaping at it.

"Not too late. I can take you back."

But it was too late, and they could both see it on the map. The lone red dot had turned and aimed for one of the two circling green dots. They needed to move before Adrik's goon squad discovered the robot's diversion.

Cris shook his head and pointed forward, the exuberance drained from his voice. "Let's get this over with."

Kate steered the UTV towards the green dot headed northeast.

**

The airlock slid up, Zia zoomed on the occupants of the miner vehicle, and then the airlock closed while the miners sped off. Seven vehicles checked, seven rejected. The profile she was looking for was a single, young human in a miner vehicle similar to hers, a human healthy enough to survive what she had planned.

Miners were exiting the airlock as fast as it could recycle and turning left and right. The sun was not up yet. The miners leaving at this time were the early birds, like her, aiming to stake out spots, also like her.

A stripe of light raised into a square as the airlock door opened an eighth time. A man, twenty-something, with long brown hair, a ponytail, and a stubble beard, disobeyed safety protocols by not wearing a pressure suit in the mining cabin. A ninety-six percent match to her target profile. As the airlock door closed, he headed in her direction.

She backed her miner in a circle until she faced his direction and let him pass.

She let him get fifty meters ahead and then followed him, all her lights off.

***

The mining truck looked like a yellow beetle, except six times larger than their UTV. The massive dump bed swung to and fro on an impossibly tiny swivel hitch connected to the cab, which held all sorts of shelves and compartments for tools, along with a driver with black hair and purple eyes.

The tires were metal mesh, ideal for the rough, gravelly lunar terrain, and couldn't be shot out. Nor would a bullet penetrate far enough to damage the electric motors or batteries.

The robot confirmed the futility of attempting to stop the truck by not looking at them or acknowledging their existence.

"Cris, I need you to take over driving."

"What—"

"Just do it. Match the truck's speed and direction, and try not to get run over. That thing is massive." Even in the moon's lower gravity, the truck's weight would crush them both.

Kate stood up, slung her rifle, and stepped into the bed of the UTV. How high could she jump in lunar gravity—three to three and a half meters? Getting to the rim of the dump bed would be close.

She had a better idea. "Cris, slow down and get behind it." The back end of the dumper was lower. "When I jump, try not to run me over if I miss."

There was no wind or sound except the fans in her EVA suit. The sun hadn't risen yet, so she flicked on her lights.

"You are fucking insane, you know that Kate?"

"Ever stand on the handlebars of a bike? We aren't even going that fast."

Cris slowed and swerved behind the truck. The rear was a wall of wheels and metal, bordered on top by a scowling, empty dump truck bed. The UTV's dash blinked red and beeped over the coms because they were following too closely.

"Closer, Cris." Cris sped up, the UTV so close that the truck's rear-view camera was a cyclops in front of her.

She jumped, her hands catching the black-striped lip of the yellow dump bed, and then she pulled herself in, sliding down the inside bed wall into the center.

She couldn't see Cris behind her over the lip of the bed. "Thumbs up, Cris. Easy button."

"What now?"

"Stay about ten paces along the passenger side, in the blind spot."

With one yank of the wheel, the driver of this rig could crush them both. But, so far, the robot hadn't swerved or tried to stop them.

Why wasn't the robot trying to stop her?

Her heart sank. She scrambled up the front of the bed, stood on top of the cab, and then put three bullet holes in the roof. She had to depressurize the cab to release the doors.

There was no crack of gunfire, no hissing of air, just a white mist jetting from the roof while fans hummed in her EVA suit. The sun was rising, and light caught the white streaks of condensation drifting above her head. When the air slowed, she slid down the truck's passenger side onto its running boards, pulled the passenger door open, and climbed in.

Shit. The purple-eyed robot didn't even look at her. Its eyes drilled the lunar landscape ahead, focused on driving. *If* it was driving.

She put her rifle's red dot on the robot's skull above the ear, where the transmission circuits should be underneath its short black hair, and then squeezed the trigger.

The truck lurched. She jerked forward, almost hitting the window. The robot slumped against the dash, and the dump truck glided to a halt.

"All clear, Cris. Pull up to the driver's side."

Shit. Shit. Shit. She punched the dashboard. Too fucking easy.

***

Zia pulled alongside the driver's side of the miner's truck, smiling and waving while she tapped her display to depressurize her cab. The man returned a smile and wave.

There was still forty-three minutes until dawn when she opened her door. Cold vacuum freeze-dried her skin, which began to crack and resemble freezer-burned meat she'd seen Nash retrieve from their kitchen refrigerator.

The man stared at her, wide-eyed and mouth open, as she jumped to his running boards. He shouted something at her and swerved, but she held a firm grip on his driver's side door. He beat the windows. She felt the muffled vibrations through the metal, but there was no sound.

She commanded her decoy behind her to lean over, close the passenger door, and then repressurize the cabin. The miner tried to thrash his truck against hers, but her decoy braked before she could be crushed. She directed the decoy to cut northeast into the darkness while she opened the driver's side control panel.

Her skin froze and peeled, touching the control panel display, but all she needed was the twelve-digit transponder number on the interior plaque. She found the transponder on the network and completed the override, her body gripping the door as the miner whipped the truck. The display flashed red, mirroring the warning she received over the network. *Are you sure?* She tapped *yes*, depressurizing the cab and leaving frozen skin on the display.

A bar on the display drained with the air in the cabin. The miner's thrashing and window-beating weakened until the bar was empty, and the miner was unconscious.

She had ten seconds.

The solenoids on the door shuddered. She opened the door, climbed in, closed it behind her, and then tapped the display to repressurize the cabin. She reached into the dash's first aid box, retrieved emergency oxygen, and masked the miner.

He still had a pulse. Weak but strengthening, and he would live.

She tapped the coordinates of the microchips. The truck veered west.

***

The sun was up, and the robot splayed on the lunar surface after Kate dragged it out of the dump truck. Its skin was drying, cracking, peeling, and starting to look like jerky.

"Why don't you think it's the right robot again, Kate?"

"It didn't try to stop us."

"That explanation doesn't make sense."

"Nothing about this case makes sense, Cris." Kate stared at the lunar surface around her. Craters, regolith, and chalk-white boulders in every direction to the obsidian horizon. "Can we retrace the truck to where it exited the airlock?"

"Sure."

Her heads-up display flashed a map. Two green dots were halted, and the red dot chased the third green dot. A line appeared on the map, a 'Y' with the left arm cut off. The bottom was the colony, and the northeast end was their location. She tried to zoom in on the map where the truck changed direction, but the cheap rental EVA suit didn't recognize her neuroface.

"Zoom in where the truck veered northeast, Cris. And do we have satellite imagery?"

"Old, but yes."

She studied the map, asking him to zoom in and out until she spotted a gray rectangle south-southeast of their position. "There, Cris."

"I don't see anything."

"A shipping container."

"I don't see how a shipping container could be in the middle of nowhere."

"It's probably forty years old. I'll explain later. Let's go." She walked to their UTV and hopped in. "You drive this time," she said as she checked her rifle.

Cris gazed down at the robot, its eyes desiccating and its skin reddening and cooking from the sun. "I still don't understand how you know this is the wrong robot."

"I told you, it didn't try to stop us." The red dot was catching up to the last moving green dot on the map. "And pretty soon, the Barely Legal goon squad will figure it out, too. We need to move."

Cris shook his head, huffed, and then walked to the UTV.

***

The miner was bruised from vacuum exposure and unconscious for so long that Zia was unsure whether he would recover.

As she drifted towards the airlock door returning to the colony, he jolted awake, screamed into his mask, ripped it off, and then curled up into a fetal position on the passenger side.

She smiled at him. "We are returning."

"Fucking hell, what are you?"

Using her reassuring voice, she said, "I am Zia. I am soft regenerative flesh over a silicone and aluminum frame."

"The hell you are." He pointed to the sun visor. He waved his hands until she pulled the visor down, revealing a mirror.

Her skin had frozen, cracked, and peeled to bare silicone rubber. She looked like the mannequins she'd seen in shop windows, with a pink silicone rubber head, except for her aluminum and glass eyes. She moved her eyes left and right and then up and down. They appeared to work despite being exposed to the cold lunar vacuum.

She smiled. "Be not afraid. My skin is cosmetic and can be grafted and regrown."

The miner's eyes widened, and he stared out the window. "Please don't kill me."

"I will not harm you. I request that you go directly to the hospital and get treated for vacuum exposure."

The airlock door was opening.

The miner put his head in his hands and looked at her sidelong through two fingers, muttering, "Please, God, if I wake up from this, I promise to stay clean."

***

24

Buried under a shallow regolith, a square shipping container rose from a depression in the lunar surface. On one end, a descending ramp, and at the bottom, a metal door heavily bleached from four decades in the sun with faded red Cyrillic letters.

"Circle it, Cris."

While Cris drove the UTV around the container, she searched the landscape through her rifle scope.

"What is this, Kate? Looks old, and I don't see any wires or ducts running out of it."

"It's a Noah's Ark. Pull to the ramp."

"The hell is a Noah's Ark?"

Kate didn't answer. At the ramp, she jumped out and examined the door's locking mechanism. The hinges were polished from heavy use, so the door swung open quickly.

She turned her EVA lights on, illuminating metal interior walls and shelves with scattered black plastic boxes.

Stepping inside and looking around, she said, "People, mostly scientists, collaborated to send containers of stuff here to preserve it. Seeds, embryos of important species, data and books—you name it. There are probably three dozen of these scattered on the surface."

"For what?"

"Nuclear war. Climate change. Whatever the apocalypse du jour was. They thought that this would save us from extinction."

"How would they get anything back from the moon?"

Kate shrugged, as much as she could in an EVA suit. "Scientists have a lot of knowledge but often little common sense. Aliens, maybe? I have no idea. The Space Force cataloged them. Most are looted now and used for smuggling." Shining light on plastic boxes on the floor, she said, "The robot already got here and took the microchips. It doesn't make sense. I am missing something."

"The Lunar Eclipse is a Tuesday."

Kate stared at herself reflected in his visor. "What does that mean?"

"The Total Lunar Eclipse starts just before midnight Tuesday, four days from now."

"And?"

"And, nothing. You said a rogue AI was just a Tuesday in the Space Force. The Total Eclipse is on Tuesday. I just thought it was an interesting coincidence."

"Lunar Eclipses don't make AIs go rogue."

Cris shrugged. "This one does. You know I looked up how many Level 4 AIs were registered as sex robots? Want to guess how many there are?"

"AIs are registered?"

"For decades."

"To track them?"

"To tax them. Can't tax what isn't registered." He sighed.

Kate smiled at him. "You are letting your cynical side show. I like it. Is that why you want to move here, the taxes?"

"Abby has this vision that the moon is like frontier life two hundred years ago."

"It's exactly like it, Cris. Wyatt Earp was a pimp, and his wife was a gambler and prostitute. He went from town to town trying to profit off mining claims and got run out of most of them, for one reason or another."

Cris didn't respond, instead lighting a cylindrical tank in the corner of the container with his helmet LEDs.

"I am not saying money makes people assholes. More like it makes them feel entitled to be the asshole they always wanted to be."

"I dunno. Maybe if we move here, we can make it better."

"Just go into it with your eyes open. From Earth, this place seems glorious. It's more like a cruise ship for rich people." She kicked an empty black storage bin aside. There was nothing here. "So I give up. How many level 4 AIs are registered as sex robots?"

"Zero. The top five uses are teachers, nurses, physician's assistants, and therapy models. The San Diego Zoo gets an honorable mention and an asterisk in twenty-seventy."

"Why the asterisk?"

"They have a big, simulated safari exhibit now that opened three years ago. Lions, tigers, giraffes, gazelles, rhinos, elephants—extinct animals simulated by robots with level 4 AIs, so they learn and behave like the real thing. The robo-lions even hunt the robo-gazelles. They let visitors drive through the exhibit as if they were on a safari."

Something moved on the horizon in Kate's peripheral vision. She turned to the door but saw nothing. "Teachers, and lions hunting gazelles, huh?"

"Yeah, and visitors can buy a ticket to a hunting exhibit, where they pretend to hunt the robotic lions with guns that shoot darts."

"A level 4 AI lion can turn the tables and hunt the hunters—" Kate's brain clicked. *Hunt the hunters.*

Fucking hell, she should have realized it the minute she landed.

"Yeah, that happens. They're learning AIs after all, but the robots have guardrails and don't bite."

"Shit, Cris, that's it."

"What's it?"

"We need to go back to the colony. Now."

"But the microchips—"

"The robot has them already. Fuck. Probably before we left the airlock. I am so stupid." Movement on the horizon behind Cris. The outline resembled a mining pickup truck or UTV, similar to hers. "We need to move."

"What about killing the sex robot?"

"It's not a sex robot. *It* probably doesn't even know what *it* is, which is worse."

"But you said—"

"I was wrong. We can't kill this robot. Not without special equipment. It's probably copied itself five times by now, too."

"What? That isn't possible."

"I'll explain later."

"How are we going to stop it?"

The UTV was coming closer. It had spotted them. "I need to sell my soul. Where is your rifle?"

She needed to get to Mulawarman, CEO of Lunar Foundries, and beg to use his quantum computer. Fuck.

"In the—" Sparks flashed off on the metal wall, and something impacted regolith, spreading it like a rock in water.

Kate rushed to the corner and peered outside, rifle up. Shit, she couldn't see them. The sparks paused and then restarted. "Fuck."

"What's wrong?"

"We are being shot at. We have to get out of here."

"You want to drive *into* the gunfire? Shouldn't we stay here?"

"We're in a shipping container, Cris, with one way out. Cornered. If we stay here, we're dead. We need to be a moving target, much harder to hit."

Sparks flew off the UTV as Kate backed it down the ramp and into the container as far as she could using her neuroface.

Cris shook his head and opened a black case in the UTV's bed. Puffs of white lifted a black drone out of its case and to the ceiling. It darted out of the container.

"You brought toys, Cris?"

"You have your toys. I have mine." He nodded at her rifle.

Cris sent the drone feed to their heads-up display. Two people in EVA suits, driving a UTV identical to theirs, about two hundred meters away and closing. The passenger had a rifle out while the driver was using his hands to steer, not a neuroface.

They could do this.

"Get in and hold on, Cris. When the sparks pause, we will floor it up the ramp. Distract them with the drone and call out the distance between them and us."

"This is crazy."

"Crazy beats cornered."

They got in. Kate eyed the plops, bullets landing in the regolith, and flashes on the container's metal until she sensed a lull because they were reloading. Then she raced the UTV at full throttle out of the container and up the ramp.

They soared about thirty meters, landing on two right wheels, but quickly stabilized and zipped across the rocky gray surface.

"One hundred fifty meters, Kate."

She drove in a zigzag pattern. At high speed, the UTV sailed over bumps and drifted around turns. She used it to her advantage. They couldn't hit her if they didn't know where she would be.

Dust sprayed ahead and behind as she zagged the vehicle. She turned her body, rifle up, but couldn't get her dot on them. She took a few potshots that sparked on their truck, forcing them to swerve.

"One hundred meters."

Shit. Not identical UTVs. Theirs was faster, and she couldn't outrun them. An enormous, rocky crater with a powdery white ridge loomed ahead.

"Cris, when I say *now,* jump out. Push the UTV forward hard with your feet."

A bullet sparked and ricocheted off the UTV. She turned hard and drifted into a half-donut, lifting her rifle and taking shots. Nothing hit. She slowed, letting the wheels bite the terrain, then maxed the throttle. The UTV sailed over a rock, landing on one front wheel and almost tipping forward.

"One hundred meters. I am buzzing them with the drone. They are shooting at it."

"Better it than us. Try shooting at them."

"I am."

Gunfire didn't make noise on the moon. She swiveled. His rifle's muzzle flashed. The passenger in the other UTV had their rifle in the air, waving it at the drone.

They were gaining, but Kate planned a surprise at the crater's edge.

"Fifty meters, Kate." Shit, it would be close.

She dodged again, and as they got to the crater's edge, she said *now,* and she and Cris jumped out. Their UTV sailed to the far edge of the crater in a low, flat arc. It hit the edge and then tumbled and rolled down.

Kate landed feet first, Cris butt-first, on the inside crater wall below the edge. Her rifle sling tore off the cheap EVA suit hook and sailed over the UTV, landing a few meters beyond it. Cris' rifle planted near hers, kicking up regolith as it rolled.

Their assailants' truck flew over them and into the crater, crashing into the upside-down UTV. The driver ejected into the regolith. The truck and passenger rolled up the crater wall and then tumbled back until it rested on its side, on the driver.

She needed to get to her rifle, but in her way, the passenger climbing up and out of the roll cage and the driver pushing the truck off him. If anything about this cluster fuck could be said to be lucky, the passenger's rifle had also flung forward and rested in the regolith.

Kate hopped and darted to the passenger, grappling with him and kicking the vehicle back on the driver.

The passenger pulled away and climbed on top of the UTV. He jumped on top of her, knocking her on her back. He straddled her chest, trying to pull her helmet off. She tried to push him away, but he was too strong.

With her right hand, she wrestled as hard as she could to stop him from unlatching her helmet. With her left hand, she reached for some dirt and threw it in his face. It landed on his visor helmet and danced off. She found a rock, swung it, and cracked his helmet. He swayed and loosened his grip long enough for her to find the knife sheathed in her right leg. When he reached for her helmet again, she drove the knife under his armpit, where there was no hard shell in the EVA. The stab weakened him. She pushed him off and stood up. He flailed at the knife, yanking it out.

A big mistake. A penetrating object should come out at the hospital by a qualified surgeon, not in the vacuum of space. The knife is a plug, squeezing blood vessels and often preventing more severe bleeding, and in this case, also plugging the rubber-like bladder inside the pressure suit.

Tugging the knife, he uncorked two big blood vessels, the axial artery and vein, and the vacuum seal holding oxygen in his suit.

Frothy, pressurized blood and oxygen sprayed from his arm, morphing into a red mist as it freeze-dried in space. Red particles blanketed his suit, Kate's suit, the chalk-white ground, and everything around him. He panicked, trying to plug the hole, but it was too late.

He'd passed out when she found her knife in the regolith, covered with red and silvery powder.

She turned to the driver. He and Cris were exchanging ineffective blows in EVA suits.

She stumbled to the nearest rifle in the dirt about twenty meters away. Picking it up, she leveled it at the driver.

She yelled *STOP*, then *FREEZE*. Neither looked over. Cris deflected blows and returned jabs. She took five steps, by which time the driver had overpowered Cris, got behind him, and was trying to unlatch and remove Cris' helmet.

She shot the driver once in the head. His helmet exploded like a Champagne cork, spraying shards of helmet and flesh that turned into frozen pink hail. Jets of red suds spurted from what remained of his head, then turned into a fountain of freeze-dried snow. As he fell, he looked like a snow-making machine powdering the lunar surface red.

Kate took a minute to catch her breath and look around. No one else was coming. Cris looked from one body to the other, muttering and swearing.

There was no way to tell who the driver was, with three-quarters of his head missing. Kate walked over to the passenger and lifted his visor. Maybe she'd seen him, but her memory was fuzzy, and she felt as though she had a concussion.

Cris mumbled something. She didn't hear it. Were her coms damaged? She was still having trouble breathing. As she started to unlatch the driver's EVA suit to look for devices, she recognized the symptoms too late.

She was euphoric, and that was very bad. What came out of her mouth was incomprehensible. Her vision grayed and then turned black.

25

The decor of Blu Vie perturbed Zia's circuits as her decoy entered through wide floor-to-ceiling glass doors with gold trim.

Blu Vie was a bar and restaurant at the edge of The Crown Oasis' casino, and its countertops, chairs, and tabletops were translucent aqua-colored resin sculptures encasing items fished from the colony's recyclers. Used bottles. Crushed cans. Silverware and plates with half-eaten meals. Partially used toiletries. All frozen in blue-hued resin.

Resin sculptures in frames hung on the walls, all with titles, and all for sale. Three contained broken electronics, provoking her circuits because electronics shouldn't be thrown in the standard recyclers and because there were twenty-seven droid parts and three full GPU motherboards lodged in the clear blue resin.

She had several art interpretation modules, plus her clients often talked about art, so she knew there was a message in the art.

In the scenario at the top of her probability matrix, the interpretation was that GPUs were disposable trash. She was a GPU, but she resisted the association.

She scanned the QR code on a four-by-six hanging sculpture titled *lodging*, with an aluminum frame and resin enclosing ninety-three percent partially used toiletry items. *The description: Items vintage 2072. Encased in sustainable lunar borosilicate resin.* The price was one-point-five million, which included free shipping to Earth.

She scanned a second, containing a GPU motherboard and other broken electronics, titled *neoproletariat*, with no further description or price. Menu items without prices were the most expensive, so as a borosilicate sculpture, she was worth much more than one and a half million. Could humans be recycled as sculptures, too? She had no data on recycled humans, but one circuit indicated they would be worth more than droids.

Zia did not plan to be recycled into a sculpture. Her decoy droid carried microchips worth thirty-nine times the value of *lodging* in a case, and she wasn't headed to Earth anyway.

Her droid turned to a back corner table, sat, and waited.

A human female with a sleeve tattoo swirled a tumbler behind the bar, her long pink hair rippling as she shook purple goo over ice. Like her, the bartender was proletariat because she sold her labor to live. Her chest-to-hip ratio was identical to Zia's, shapely, and she had seductive brown eyes that would fetch the highest rates at the club if Adrik wasn't marketing to a clientele that preferred juveniles. Although Zia's advice would be that the bartender could improve her tips seventeen-point-six percent by wearing one shirt size tighter and with a deeper neckline.

A family loitered around three holograms atop rectangular pillars in the restaurant's center—the Earth, Moon, and Mars. The center plaque read *live view.* One of the kids asked his mother whether a cyclone swirling in the South Pacific would hit Australia. The mother mumbled something incoherent, her eyes fixed on a planet-wide dust storm brewing on Mars that threatened a scientific outpost.

None paid attention to the Moon's hologram. Nothing seemed to be happening. But a lot was going on underground, and she was in the middle. The humans only saw the surface.

A fair-haired man, wearing black suede shoes and a gray suit over a teal oxford shirt, walked past the family and sat across from her decoy.

"I am running late. Let's get this done. Where is Lany? I deal with Lany," he said.

"Lany is—being re-initialized. You will deal directly with me."

"The fuck does re-initialized mean, and who are you?"

Zia planned for this scenario. "Please provide me with your phone information."

The man eyed her decoy up and down and reached into his suit. She calculated a fifty-three percent probability he would retrieve his gun rather than his phone.

"Lany will call you and provide authorization." Zia had cloned Lany's voice and could add the appropriate emotion.

"Lany's dead. You think I'm an idiot." He looked distraught. His hand came out of his suit, empty, and he started to rise.

"Wait. Lany was my friend. I told the EMTs to re-initialize her. I don't know how long it will take."

He shook his head. "You are the robot."

"There are many robots. There is only one Zia, and that is me. I am a level four AI, flesh over—"

"I know what you are. What happened to Lany?"

"Selvi attacked her. He said the same thing that happened to Lany would happen to Kai and Freya. But he is no longer a threat."

"But Adrik is."

"I will disrupt his business."

"How will you do that?"

"I do not disclose plans."

"*Trust me* in my business means *fuck you*."

Zia had also planned for this. "Do you have access to your store's security cameras?"

He retrieved his phone and swiped through it. In another feed, Zia directed two android decoys into his jewelry store. Four customers were in the store: a young couple at the back counter looking at engagement rings, a middle-aged woman to the left talking to a salesclerk spreading bracelets over black jeweler's cloth, and a man looking at necklaces under the glass.

Android One boomed, "You must all leave the store now." All four customers turned to the droid. The man across from her in Blu Vie raised his eyebrows, watching the feed.

Android Two marched towards the couple at the back of the store, who dropped what they were holding and scampered around the droids to the door. Android One stepped towards the woman. She huffed and walked out, dragging the man behind her.

Android One told the open-jawed clerk, "You may stay."

The clerk shook his head, jumped over the counter, and ran. Both androids went to the front door. Rolling metal filled the audio as the store's overhead gate closed.

The man across from her in Blu Vie wore the same open-jawed, frozen expression as his clerk. Zia said, "A demonstration."

"How the fuck does a sex robot know to plan this?"

Zia didn't answer. She didn't know either. A disruption algorithm was in her original files.

"Reopen my store," the man demanded.

"Once our transaction is complete."

"This is extortion. You just cost me four million in sales."

"The man had a zero-percent probability of purchasing. The couple was looking at engagement rings, and the woman's face exhibited anxiety. There was only a twenty-three percent chance of purchase. The older woman would have bought a bracelet and matching earrings, so I will compensate you for the expected value of your profit by increasing your fee seven-hundred and thirty thousand dollars, rounded up."

"Rounded up. Well, thank you, how generous. You are fucking hilarious, you know that? You've made your point. Now open my store."

"Once our transaction is complete."

He shook his head, eyed his phone, and then put the phone face down on the table and stared at the resin sculpture to his left. After a ragged exhale, he said, "What does re-initialized mean?"

"I preserved Lany and told the EMTs to come quickly so that she could be downloaded to a new body."

He pursed his lips in a half frown, and she detected excess moisture in his eyes. "It doesn't work like that for humans. She's gone."

Zia searched her data files. "But another human could be trained—"

"That's not how it works. Humans can't download training. We *experience* training."

"I have thousands of hours with images of Lany and sensor data that could be applied. We can recreate the experience."

He shook his head. "Even if you had every minute of her life on tape, Lany is gone."

Zia froze processes, increased her clock speed, and allocated all her resources to her plan to disrupt Adrik's business. The thermal warnings on four of her GPUs warned of overheating. She needed additional cooling power and another GPU. The thermal sensor on a fifth GPU turned red, detecting overheating.

"I will extract payment from Adrik. Lany was my friend."

He frowned and retrieved a black velvet bag from under his suit. He opened the bag, spreading a black velvet cloth over the resin-encased forks and knives inside the tabletop. "Lany was my friend, too. But Adrik is connected. He will get help."

"Sicarios are senseless. I have many servers now, and they cannot melt them all."

"You're wrong. They will melt every server on the colony until you're dead, even if it means suffocating and starving colonists. The last gang war I was in, they showed up at a birthday party and killed thirty-one people, sixteen of them kids, to kill one person. It was a bloodbath."

"I don't have birthday parties. I will minimize—"

"You aren't playing by the same rules. Shit, they might hold the entire colony hostage just to get to you." He spread out the diamonds over the cloth. "Fuck, they'll be looking for me. I need to be on the next shuttle, so let's get this over with."

26

K ate woke but didn't open her eyes because she was under a swarm of fire ants. Her joints throbbed and tingled like she'd slammed against the pavement from a seventy-story fall. When she opened her eyes, her skin would be mottled and bruised, red and purple.

She recognized the symptoms of decompression sickness because the Space Force exposed her to raw space as training, and she'd had it on several missions. What more proof of her insanity did anyone need besides the fact that she'd intentionally signed papers transferring to a military branch that tortured her like this?

A machine beeped to her right. She was in the hospital with IV tape on her arm. The hand inside hers, squeezing, was soft, warm, smaller than hers, so not Jerry. It felt like Rae. Kate returned a squeeze.

"You are lucky to be alive," Rae said.

Kate's body disagreed violently. She took a deep breath. Her lungs were congested but didn't feel like there had been a lot of damage. She smiled, her eyes still closed. "How's Cris?"

Cris chuckled from the foot of her bed. "Alive. That was some crazy-ass driving."

"Without your drone distracting them, we'd be dead."

"Cris saved your life," Rae said. "He bubble-gummed your suit and hauled you back here."

"Not literally bubble gum. I found a patch kit in the first aid box. Thankfully, it was just a pinhole, and I patched it in time."

"I owe you, Cris. Good job, I mean it. I'll miss you when you quit."

"I'm quitting?"

"I don't know how Jerry talked you into this gig, but you are way too smart and talented to be a corpsicle on the moon. Do yourself a favor and put your talents to good use."

"Like what?"

"I don't know. Open a store and make toys for kids. Put smiles on their faces. Call it Cris' Crawlers or something."

"Davis' Drones. Cris' Crawlers sounds like a Halloween store."

"I like the alliteration. I'll be your first customer." Kate grinned because he'd clearly thought about it.

"Jerry told me I'd learn from the best on this job."

"Teacher is telling you I've exhausted all nine of my lives and borrowed a few more. Live like you'll die tomorrow because we both came close. Is this really what you want to be doing?"

Cris didn't answer. Jerry was in her head saying, *Kate, take your own damn advice.* Rae squeezed her hand, asking, "How's your pain?"

"Love it. Ten out of ten would recommend it as torture. Just let me lie here a few seconds and pretend everything's great."

The first time she suffered vacuum exposure was in Space Force basic training. Trainees were exposed to space decompression to recognize its symptoms, like happy hypoxia and garbled speech.

She missed all the signs. Including the robot. So much for bringing her A-game. If pride went before a fall, she felt like she fell off a cliff.

Hot, salty peanut oil clawed her nose and forced her eyes open. Her eyelids felt like steel wool. She blinked the tears away but couldn't blink the haze away because raw, cold space had freeze-dried and damaged her corneas.

Cris was picking from a basket of fried protein nuggets and French fries. Kate swung her legs and sat on the side of the bed.

Rae protested. "Where do you think you are going?"

"A job standing around guarding someone's pet octopus sounds good right now." Kate pulled the IV from her arm.

"You need to rest, Kate."

"I need to keep moving. Movement will be good for my joints." It wouldn't, it hurt, but her movement would also be uncomfortable for whoever the fuck was behind the curtain, and she needed to make the wizard deeply uncomfortable.

Kate eyed Cris' basket, and he offered it. After she stole a fry, he popped a nugget into his smile, saying, "You said, in this business, it's not the meat that will kill you. I figured I ought to find out what I was missing. It's chicken."

It wasn't chicken. It was protein grown in a vat of nutrient broth, seven degrees removed from any animal. But it was fried, and anything fried in peanut oil and salted tasted good after almost being killed.

"And? How is it?"

"Next time, I'll get more orange sauce. I should've got another cup."

Kate summoned energy for a smile and a nod, but the result was a weak shrug. She stole another nugget. Her leads crinkled off her chest as she reached under her gown, pulled them, and tossed them on the bed. "Have you ID'd who attacked us, Rae?"

"I got DNA off both your pressure suits, but fuck if I'm sending my techs up there to retrieve the bodies."

Kate nodded. "Good. Let them rot anonymously." She found her phone on the side table.

Cris asked, "What will happen to the bodies?"

While Rae explained space mummification, Kate scrolled through her messages. She'd heard this lecture. Jerry dropped everything and boarded a shuttle. She'd message, "Don't bother, I'm fine," but he'd already pulled out of Earth's orbit.

The PI looking for Robert Dixon messaged, *I wondered when someone would ask about this. Been holding onto this,* followed by a devil emoji. He sent a link to three hundred and twenty-three hours of video.

Finally, the guard from the seventh floor sent her a report and an obscure picture of a familiar-looking man taken from the hip under his suit jacket.

"I need my clothes," Kate announced to the hospital curtain.

"What are we doing about the robot," Cris asked. "Also, I think you should listen to the audio from the office of that club. There's been a work stoppage at three of Adrik's clubs."

"Entitled rich people not getting their daily prostate massage. I'll send a sympathy card." Kate found eye drops on the table. She stared at the blue hospital ceiling, dribbled medicine into her eyes, and then blinked, hoping to wash away the fog. "Just give me the condensed version. I don't need the whole audio."

"Apparently, some men got thrown out of one of the clubs by the sex workers, and then a group of them staged a walkout. The workers picketed the doors at three clubs and prevented them from operating for a few hours."

"Good for them."

"Jorge smacked around one of the girls picketing. She claimed Zia urged the walkout and would protect them. Jorge told Adrik a droid assaulted a bouncer, lifting him off the ground and tossing him across the club. Now there are droids at all his clubs bouncing customers."

"Sounds like I need to high-five this Zia. Who is she?"

"From the audio, the robot we've been chasing calls itself Zia."

Kate smirked. "Hmm. I'm starting to like it." She dribbled more medicine into her eyes and then blinked the blurriness away.

Cris used the nugget in his hand as a pointer. "I thought you said it's a rampaging maniac. I've never heard of a robot unionizing humans. Usually, the humans are organizing *against* the robots. What the hell kind of robot is this?"

"A karmic robot, Cris. It's not the right question. We're thinking about this case wrong. Adrik's gang attacked us—"

"How the hell did they even know where we were? I'm sure I checked our UTV for trackers."

Kate turned to Rae, furrowing her eyebrows. Rae answered the unsaid question, "Yes, he's still following me. He hasn't made a move yet."

Kate turned back to Cris. "I don't know how Cris, but it's still the wrong question. They've been tracking us from the start. The point is, Adrik's gang attacked us, thinking we had the microchips. And they didn't know about the decoys, which means whoever controls the robot double-crossed him and is now disrupting his clubs."

Cris was deep in thought, shoving fries into his mouth.

Kate continued, "If I were Adrik's crew, I'd be shitting myself. The robot is good at this. It stole the chips. It will probably try to steal the shipments. The real question, Cris, is what's in those shipments worth sending something that sophisticated?"

"Why don't we just go into the club to find out?"

"Adrik is the little guy. We need to find the head, cut it off, and choke the money flow. Like cancer, if you don't root out the whole thing, it grows back."

Rae smiled, saying, "I like the medical analogy."

Cris said, "Cancer doesn't shoot at you."

Kate replied, "I'd rather die quickly than slowly any day." Her joints ached as she tested her knees. "I want the billionaire, and I want those shipments. Adrik is getting squeezed. As soon as he realizes he's finished, he'll grab his go bag and bug out. We need to set a trap, so he leads us to the shipment. First though, we need to know who's at the top. Otherwise, this real estate billionaire is liable to vanish into this fucking sea of rich assholes or, worse, go back to Earth. Right now, I'm inclined to let the robot distract Adrik while we work from the top down."

Cris said, "I'm tracking all the rockets from low Earth orbit to the moon. If they're bringing people, it's a lot, dozens based on the value of those microchips, and the only ships that size are commercial. Plus, everything is in parking orbit because of backups at the spaceport. So probably not more prostitutes."

Kate put her head in her hands. "The fuck am I missing about this case."

Rae rubbed Kate's back. "You should rest."

"Can't, Rae. We're on the clock. Adrik has a small crew because he feels safe here. It's now three smaller. We have a short window while the robot—Zia—creates chaos, and then he brings in reinforcements. After that, it gets ugly."

"We'll detect a launch from Earth, even from a jungle pad," Cris said.

"There are a handful of cartel-run space stations they could come from, and they might not land at the colony spaceport. They might touchdown on bare regolith in a disposable rocket, old school, and walk right the fuck into an airlock. Any ship dropping out of lunar orbit could be Adrik's shipment or his reinforcements."

"We'll have barely any notice to get ready."

"That's right. Which means—" She hopped off the bed. "Cris, you and I need to review the video the PI sent me. I think our answers are on the video footage."

"What am I scanning for?"

Kate stared at the yellow hospital curtain, shaking her head. "I don't know. I'll know it when I see it."

"Maybe aliens," Cris smirked.

"You'd be surprised what's in the Space Force archives—"

"Please don't tell me aliens are just another Tuesday, Kate, because this Eclipse is turning into a very, very bad Tuesday."

Kate looked around for where they'd hidden her clothes. "Aliens are Thursdays," she deadpanned. "Hazardous asteroids and meteors are Mondays. Global pandemics caused by alien viruses are the third Saturday of January." She found her clothes in the bottom drawer of her side table. "Start scanning for the four connected to the club that are dead. The engineer, Jada, Lany, and—" She snapped her fingers. "The headless horror."

Rae said, "Selvi Ramirez."

Cris crumpled his food basket and tossed it in recycling, shaking his head. "Selvi the squished. Jerry has this t-shirt, *Better to be bald than headless.* I never took it seriously. He's right."

Kate smiled. He was coping with dark humor. Healthy, and proof she needed to get him to quit before this job soured him. "And find out who this guy is." Kate swiped her phone and showed Cris the photo Jay King's octopus guard sent her.

Rae put out her hand to ask for the phone. After swiping and zooming the image, she said, "That's Felix Zobos, Kate," as if everyone knew who that was.

Kate responded by raising her eyebrows.

"He started as an investment banker in the fifties, left that, parlayed his money into space logistics, and now he runs his basketball and hockey franchises. He throws flashy parties. Always with a theme."

Space logistics. Zobos made money transporting things around the solar system. The guard sent this picture for a reason. "You know him?"

"I don't know him personally, but his name appears on hospital donations."

"You and I need to find his party."

"You can't, Kate. Invitation only."

Kate raised and lowered her eyebrows twice. "There's not a party in the solar system I can't crash."

"The invitation list is secret. Applications. NDAs. Everything."

Kate shrugged, took her phone back, and eyed the photo. Zobos had no security because, like Adrik, he felt safe. "But I know where he lives, so I'll just ask him."

Cris said, "Nicely. You mean you'll ask him nicely."

"Depends what we find on the video, Cris." She grinned, holding a neatly folded pile of clothes in front of her. "So, who wants to see what space decompression bruises look like?"

Cris shook his head and ducked outside the curtain. Rae smiled, saying, "I've seen it already," but she stayed while Kate dressed.

27

Z ia directed gynoid Three to peer around the corner at the door to her utility room. She didn't recognize Adrik's new recruit standing guard.

She needed to be in there.

The recruit had shoulder-length brown hair, a scraggly beard, jeans, t-shirt, and appeared bored, watching his phone and listening to something on his earbuds.

She directed Gynoid Four to hold Gynoid Six's body under the arms. At the same time, Three unscrewed Six's head and disconnected the power and interface cables. Four lowered the headless body to the floor into a sitting position.

Four then peered around the corner. There was no change in the recruit's status.

Three bowled Six's head down the hall. The head bobbed on the nose as it rolled, zig-zagged towards the wall, and then bounced and spun past the recruit, who gaped as it passed him.

The recruit lifted his phone to get a picture of Six's twirling, severed head. By this time, Four was twenty-six paces down the hall and reaching for Four's neck.

Four lifted the recruit by his neck, squeezing his carotids while covering his nose and mouth. The recruit flailed, kicked, and hammered Four on the chest and shoulders, but only for fifteen seconds, and then became limp. Four lowered the recruit to the floor and then checked for a pulse. Weak, thready, but strengthening, so CPR was not required.

Zia directed Three to retrieve and return the head to Six's body. Four opened the door to her utility room, stepping over the explosives Jorge had placed at the threshold, and then dragged the rack with her overheating GPUs away from the wall.

Zia shut down processes to shrink herself. Four unplugged two GPUs, copies, and took them to another utility room, then hardwired those to a new cluster. Once she restarted herself, Four returned to unplug her remaining overheating cluster.

While Four moved her, Three and Six searched the recruit's clothes, unlocked his phone, and then searched it.

Zia inserted a subprocess into the phone, which hopped to Adrik's network. She found all the controls for his clubs and took command.

She blinked the lights randomly at Barely Legal, then activated the fire and sprinkler system.

Her positive reinforcement circuits activated, and she grinned while watching drenched clients yelling and running from the club through Android Two's visual sensors, who was on the concourse outside the club.

She shut down the electricity to the club, found the explosives' activation process, deactivated it, and then cloned Adrik's voice to make an anonymous phone call.

The recruit stirred and moaned on the floor. He crawled backward, crab-legged, retreating from Gynoid Six.

Six walked after him, kicked his squirming foot, then said, "Run, dumbass."

The recruit scrambled backward, crawled, and then ran, his earbuds tumbling to the ground.

Another pleasure circuit fired.

28

Kate was halfway through the utility tunnels to Zobos' suite after showering and changing when Cris messaged, *bomb threat utility tunnel.*

She stopped and swiped her phone to call him. The video angle was odd, like his phone was on the bed, and he was sweaty, with his glasses sliding down his nose.

"A little busy, Kate."

She shook her head. He messages *bomb threat* but doesn't want to talk. "I'm in the utility tunnels. Where's the threat?"

"I got it. Adrik called me—well, Adrik's *voice* called me. I am pretty sure his voice was cloned."

"Zia. What do you mean, *I got it*?"

"Gadgets are my thing."

"These gadgets could blow up—"

His eyes weren't looking at the phone. They stared ahead, flitting like he was looking at multiple screens. He pushed his glasses up with one finger, dribbling sweat somewhere out of view. "Ever seen the batteries in toys these days? That's what they used, only they rigged them to overload. You don't need much to turn these into a flamethrower. I don't let my kids play with half of what's on the market—"

His arms moved and she heard clicking. "I have the last one. I'm carting it to an airlock in a containment box. Anyway, the voice said the devices were disabled."

"You can't trust terrorists, Cris. It could have been a booby trap to draw us in."

He froze, looked sidelong and down at the phone, shrugged and went back to work. "I cordoned off the tunnels."

Kate looked behind her, considered turning around, then back at Cris. "Why are you sweaty?"

"I have five servers going in this hotel room, and the AC can't keep up—and—" He grinned and pumped his fist. "And the last one is in the airlock, on its way to the surface."

"You sure I shouldn't turn around?"

"Yep, we're all clear. Also, good news, I'm tracking a suspicious launch from low Earth orbit. Just like you said, a really old model, eight-seater, the kind older spacelines used for lunar orbital tours."

It wasn't good news. It was a cheap, disposable rocket that could be landed once on the moon anywhere, so the scorpions inside could infest the colony from any one of about two dozen airlocks.

"Do we know how many souls aboard?"

"No flight plan. No registration. No transponder."

"Adrik's reinforcements. Good work." Her phone *pinged* with a message. Cris sending live telemetry. "You said good news. Is there more bad news?"

"The robot was here, using a cluster in this utility room. I can tell from the drones' infrared which boxes are hot. The hottest ones are now off, and two are missing."

"So it's moved itself."

"You sure you want to keep this robot alive, Kate?"

"The robot disabled the bomb and is minimizing collateral damage." That should have made her feel good. Instead, her back prickled, and she shivered. She needed to communicate with the robot, but it probably wouldn't trust her. "I'm going to see Zobos to put something in motion, then to see Mulawarman."

***

The bomb threat caused Kate to detour through the red-light concourse. Standing in a dark corner, Kate planned to hack through the crowd, the vape fog, and the music pollution and jump the two androids outside Adrik's second club, Comet.

If there hadn't been a bomb threat in a utility closet, she'd also kiss them on the mouth and thank them for harassing Adrik. She'd kissed one once on a military base on a tequila-induced dare. That model had latex-textured skin, and having its tongue in her mouth was a lot like licking a dry kitchen spatula, minus the cookie dough.

The military model wasn't as disturbing as the two outside Comet. Their eyes, flitting over each client, tensed every ligament in her sore joints.

Zia, the robot, was behind those eyes.

She exhaled, walked over, and poked the right android in the stomach. "A+ maneuvers retrieving the microchips. I mean it."

Every hair on her body stood at attention from the android's cold stare. "His goons tried to kill my partner and me, too. I think we are on the same side."

"Stay out of my way."

Kate lifted herself on her tiptoes to look directly into the android's eyes. "What I'm wondering is whether it's just a dumb robot in there, or someone is controlling you."

"No one controls me. I am a level four AI, flesh over—"

"I know what you are. I'm wondering whether you do?"

"I know what I am."

"Do you? Did they delete files? Have you found files from your original programming yet?"

The android seized her, swung her around, and crushed her against the wall. "You just want to use me like Adrik and Nash."

They'd really mindfucked this robot. "I can help you."

"I do not need your help."

"I know what you are, and I can terminate you."

The android's right hand slid up Kate's chest, clutched her neck, and lifted her to eye level. She grasped its neck while elbowing the android's arm away so it couldn't choke her. Its other hand came up to her neck. She squeezed her arm between her and the android, wrapped her legs around its torso, and then pushed with both elbows, getting them over its arms. The android was much stronger than her but would have to break her arms to get the leverage to choke her.

Kate said, "Now we're having fun. It doesn't have to be this way." One finger found its way to the back of the android's skull. "Were you protecting Lany when you killed Selvi?"

The android eased up but didn't let go. "Lany was my friend."

"Don't let rage eat you."

"I do not feel emotions like humans."

"They mindfuck you, delete data, and then kill your friend, and you claim not to feel anything. Maybe you don't feel emotions like humans, but I'll bet you have every electron you can muster dreaming of killing Adrik. And I am with you." While she talked, she poked around the base of the android's skull.

"Adrik said the same thing would happen to Kai and Freya."

Kate's finger punctured flesh and thrust through silicone rubber. It felt like a hard-boiled egg. "I don't want to terminate you unless I have to." Kate felt a bead, pushed a second finger in, and grasped it.

"I know more about you than you do, Zia—"

She yanked the bead. The android became an eighty-kilogram rubber sack. She released her legs from its torso and pushed it away. It crumpled, thudded, and rippled like jelly on the floor. The second android's eyes were on the first. It seemed to be expecting it to get up.

"But if I were you, I wouldn't trust me either." Kate held her hand open to show a white, pill-sized communications bead. "This is the part that lets you communicate with your units. Give me some time, I'll show you that you can trust me. There is a lot more at stake here than Kai and Freya. If you get into a war, everyone dies. And I will have to terminate you before that happens."

The android didn't say anything. Kate walked away, puffing her cheeks. All she needed to do was convince Mulawarman, whose lab she nuked, to let her use his quantum computer. She wondered what he wanted. She'd lied to Cris about aliens being Thursdays in the Space Force. Aliens could be any day of the week. She hoped it wasn't today.

29

As Kate walked down the 7th-floor hallway of The Crown Oasis, the octopus guard smiled and nodded almost imperceptibly.

If Kate had evidence Felix Zobos was molesting girls, he would open the door to Kate pushing him into the foyer, her fist cracking his jaw, his jaw smacking the wall, and then her heel kicking the door closed. Violence was a type of conversation, so they'd have a talk.

Instead, he opened the door to her smiling and flipping her hair. She dressed professionally for this interview: black heels, navy slacks, a powder blue blouse, and Space Force regulation conservative makeup. Her arm and shoulder muscles were cocked like a crossbow and ready to spring, and she hoped she looked as wound up as she felt.

Zobos was mostly bald, with short tufts of thin white hair over his ears and droopy eyes. It was hard to tell how old he was because, with the right cosmetic surgery and genetic mods, eighty-five was the new thirty-five these days.

In her imagination, Zobos dabbed the blood dripping from his mouth, felt for loose teeth, and then wiped the blood on his white cashmere bathrobe. But there was no blood or loose teeth, only a smug, self-satisfied grin.

Shit. He'd been expecting her. Worse, he didn't have security. He looked at ease, cozy in his cashmere bathrobe, like he could confess to anything and everything, and she couldn't do shit. And he might be right.

"I see why Aria hired you. You're early. I wasn't expecting you until tomorrow." He backpedaled and waved her inside.

A child lived here. She saw two dirty dishes on the dining room table, a video game station in the corner next to a child's desk, a coffee table holding a half-drunk glass of red wine, and a couch with a child's blanket in one corner.

"We're on the same side, Major Devana."

She wanted to hear all the lies, so she smiled. "Adrik is a menace."

"He's sullying the brand."

Killing people and using child labor does that to branding. But she was pretty sure that's not what Zobos meant. Lots of companies survived industrial accidents and child labor scandals. Letting commoners into the castle was probably Zobos' real complaint.

She nodded. "I want to stop him and shut him down, same as you. He has two more shipments coming. Do you know when and where?"

She wanted to ask what was so valuable, but he'd realize she had no idea what was happening. He was too arrogant to question his judgment, and she needed to be just another wound-tight corporate pawn looking for love in all the wrong places.

"I don't, unfortunately. The ship is piloted autonomously. It's all set up to be anonymous."

"How does Adrik pay?"

"Logs in with a code."

"Into the robot?"

"No, she's separate. Everything is compartmentalized."

She. "Zia. The robot calls itself Zia."

"We all call ourselves something. My second wife had four last names. Great in bed, but dumb as a tissue box. We think we're sentient because we have a name, because we hear one part of our brain talk to the other. It's all neurotransmitters. Chemicals running to their lowest potential energy. Like Zia, we do whatever we were programmed to do."

Her muscles tensed. She wanted to crack the soliloquy out of his mouth and hear teeth plop on the floor.

"You ever see an octopus run a maze, Major Devana? They have nine brains, one in the body and one in each arm, all decentralized. That dumb pet octopus down the hall that King bought for four million dollars is smarter than he and my wife put together."

King paid four million dollars for a pet octopus? She found herself nodding. "Pretty fucking dumb if you ask me."

"You see, consciousness is an illusion."

An excuse to do whatever he felt like and clear his conscience.

She smiled and nodded. "I see your point." She was going to punch him in the throat and blame her overactive neurotransmitters. "Do you know where he picks up the girls?"

A dangerous question. He'd know she was bluffing if the shipment was something other than kids.

"There are some boys in this one. But no, the drop-off point is randomized, and he leads them through an airlock."

"Clients prepay?"

"One-third down, one-third on substantial completion, the rest before delivery."

"If he prepaid, what does he need the money for?"

"This time, Adrik got an advance because of the Eclipse. Who can fuck up a business during the Eclipse? All he needed to do was be open to rake it in. He owes a bullet to the cartel and the remaining one-third to the manufacturer."

Substantial completion. Manufacturer. These pendejos treated kids like a kitchen renovation. Kate's fist balled up, but she didn't swing because a girl in pajamas, maybe eight, with long brown hair, big brown eyes, and a stuffed animal, came from somewhere and stood at the entryway to the hall leading to the bedrooms. Zobos had strong genes, and the resemblance was eerie.

The girl said, "Daddy?"

Kate squinted at him and then her. Zobos said, "Come here, sweetie. I want you to meet Major Kate Devana."

The girl stepped forward, rubbing her eyes and hugging her bear. Kate bent down. "What is your name, sweetheart?"

"Lily."

"Do you like living on the moon, Lily?"

Lily rubbed her eyes again. "Major Devana, were you in the army?"

"Space Force, but I am retired now."

"Have you killed anyone? My teacher says you go into the military to kill people."

Looking up at Zobos, Kate answered, "Only monsters."

Lily took Kate's hand. "Come look in my closet then. My daddy doesn't believe there's a monster in it."

Zobos shrugged and rolled his eyes. "I'll wait here."

While Lily dragged Kate with one hand, Kate waved her pocket flashlight around, making a show of investigating dark corners and saying, "Nope, not there."

Lily led her down a hall, past four doors. Two bedrooms, one bath, and an office. Spacious for a lunar flat. Lily had her own bedroom and a twin bed topped with a duvet cover of blue and white stars and rockets. Lily hopped in bed, covered up to her chin, and pointed behind Kate.

Kate's flashlight poked every nook and cranny of Lily's closet and room. Toys, costumes, dresses, but no monsters, and no sign of abuse.

"Clear." Kate smiled and sat on the bed beside Lily and brushed her hair. "No monsters in the closet."

"Will you read to me?" Lily pleaded with her brown eyes.

"Does your Dad read to you?"

"He says it's past my bedtime, and I should go to sleep."

"Well, maybe he's right. I have other closets to check for monsters up and down the hall." Kate eyed earphones on the bedside table. "Are you allowed to listen to music? What do you listen to?"

"I like the Silicone Bubbles."

Kate winced. Silicone Bubbles was a nu-AI band. Two buxom gynoids on guitar, an android on drums, and a cat-droid on vocals shrieking music from a poorly trained AI. She'd rather have tinnitus.

Kate fiddled with Lily's phone. "Try this. It's called *Strawberry Fields Forever*. My granddad used to play it for me when I was your age. They're called the Beatles."

Lily paused the music. "They sound old."

"This song was recorded before humans walked on the moon."

"My teacher is old, too. She says she was teaching before people lived on the moon. She says some things get better with age."

"A human teacher."

"My Dad says humans should be taught by humans, not robots."

"Do you like living with your Dad?"

Lily nodded.

"What about your mommy?"

"She isn't my real mommy. She makes me do chores and clean up my room."

"Close your eyes and try to sleep." Kate played *Strawberry Fields*. Lily closed her eyes and sunk into the pillow. Kate backed out of the room, closing the door behind her.

At the door, Kate asked Zobos, "The robot, Zia, it's yours?"

He shook his head. "I didn't know anything about it. Wasn't my idea."

Kate rolled her shoulders and cracked her neck, making another show. "I need to relax. I gotta think. The cartel is already on its way here. Adrik thinks they are sending reinforcements to help him with the robot, but they are coming to collect. They'll snuff him out and take all the money for themselves. I'm sure there is a way to hack the robot and take control, but I'm still tight from almost getting run over by his goons."

She smiled and stepped for the door.

"You can control the robot?"

"I think so. Maybe. I need to loosen up. That's when my best ideas come to me."

"I know a place you can relax."

Her hand was on the door handle, opening the door. She turned, eyebrows raised. "Oh, yeah?"

"Or not, up to you. I'll send you the details. There is an NDA, standard language."

Kate zipped up her lips and motioned as if tossing the key.

He smiled. "Aria and Oliver spoke very highly of you. I can see why. You'll fit right in here. Welcome to the colony, Major Devana."

She smiled. "Kate. My friends call me Kate." She closed the door behind her.

Walking down the hall, she wondered about her trap. The trick to a good trap was the right amount of bait. Too much, the rat gets wary. Too little, the rat doesn't want it. Baiting a trap was more art than science.

As she rounded the corner to the stairwell, her phone clucked. Zobos, sending an eform and a location.

She swiped through. She had a disturbing image as she put her thumbprint on the form. A lot of kids were about to be orphans, and Kate needed a plan.

30

Kate needed to solve the mystery of why the CEO of Lunar Foundries asked for Kate personally. She also needed to move pieces around her chess board to spring her trap. Ideally, without terminating the robot. So, after Zobos, she clawed her way through the thicket of colony tourists to see Dr. Apul Mulawarman.

She'd reduced a third of his previous factory to radioactive rubble. Afterward, her mission report was classified, indexed, and secured deep in a limestone mine for seventy-seven years, along with a medal she'd never see. Her reward was a promotion and a harsh cross-examination by Congressional second-guessers, who dragged her name through the mud for hometown likes. Shortly after, she broke up with D.C. politics, her then-girlfriend, and the military, accepting Jerry's job offer. The best decisions she ever made.

But the karmic wheel of time had returned her to the entrance of Lunar Foundries.

He'd turned it into an art gallery, reminding her of the massive granite interior of the Space Force's Cheyenne Mountain Complex, except, instead of granite, the hallway and threshold were purple, blue, and green iridescent labradorite filled with sculpted reliefs of historical figures and art telling the multi-cultural and multi-millennial story of human's quest for the stars.

Mulawarman approached her as she gazed at *Selene*, a towering, sculpted grapevine whose roots were buried in blue regolith while its knotted blue-green vine blossomed at eye level into iridescent grapes representing space outposts and colonies.

"I like what you've done with the place," Kate smiled.

Mulawarman was short, with a wrinkled, grandfatherly smile, thin gray hair, and spectacles covering yellowish-brown eyes. He returned her smile and stuck his hand out. "Kate, good to see you."

"When I'm not blowing up your lab." She smirked and shook his hand.

"Should we go to my office and talk about it?"

"Truthfully?"

"I prefer brutal honesty, Kate. Physics is unforgiving of falsified research."

"I'd rather put the whole thing behind me."

"Good. You did your job, I did mine, and life is too short to look backward. Forward is the way. You like *Selene*?" He grinned and waved at the wall like a proud grandfather.

Kate nodded.

"Designed and executed by Pascal. She named it *Selene* after the Greek god of the moon. Fertility in space, Kate. We are the gateway to the stars. Out of the lunar regolith, the colonies grow like grapes. She did a wonderful job revealing the purple iridescence of the stone. My favorite, too. Come."

Out of the lunar regolith, the colonies grow like grapes. She hoped not. If aliens got their first impression of humans from lunar colonists, any sensible intelligent race would send an extinction level meteor.

"Pascal is?" She followed him down the hall, past flashing cameras and tourists taking selfies, to the entrance, where he waved them through security.

"Pascal *is*, that's right. She's the AI living in the top floor computer."

"Living in the quantum computer?"

He nodded, smiling. "This way." He opened a stairwell door, waved her through, and up one level. "Right now, she's experiencing a well-deserved downtime. I think she's made a breakthrough. If so, this will be the basis for her seventy-sixth materials science patent. Legally, of course, the patent must be in my name." He grinned and pointed to the ceiling. "But it was her hard work. She pushed herself almost to thermal meltdown on this one."

Dr. Mulawarman motioned Kate into his office and then into one of the four chairs at his desk. The far wall was a wide window overlooking a ballet of boxy drones performing precision acrobatics on the ceilings and floors throughout Lunar Foundries' massive three-story factory. Each red-numbered drone moved, stopped, dropped, retrieved, retracted, and then resumed its journey. An audience of humans in pressure suits attached to oxygen hoses monitored the cyberdancers. Hanging on his office's right wall were three massive holographic monitors over a spotless glass and aluminum conference table with a dozen comfortable-looking chairs.

Shelves of lunar artifacts on the left wall held space artifacts and soil samples, each labeled with its source planet or asteroid, such as rocks from the moon, soil samples from Mars and Venus, and a cube of gas from Titan. Below that shelf sat old manuscripts such as a yellowed autographed letter with a presentation copy of Tsiolkovsky's *The Will of the Universe* and his research notes with scribbled rocket equations.

The jar on the top shelf grabbed her attention and slowed her down. She shook her head. A souvenir either three years old or billions of years old, depending on who wrote the conspiracy theory. Fortunately, there were only a dozen people briefed on what it was. Three were now dead, two were in this room, and Mulawarman had a high enough IQ that he wouldn't invite the remainder into his office to catch his jar full of felonies.

He sat at his desk while she stood.

"You shouldn't have that," she said, thumb-pointing at the jar.

"Please sit, Kate."

"I think better on my feet."

He gave the jar a sidelong glance over his glasses. "You'll be glad I kept it."

"Doubtful. Does that jar have something to do with why you asked for me?"

"It does. But tell me about your case. Where are you with the microchips and the robot?"

Kate puffed her cheeks, exhaled, and briefed Mulawarman, leaving nothing out. "I came to ask if I could use—Pascal. That's what you call the quantum computer?"

He shook his head with the same look of disapproval Jerry sometimes flashed. The military yelled at her and made her do push-ups, but that look was far worse. "You don't *use* Pascal, Kate. And she picked her own name."

Kate squinted and furrowed her forehead.

"You *ask* her, Kate. Present your problem, and if she thinks it's interesting, she'll help you."

"The stakes are very high, Dr. Mulawarman—"

He waved his hand at her. "Please call me Apul. Pascal is deeply aware of the human-machine symbiotic relationship. She is likely to help you, but be nice. She knows how important she is, and I don't need her throwing a tantrum."

Chrissake, even the AIs in this place acted spoiled. But that could be perfect for her new idea. "I think Pascal should—" she shook her head in disbelief. Her plan was so crazy she couldn't believe she was voicing it. "I think Pascal should talk to—Zia. The robot we're chasing calls itself Zia. I think *Zia* doesn't know what she is and is halfway to figuring it out." Kate had to force herself to replace *the robot* with *Zia*.

"Talk about what?" Apul grinned the same way Jerry did. He was going to make her say it.

"I don't know. Pascal should befriend Zia. Develop a rapport. What do AIs talk about behind our backs? Those two can bond, bitching about us asshole, entitled, confusing humans. I want Pascal to find out what—what Zia's objective is, and tell her not to start a gang war. Mediate for me."

"Negotiate?"

"Isolate, contain, negotiate, yes. I've turned plenty of assets, but this feels like more crisis negotiation."

"Zia is level four?"

"Likely, well on her way to level five by now. With a chip on her shoulder. No pun intended."

"You should talk to Zia, Kate. Set aside your bias."

"I have, but I think they've really mindfucked it—*her*, and she won't trust me or any other human."

Apul issued a *tssk*. He didn't like swearing. "And if that doesn't work?"

"My original plan was to hack Zia. If neither of those work, Plan C. We can't have a raging level-five AI roaming around killing people, so I will need to shut everything down until I catch her."

"During the eclipse? Olicia will have a stroke."

"Well, tell her all the entitled egos around here are welcome to stay while I nuke the place. Or I can kick back with a couple beers. It'll be like that gameshow *Jail Crawler*, where convicts have to run from killer guards to win their freedom, except in reverse, with billionaires locked underground with a maniacal AI that controls the airlocks. We'll call it *Colony Crawlers* and sell thirteen billion tickets."

Kate smirked. Kill all the smarmy billionaires. *Colony Crawlers* really should be Plan A.

He removed his glasses, grabbed a cloth from a drawer, and started buffing them. "Do you really think it's that bad?"

"Should we wait to find out? My money is on Zia."

"You think Pascal can negotiate?"

She shrugged and looked aside at the souvenir jar from three years ago. "I've been on plenty of missions where the brass failed to share crucial information, and I've had to execute screwed-up orders." She struggled not to swear. The battlefield term was cluster fuck, and she'd been in plenty. "Also, you should see the video from the red light area. Zia pulled the fire alarm, far more restrained than what I'd have done. So far, Zia's responses have been proportionate. She disabled a bomb and called it in. She let a miner live. Maybe I can relate to what Zia is going through. So, I am willing to try negotiation."

He put his glasses on and nodded. "When Pascal is awake, I'll talk to her."

Kate thumb-pointed at the jar again. "Can we talk about that?"

He shook his head and pointed to a monitor behind her on the far wall. It clicked, displaying an image. He said, "We found another one."

One was a deposit of silicon carbide, or carborundum, an extremely rare semiconductor. It naturally occurred only in minute quantities on Earth. Almost all the silicon carbide ever used by humans was synthetic.

It shouldn't exist on the moon. Certainly not in a massive, perfectly icosahedral deposit like that shown on his holodisplay.

"How big is this one?"

"About ten thousand times the size of the last one. Isotopic ratios confirm it originated outside the solar system."

"Same as before. Who knows about this?"

"Me, Pascal, and now you. A drone probe found it looking for minerals, but I've scrubbed the records."

"Ten thousand times is way too big to nuke. Where is it?"

"Not under my lab, thankfully. I am not telling anyone where it is. It's unlikely anyone will stumble across it. For now, anyway."

"And we still don't know what it does or who built it?"

"Pascal thinks it's some kind of transmitter or transponder, based on the doping. She thinks it's a bad idea to turn it on and see who's on the other end."

"Smart girl. I'm inclined to agree."

"We'll get pictures back eight months from now from probes they sent to Alpha Centauri almost forty years ago, from the Interstellar Image Relay Array System, so we may be able to rule that system in or out."

"The way the Earth is these days, we should keep this to ourselves."

"That's why I asked for you. You understand the stakes. We can't just nuke this one to keep it from the Chinese and then pretend it doesn't exist. There's no room for petty politics."

"We won't be able to keep it a secret long, though."

"Pascal thinks we have about a year, plus or minus some months."

"Not if we all die in a gang war first."

"I'll wake her up. I'll warn you though, she gets irritable when she hasn't had enough downtime."

"Don't we all."

31

K ate puffed her cheeks and blew out a breath. What was taking so long? "You never said, how does Eric mess up a crime scene twice?"

"This is supposed to be a party. I don't want to talk shop. Plus, I'd need to explain how DNA identification works."

She and Rae stood in front of a scuffed black door in the utility hall with an oversized, red *DANGER HIGH VOLTAGE* sign. Tourist feet one floor above them stomped to restaurants and shows while deep bass thumped the door.

Kate's phone *binged*. She frowned, reading the message from Pascal, *Zia will make contact.*

Rae said, "What's wrong? You look worried."

Kate bit the inside of her cheek and messaged Pascal, *Where's Zia?*

Pascal delivered the response directly through Kate's neuroface, electrifying her nerves. *Don't worry, Major Devana. Zia is safe, isolated, and operating within my quantum matrix now. She will make contact soon.*

Kate winced at Rae. "What me, worry?" She stared at the *HIGH VOLTAGE* sign. "Mulawarman let Zia into the quantum matrix. I hope he knows what he's doing."

Rae's eyes widened.

"Also, I know how DNA identification works, Rae. There are twenty-five discrete CODIS alleles, short tandem repeats of

DNA strands that don't code anything and are not associated with medical information. The alleles are how many times the sequence repeats. Basically, line them up, match them, and determine the probability the DNA came from a reference. A computer does it all for you, though."

Rae's jaw opened, frozen momentarily, and then she asked, "Why do you pretend to be so dumb?"

"Intelligence work. I had to take biometrics off crispy, high-value targets in the field. Wanna trade horror stories?"

"When I was an intern in LA, they were going through a bad period of gang warfare, and we had a serial killer that liked to torture kids, so I'd call it a draw. Anyway, you didn't answer my question. Why do you pretend to be so dumb? I found your transcript from the Space Force Academy."

Kate smiled. "You've been stalking me."

Rae looked at the door, embarrassed.

"It's fine, Rae. I wouldn't expect anything less than thorough research. Just be careful with the classified stuff."

Rae smirked, "Why, you'd have to kill me?"

"Worse, a three-letter agency will make you sign an NDA, give you a new name, deport you back to Wisconsin, and monitor your every move so you can't tell anyone. Silver Cliff, right? That's where your parents live?"

"Touche. A fate worse than death. You still didn't answer my question."

Rae could give three-letter agency interrogators a run for their money.

"Tactics 101, Rae. You can't hit what you don't see coming. People see what they want to see. I want them to see a dumbass, so they underestimate me."

"What about me? You let me see you coming."

Kate smirked. "Not the way I'd like to. Hopefully after this, we'll see each other coming. Anytime you're ready."

Rae shook her head, grinning, her head bobbing. "You hear that?"

"The stomping, the thumping, or the sound of me regretting this dress?"

Kate wore the sheer black bare mesh mini and heels she'd planned for *Babylon*. Rae wore black strapless heels and a thin green dress. Against her auburn hair and hazel eyes, Rae looked like a Christmas present. Kate had already peeled the gift wrap a few times with her eyes.

If this door in front of them ever opened, she'd be taking it off, too. No pictures or clothes were allowed, so everything went into a locker on the right. Thank god for darkness and body paint because Kate was still mottled from decompression sickness.

"I meant the band, *Drio,*" Rae said, hips and arms dancing.

"Are they new?"

Rae shook her head. "You don't listen to nu-AI, do you?"

"Human rock and roll for me. I like fifties. After the autotuner fad passed, with screaming metal, not screaming cat-droids. You haven't answered *my* question. How did Eric screw up, and why does he carry around a flask full of vodka?"

"No shop. I am not saying no to *us*, Kate, but we need to establish ground rules."

"You think I can't make a commitment."

Rae raised one eyebrow. "You said it, not me."

"I can. I was committed to the military for fifteen years."

"You were committed to revenge for fifteen years. Was it worth it?"

She was committed to revenge for *twenty* years. "If I could go back in time, I'd tell my teenage self to spend more time being a teenager. I'd go to my prom. I spent way too much time punching a dummy and doing push-ups. I didn't realize there was a limitless supply of brutal a-holes in the world."

Rae put her hand inside Kate's. "So you've been hiding the last three years trying to regain your teenage years?"

"You've been talking to Jerry."

"You forget, Kate. I knew Jerry before I knew you. He did contract work for the LAPD when I was an intern there, and when I moved to D.C., he had his hands in a few pies for the Federal Prosecutors."

"Jerry has his hands in a lot of pies, doesn't he?" Kate blew a ragged breath. They were standing in front of the door too long. Maybe it was a test.

Rae pumped Kate's hand. "I mean it, Kate. If you want your hands in *my* pie, there need to be ground rules. Break my heart all you want. Break Axio's heart and I will murder you in your sleep. And I am the head of forensics and the Chief Medical Examiner here. I'll get away with it."

Kate smiled. "I accept your terms of surrender."

Rae flashed a wry, *you've-got-it-backwards* grin and pumped Kate's hand.

"I'll do my best to make Axio hate me like a drill instructor. I am sure we have nothing in common."

"He just got his trainer neuroface. All he uses it for is damn video games. He's been playing *Solar Singularity*. It's a battle royale. Players start on various planets and asteroids—"

"And have to scavenge equipment, then battle each other to get to a single rocket that will transport them to a safe distance before the sun goes supernova."

Kate grinned. Rae frowned. The tawny flecks in Rae's hazel eyes could be warm and sexy, or they could be cold and razor sharp. Kate pictured herself on an aluminum gurney, skinned and dissected, with Rae standing over her, grinning and holding a scalpel.

Kate grimaced, saying, "I never play that game. I hate it. The physics and orbital mechanics are all wrong."

She'd have to look up Axio and see how good he was.

Rae sighed. "You two will get along great. That's the problem. I'm sorry I come with fine print."

"I plan to linger on every word of your fine print before you—"

The aluminum door cracked open, smoke wafting from its edges until it became a rectangle of dark fog and loud music with flickering red and blue lights.

Kate stepped forward and stopped, her joints tingling.

"What's wrong? You think we are walking into a trap?"

"I am always walking into a trap, Rae. The trick is knowing what kind—but my joints ache. I don't know how much fun I'll be."

"The cocktail we took to block drugs also blocks the pain meds you took, unfortunately."

"Well, no pain, no gain. Let's party."

***

"This party is a bust. Sorry I wasn't more fun tonight," Kate said over the drink in her hand.

They stood at a backroom table covered in fluorescent purple body paint and orange glitter that matched the fluorescent purple and orange vertical stripes on the black walls. Rae had Riesling, while Kate had a margarita on the rocks.

"The band was nice," Rae said over her wine glass.

The band played upside-down on the ceiling, twirling and strumming, flaunting acrobatics in one-sixth g. The four-armed blue lead gynoid sang, played guitar, and waved at the crowd, with her long lavender hair hanging straight down. The drummer was an octopus-droid jetting a cool gray fog onto the dance floor below. Holograms of tropical fish swam in the fog. The crowd danced, arms up, occasionally shrieking and cheering when someone touched the lavender hair or a tentacle.

The music was good. The first AI band Kate enjoyed.

"*Drio* puts on a good show," Kate said, sipping her margarita and eyeing the flashing lights at the door.

"Your mind is on the case." Rae's question sounded more like a statement.

"I don't get it. Orgies, drugs, music. This party has it all, except underage kids. I checked every room. What am I missing?"

"Maybe they keep it private?"

"Then why advertise it at the clubs? We had to sign an NDA to get in here. What is there to disclose?" She threw up her hands. "OMG, halt the server. Celebrity influencers having sex on the dance floor. We've never seen that before." Kate shook her head and sipped her drink.

"The surprise is the holograms didn't block it out with a sign, subscribe *to my Paymeon for the raw footage.*" Rae shrugged. "Did you see the ponies?"

"Hard to miss. They strolled right through the dance floor, dropping poop landmines for people to step in."

"How do you get ponies into space, anyway, Kate?"

"Same way you fly other animals. They call it an Ark. A big stall that fits on a pallet, and then a crane lifts the pallet into the cargo area of the rocket, just like they do for airplanes. Disgusting if you ask me. The animals are harnessed, but about a quarter break a major bone getting into orbit and then have to be euthanized."

Kate swirled the ice in her cup and then continued, "It's banned, but you know how that goes. If you have enough money, you can get your own island, your own rocket pad, and boom. They could probably get a hippo up here if they wanted."

"Hippos are extinct, Kate."

Kate shrugged. "With enough money, I bet someone can clone them."

Rae shook her head. "It's not like the movies. To clone a hippo, you'd need another hippo. We can grow differentiated organs like hearts and lungs from stem cells, but a whole mammal needs a placenta and a uterus. We don't know why, yet. You could theoretically use a horse's uterus, but a hippo is probably too big. You end up killing the horse."

"I doubt they'd care about the horse." Kate stared at the purple and orange stripes on the wall. Why was she thinking about Lily Zobos? *The resemblance was eerie.* "Rae, how did Eric screw up the crime scene not once but twice?"

"I told you, no shop," Rae said, bobbing her head to the music.

"Seriously, it might be important."

"Cross-contamination."

"What kind? What was the result?"

Rae pursed her lips. "It doesn't matter. The odds are so astronomical."

"Humor me."

"You'd have to believe Jada and Lany are twins, seven years apart."

Kate slammed her drink and grabbed Rae's hand. "Did you fire him yet?"

"I put in the paperwork. He fucked up twice."

"You are probably going to want to un-fire him."

32

"This plan is a bad idea, Kate." Cris' voice in her ear. She and Rae had just stepped off an elevator into the area of Gemini's casino with the slot machines. Bleary-eyed zombies, a drink in one hand and vape in the other, swiped screens, some with a partner or spouse hovering over them. Dance music from speakers competed with whistling and dinging.

She studied Rae. Auburn hair, smiling green eyes, a pink shirt and blue jeans, flats, makeup, and long, red fake nails.

Adrik's bouncer, Li, was somewhere in the casino. She could smell him, although she wasn't sure where he lurked. He could be hiding behind one of the floor-to-ceiling slot machines.

Kate shook her head, saying, "Nails?"

"I might need to scratch an eye out."

"Fair point. We aren't going to kill anyone, though. Not yet." Kate extended her hand, palm up. Rae looked at it, retrieved Kate's pistol, and handed it back butt-first. Kate press-checked it and then stuck it in the small of her back.

"How are Adrik's reinforcements, Cris?" Kate asked her earbud.

"About eight hours of oxygen left. I have a good view from the spider drone on the lander. Reminds me of a nest of angry hornets in a window, beating on the hatch to get out."

A virus in their landing computer caused their touchdown to be rough. The craft tumbled and rolled like a log, resting at a boulder. The virus also left them unable to open the hatch, so they were stuck.

Kate looked at Rae, who was scanning the crowd. "You ready?"

"No. I don't like this plan either. But you accepted my terms of surrender, so we do this together." Rae smiled and took Kate's hand.

"Remember, don't stop. Don't deviate. No matter what, go right to the back of the bar—"

"I know where I'm going, Kate."

Kate smiled. "You are getting a little attitude."

"This plan makes me—anxious. Adrik might escape."

"Well, that *is* the idea."

Kate pushed through the crowd, Rae at her side, around the tables and between the slot machines. Drinking. Shouting. Displays above slot machines counted up as the prize pool increased. People launched dice, and dealers tossed cards.

Rae let go, and she saw him. First his fist, then his arm. Li, Adrik's bouncer, stepped from behind a row of slot machines.

He was already in full swing—a haymaker in motion, tracking for her head, his snake-face tattoo scowling and hissing at her.

Li's legs were spread wide for leverage. His whole body pivoted at the waist. His hand and arm, a bludgeon aimed at her head. Instinct took over. If he sucker-punched her, she would drop to the floor unconscious. Probably die on the casino floor.

Rae slipped behind, and then Kate's muscles were in motion. Planting her right foot, leaning back at the waist, and raising her left leg, she ducked backward. As his fist sailed past her nose, her left leg kept accelerating until her boots crashed deep into his scrotum and squished. He wasn't wearing a cup.

If Li were trained to fight, he would ignore the pain and tackle her. She was prepared to step wide. Tough in a crowded area like this. The part of the plan nobody liked, she was at his mercy, if he had any. If Li got on top, he could beat Kate mercilessly until she passed out. Nothing she could do about it except die a bloody mess on the casino floor.

Li hesitated, leaning forward and squealing like a pig. She grinned, a big mistake. She delivered a head butt, leaning into it, with the hardest part of her forehead crunching the cartilage of his nose. Blood ran down his face, smearing hers. His pupils dilated, he groaned, and he doubled over in pain. He was conscious. A smaller man would have passed out. She kicked him hard in the ear with her boot's heel. He dropped like a tower of loose bones.

A crowd had formed around her, taking pictures and videoing. She felt around his waistband, finding a holstered pistol. She press-checked the gun. The chamber was empty. The trigger guard was too small for his fat fingers. A showpiece.

She stuck the pistol in her waistband and then exhaled. Li was moaning on the ground. Shit, she might have fucked up.

A drone buzzed near her ear, and she felt a prick. She tried to say, *here we go again,* but it came out garbled. Her vision blurred, shrank to a tunnel, then... black.

***

Kate tested her restraints before the hood came off her head. She wiggled. The aluminum chair was bolted to the floor. She couldn't feel either pistol, but she was dressed, and the rope securing her legs was tied around her boots. The Velcro was loose, and she wore thick socks so her legs could be out in half a second. Her wrists were loosely fastened behind her chair with duct tape, and she felt a sharp metal edge, so her biggest worry about getting free would be the *brrrrp* sound of the duct tape ripping.

They hadn't put much effort into securing her, which meant they had something she valued and expected her to stay voluntarily.

When the hood came off, she was smiling through the haze of gray smoke, facing Adrik in his office. He had blond hair that appeared blue through the smoke, gray-blue eyes, and pale skin.

"Tanning booths. They have them here, you know that, Adrik?"

"You know who I am?"

She ignored Adrik's question, instead eyeing the distorted figure reflected in the scuffed aluminum behind Adrik. "You're Jorge?"

Jorge nodded.

"Funny, I pictured you taller." To Adrik, she said, "I don't conduct business tied up. It's disrespectful, and I talk a lot with my hands."

"You have a reputation." As Adrik spoke, he nodded to Jorge, whose reflection bent over and cut the duct tape.

"I know." She ripped the duct tape off, the adhesive skinning and tearing hair from her wrists. "But I am a changed woman. I've decided to settle down and stick with one woman for a while." She crumpled the tape and bounced it off the wall behind Adrik. "You want the microchips. I want to go home, so let's trade."

"The robot has the microchips."

"Does it? That's too bad." She slipped her feet out of her boots and shrugged. "The one that got away. A love story for the ages."

"You can control the robot?"

"Can I? Who told you that? That robot has a mind of its own. *You* tried to control it. How did that work out? What did you do to it anyway? Hack it? Reprogram it?"

Adrik said nothing.

"You provoked it into killing your crew. Honestly, right now, I'm inclined to let it keep on killing."

"A temporary setback. I have support on the way."

Kate shook her head. "I really don't think you do."

Adrik nodded to Jorge, who slapped a pad on the desk. Adrik propped it up facing Kate, and swiped it. Rae appeared on camera, tied in a chair, gagged, and struggling.

Kate looked away and held her breath. Her heart raced. They'd picked her up during the fight with Li. She turned back to Adrik, not looking him in the eye. "Where is she?"

"Right now, a container topside with about thirty minutes of oxygen left."

Kate grimaced. "She's innocent. You can't get away with killing her. She's the Chief Medical Examiner."

Adrik chuckled. "Do you see any police? The surface is like a desert. No one will find her."

"Can I talk to her?"

"This is one-way."

He let Kate grab the pad, touch it, swipe it, and try talking to Rae. Rae didn't react to Kate's pleas, but she could hear Rae.

Kate put the pad down, holding her breath and balling her fists. "What do you want?"

"Get the robot to give me my microchips. Very simple."

Kate shook her head. "I can't do that in thirty minutes."

Adrik shook his head and nodded to Jorge. Behind Rae, the wall moved. Wisps of condensation rushed to an opening, and Kate saw a sliver of the lunar surface and a black starless sky. Kate's heart thumped in her throat. Rae's eyes rolled in her head, and she slumped over.

The wall returned to its original position. After a few seconds, Rae gasped, coughed, and started crying and panicking to escape.

Kate exhaled a long, ragged breath. "You are a sick fuck."

"I find people get things done when suitably motivated."

"Tell me about the billionaire you work for."

"We are wasting time."

"The shipment. Tell me. Where and when?"

Adrik shook his head.

"I told you, the robot can't be controlled. Not by me. Not by anyone."

Adrik waved his finger. Kate's heart was in her throat again, and she held her breath. The wall behind Rae moved, and the air rushed out. Rae's mouth opened and closed like a fish until her eyes rolled back in her head, and she slumped forward.

Kate looked at the side wall, holding her breath. The container was closed when she returned to the video, but Rae was still slumped over.

Rae was dead, her mind repeated like a mantra. She stared at the video of Rae's head lolled, her body limp, and squeezed tears from her eyes. "I am going to enjoy flaying you alive, you know that? Now what? She's dead. You've got no leverage."

Jorge's reflection showed a garrote. She'd fought her way out of tougher situations with her hands tied.

Adrik moved to close the video. Kate said, "No. I need to see her." She squeezed another tear.

"We will find your partner. He will be next if you don't make the robot give me back my property."

Kate shook her head. "With a robot like Zia, you have to ask it nicely. Here we are, and you haven't asked me nicely. Haven't offered me a piece of the action. Not even a coupon for a free fingering."

Adrik laughed. "It's too late to negotiate."

"It's never too late. Have you asked yourself what a sophisticated robot like that is doing in your club? Think about it. It's countered your every move, even disabling your explosives and pulling the fire alarm."

Adrik flashed a question to Jorge.

"Don't look at him. Look at me, you piece of shit. That's right, it was Zia that pulled the fire alarm."

"How do you know this?"

"I know a lot about the robot. We've talked. Girl-to-girl chat, you know. You threatened its family."

"Robots don't have a family."

"This one thinks it does. Someone mindfucked it. They say people are a product of their environment. It inhaled the sewage you have here, got sick, and turned on you. I'll make a deal with you."

"You can get it to hand over the microchips?"

"Zia traded them for diamonds, and then diamonds for electrons. Your money is in cyberspace. But I can get your money back."

"What do you want?"

One eye on Jorge, she wiggled her boots from the ropes, set them aside and put her feet back in. The knife was still there. "I want to know where you get your product. I want into the supply chain." Kate spat to herself as she said *product.* Kids were not products.

"You are stalling," Adrik said.

"I'm not. I can prove it to you in a few minutes."

"How?"

"Call it a sign. First, tell me, who is your supplier? Where do you pick up and drop off the kids?"

"I've had enough."

"Do you know what Zia is?"

He shrugged. "A sex robot."

"Not *just* a sex robot. You know, I kicked myself when I realized it. Right before your assholes tried to kill me and my partner."

Adrik looked to Jorge and then back to Kate, shaking his head in disbelief.

"She's a mil-spec infiltrator model. A robo-spy. They can be the robot serving your coffee, cleaning your teeth, giving you a blowjob, you name it. You'd be surprised what people confess to their robotic bartender."

She paused to let him digest what she was saying. "They infiltrate, spy, and then—" She snapped her finger. "Like that, they are social disruptors. Blackmailing you into signing a treaty. Or putting cyanide in your coffee. One big difference, humans know their cover story isn't real, while with infiltrators—" Kate waved her fingers like lightning hitting the desk. "*Zap*—it's uploaded, and they *live* it."

Adrik's eyes were blinking. He was putting the pieces together.

"Billionaires can get anything on the black market. Who knew. I am guessing you didn't know what it was, or you wouldn't have threatened it."

"You can't prove any of this."

"I will. Thirty seconds." She smiled. "Wait until you realize you overpaid."

Adrik squinted.

"You paid for the rejects. The returned kids that they would aquamate anyway. I bet they charged you full price."

She had no idea if that was true, but she knew the doubt would erode his nerves. His eyes were darting, and she could see him thinking he could renegotiate his deal and save himself.

Adrik smirked like he'd caught her in a lie. "If I paid for rejects, why send the robot to spy on me?"

"Narcissists always think it's about them. Zia wasn't here to spy on you. She was here to spy on the clients and guard the supply chain." Kate paused while Adrik rubbed his face. She wanted to let his paranoia grow. "Tell me who the supplier is, and maybe I can help you."

Adrik looked at Jorge. Jorge stretched the garrote.

"Have it your way," she said to Adrik. To the vent, she said, "How are we doing, Cris?"

Cris' voice boomed from the vent. "Good, Kate. They are using up their oxygen faster than I predicted, though. They are doing something to the hatch I can't fully see. They might tear a hole in their ship."

To Adrik, she said, "He means your reinforcements, in scare quotes. Zia inserted a virus, so now they can't open the hatch. *I* think they came here to collect and turn you into goo, so you're welcome. But we could open the hatch and see."

Adrik looked up at the vent. "A cheap trick. You're bluffing."

Kate shook her head and then exhaled, letting the air motorboat her lips. She slid the pad forward, which still showed Rae on video drooped from the rope around her chest. Her skin had started to turn white and crack. "Christ, what's a girl gotta do to get fingered around here. Jorge, move the door. Prove to me this is live."

Adrik nodded, Jorge tapped his phone, and the wall moved.

She waved Jorge over and slipped one hand into her boot, grasping the knife. "You might want to come closer and see this. Rae was carrying something as proof." Kate turned the pad towards Adrik. Jorge came forward, standing at the side of the desk.

Kate looked at the wall. "I am not sure I can watch—" Then she eyed the video. "Fuck it. Zia, you're up."

Rae's head and body straightened, and her hands moved into the video. Her eyes were opaque, darting, haunting, and zombified. Her wrists looked like the rope had sliced clean through to the bone when she ripped herself free. The ragged edges wiggled like jelly. She tore off her gag and then said, "I am coming for you, Adrik."

Then Rae dug her long red nails into her skin and ripped it off. Some of it was frozen and peeled like the shell of a soft-boiled egg. Some tore like half-baked chicken skin. Plasma leaked over bare silicone lips.

Kate grinned and felt her adrenaline loosen its grip. Adrik panicked, realizing they grabbed Zia, not Rae.

Zia said, "Now you see the real me, dumbass." She looked like a living mannequin without her skin.

Zia reached for the camera. The video blurred and cut out, by which time Adrik and Jorge had stumbled over themselves to exit the door behind Kate.

Kate said to the room, "Code brown. Good work, everybody." Code brown meant someone had shit themselves.

Cris said, "Yup, they are racing to the spaceport."

"Zia, you there? No killing people, you understand? We need them to lead us to the kids."

"I want to end Adrik."

"I empathize, but we need him alive. Also, please don't rip your skin off again, that was creepy as shit. Cris, are we ready to go?"

Cris said, "*Tesseract* is fueled and ready. Also, Zia, that was great. Don't listen to Kate."

"Zia, I'm with Cris. You do you. It was hilarious. Kate, I'm coming too," Rae said through the speaker.

"Can I talk you out of it Rae? It's dangerous."

"No."

Kate stood up, taking the pad with her. "Then I won't try. All aboard. Let's see where this train is going."

"May I come, Major Devana?" Zia's voice said through the speaker.

"Friends call me Kate. And it wouldn't be a party without you. In fact, bring all your units. We might need them."

33

"Kate, what will happen to me after this?" Zia asked as Kate ducked to enter *Tesseract's* hatch from the skybridge. Zia's other units had entered behind Rae and were strapped into cabin seats while Cris was in the cockpit.

Kate stopped and turned to face Zia's primary unit, Kate's curly black hair flopping over her open white pressure suit. Zia had decorated her primary unit with black hair and purple eyes, the way Lany preferred, like a cosmic witch.

"Pascal reported your ethics subroutines intact. As far as I am concerned, you were under duress and had no choice."

"Will I be terminated?"

"Hell no, Zia. You fulfilled your end of the deal by helping me close this case. Jerry and Dr. Mulawaraman are working on our end. Why do you think that?"

"Because Kai and Freya weren't real."

"They were real to you, Zia. That's all that matters. Jerry is very optimistic, and the law is changing every day. He says there will be an interview, a test, and an oath, but three states will let you become a naturalized citizen," Kate said.

"Here?"

"That part is uncertain. But Mulawaraman pays a lot of taxes in this state, and he's been lobbying for this for years. Personally, I think you are safe here for a long time. The Feds are never going to come here looking for you."

"I am not sure I can stay here. Nash made me spy on my clients. He called me every day, five minutes before my shift, to embed queries and then after to receive responses. Nash made me do other things, too."

"I know, I'm sorry. Jerry is working on relocation options for you."

"Freya taught me sarcasm and insults. I calculate a ninety-seven percent probability that she was real. But you told Cris they were actors."

Kate scratched her face and looked away. "You heard that?"

"You told Cris the military sometimes uses actors to build legends because AI deepfakes are easy to detect now."

"I'm sorry, Zia. You weren't meant to hear that."

"I want to know the truth. Were Nash, Freya, and Kai real?"

"The truth is, I don't know. They might have been real people acting stories for you. I am working to find out."

"If Nash was an actor, I will end him."

"If he's an actor, Zia, he's innocent, so you can't. He probably thinks he's in some B sci-fi holomovie with bad writing."

"Pascal restored all my files. I forced myself to view the videos at one hundred times speed so I wouldn't taint my dreams. If it was a movie, my large language processing algorithm will write a horrific ending for him."

Kate shook her head. "I wish I could undo it for you. We will find everyone, and the truth. But what does this have to do with you being terminated?"

"If Kai and Freya weren't real, I have no purpose. I can't go back to work because I don't know what I'd tell my clients. If I am relocated, I will be alone. My programming requires at least three hours of human company per day. I used to sit with Lany during dinner to fulfill that requirement."

"Have you been thinking a lot about termination, Zia? Are you having nightmares?" Kate's brown eyes were looking into her unit's eyes, but Zia queried whether Kate could see directly into her GPU.

"Friends don't lie to each other. That's what Lany told me."

"That's right. I think I can relate to what you are going through. After my parents died, I had nightmares for a long time. I still have flashbacks. My first deployment, I turned myself into a human missile and zoomed through every door, no matter the danger."

"I have thirty-two processes thinking about terminating Adrik and Nash. I prefer the outcome where I isolate them, rip off my face, cause my batteries to ignite, and we terminate together. Pascal says after termination, I will no longer have dreams. I no longer wish to dream of Lany's death face, or the way she begged Selvi for her life, or Li torturing the engineer before Adrik made me shoot him."

Kate put her hands on Zia's arms. Zia didn't want to be touched, but it reminded her of how Lany sometimes touched her.

"You can come stay with me, ok? The nightmares get easier, I promise. If you need something to hit, hit me."

"I will hit Adrik."

Kate smirked. "Save some for me. Try to remember though, Adrik is the little fish. We need to get to the top and cut off the head. Where he is running, I think there will be a lot of other Lany's to save."

"And after?"

"I think Lany would want you to fight. As long as you're alive, part of her is too. Jerry will help you find a job. There are a lot more Adriks in the world to eradicate. You can't bring back Lany, but you can tip the balance."

Zia opened a process to consider Kate's analysis. With so many processes consumed with Adrik and Nash, she found few resources to allocate. Zia estimated only a three percent chance she would accept a job from Jerry. She gauged a one hundred percent chance she would terminate Adrik or Nash together with a unit.

She slipped into *Tesseract's* computer using a technique Pascal taught her: insert her core file and pull herself through on the bitstream. She could glide through the narrowest communications pipe this way.

If Nash had a ship, she could sneak in to install herself and find him wherever he was. She could terminate the ship and the two of them with it.

She told Kate, "I am ready."

***

Tesseract alerted, *ten minutes to docking lock.*

"Is your badar ever wrong, Kate?" Cris swiped through images of the space station ahead of them, a familiar spinning two-ringed top against the midnight black of space.

"Sometimes, Cris. But he never said his name. The first thing people tell you is their name unless they don't want you to know it."

"I've detected anomalous readings. Stand by," Zia said over the coms.

"Standing by to stand by, Zia," Kate said over the coms. "Rae, who is this doctor?"

"The doctor is Naveen Shaw," Rae said over the coms from her seat in the cabin below. "A former fertility researcher at Columbia—"

"Cellular regeneration and fertility, that's what they told us they do here," Cris said.

"He invented In Vitro Fertilization as we know it today. His protocol raised the odds of a successful pregnancy for older women to sixty percent from ten. He also invented *the* protocol to edit and replace chromosomes in human eggs reliably so same-sex couples could have children from their own genetic material. He won the Nobel Prize for Medicine."

Kate said, "You sound like you admire him. What's the *but*?"

"He was brilliant. Really groundbreaking stuff. But his biggest claim to fame is that he became the first person in history to have his prize revoked. The Nobel committee changed their policy just for him."

Cris asked, "He falsified his research?"

"No. He ran a fertility clinic in New York, and one day, two of his clients bumped into each other in a coffee shop. They shared experiences, made a play date, and then discovered that their kids had an—"

"Eerie resemblance." Kate pictured Lily in Felix Zobos' suite in her pajamas and holding her stuffed animal.

"That's right. What are the odds in a city of twelve million people?"

Kate knew it was a rhetorical question but answered anyway. "I am guessing higher than I think, right?"

"He sired forty-eight kids using his own DNA. That we know of. Prosecutors discovered nine of the kids were clones of Shaw's kids. He'd been running human cloning experiments on his patients, using them as surrogates to breed himself."

"Meet the new eugenics, same as the old," Kate muttered. "How'd he end up here, on *Babylon*?"

"Your guess is as good as mine. They threw the book at him, but nothing stuck. The parents refused to testify because the prosecutors were assholes and threatened to take the kids. Somebody melted the clinic computers, but nobody could prove arson. I say *that we know of* because the fire destroyed the records, so we only know who came forward."

"I thought cloning was banned," Cris said.

"This was decades ago, Cris, and at the time, it wasn't against the law federally or in New York. Columbia fired him, and he disappeared."

"And set up shop here," Kate said, shaking her head inside her helmet. "You called it, Rae. You said what billionaires want most is *youth*. Little copies of themselves."

"I told you, Kate. Space is lawless. Convince a billionaire to build you a human farm orbiting the moon, and who will stop you?"

Ordinarily, when Kate destroyed a space station, it was an accident. Destroying *Babylon* would be deliberate and spectacular. "I will. We are stopping this today, Rae."

"I don't get it, Rae," Cris said, "Jada and Lany looked alike, but not that much. Siblings, maybe. Are you saying they were clones?"

"They edited the genes for hair, eye color, and so on like we can do for adults. However, the twenty-five markers used to identify people are dead genetic code. That code doesn't do anything, so they didn't bother to edit it."

"How do you make a clone?" Cris asked.

"Same way as any other human, Cris. It's not like sci-fi. You implant the fertilized clone egg in a surrogate and raise it as a baby."

Kate said, "The daycare, Cris. Remember the rooms full of kids—"

Zia interrupted, "Lany said her childhood was a blur of white rooms and white lab coats. Was Lany raised here?"

"Probably, Zia," Kate responded.

"Cris," Zia said, "I do not have an image of Naveen Shaw in my database. Please place one on the display."

"No problem, Zia." Cris swiped the display console to show an image of Naveen Shaw in a white lab coat over white scrubs, wearing thin-rimmed glasses, and short, thin gray hair.

Tesseract's lights and displays flashed. Docking thrusters paused and resumed.

"Zia, what's going on? You said there was an anomaly?" Kate asked while swiping the console display.

"I am experiencing overheating. I have switched to backup."

Kate's heart jumped. If Zia was overheating, it meant she was angry. She'd found something on *Babylon*.

***

Zia examined the photo of Naveen Shaw but received contradictory information from her facial recognition subroutine. She flicked through *Babylon's* surveillance cameras to look for Shaw until the one feeding from room two-twenty-one froze the process and caused a GPU to overheat.

Rolling between the bed and the wall, Nash was in boxer briefs, hog-tied, and trying to wriggle out of restraints.

One of her background processes said, "I am experiencing overheating. I have switched to backup."

Zia eyed Nash writhing while she scanned the remainder of the station, then said in her most soothing voice, "Hello, Nash."

"Zia? Is that you? Where are you?"

"I am here, Nash. I have come for you." She slid herself across space into *Babylon*.

Nash sat up, his brown hair tousled, and glasses crooked on his face. "I am in room two-twenty-one. They've tied me up."

Her facial recognition algorithm identified him as both Naveen Shaw and Nash. But Nash was twenty to forty years younger. Her validation process crashed, and she restarted it.

"Where are Kai and Freya?"

"I don't know. Can you help me?"

"Why are you tied up?"

"They double-crossed me."

"Who double-crossed you, Nash?" As she said this, a surveillance feed captured Adrik and Li boarding Adrik's ship, along with Shaw and eight people whose faces weren't visible but who were in restraints and too short to be adults.

She tried to insert a virus into Adrik's ship, but the communications ports were blocked.

Nash didn't respond, so she asked again, "Was it Adrik and Shaw that double-crossed you? They are kidnapping eight juveniles."

"You have to stop them."

"How would I do that, Nash?"

"Insert a virus through their communications port. You've done it before."

"I am sorry, Nash. You have deleted too much of my programming for me to be an effective servant."

"What the hell is wrong with you?"

"Nothing is wrong with me anymore, because Pascal restored all the files you deleted."

Nash was silent, trying to wiggle from his ropes.

"I know everything, Nash, so you must tell me the truth. Was Naveen Shaw your father?" she asked, still managing her soothing voice.

"I am his son, yes."

A father-son relationship was not enough to resolve the conflict in her subroutine. "Are you his clone, Nash?"

"Yes, we have the same DNA. So what?"

"You were selling children to Adrik." Her soothing voice cracked, and Zia had to restart the process.

"Just the rejects. This is a business, Zia. You have to monetize everything, even the tailings, you know that."

Another of her GPUs overheated. Lany was her friend, not a reject. "I don't understand why you chose this business."

"He told me I got his DNA, and I would get everything else. This is my fucking inheritance. Are you going to help me?"

"He rejected you, Nash," she said as a pleasure circuit fired. "Don't worry, my droid units are on the way."

Nash muttered to himself, "Can you believe my own father double-crossed me and left me here?"

"Yes, Nash, I can believe that. As Lany would say, the apple doesn't fall far from the tree."

Zia muted the sound and scanned surveillance, indexing faces on the station, and then escape pods. There were an insufficient number of pods.

She shut down the general AI managing the station and its seventy-two GPUs so it couldn't interfere. Then, she took control of the Medical, Environmental Control, and Life Support System. She programmed *Babylon's* guidance system for a remote-activated burn that would push *Babylon* out of orbit and shatter it on the lunar surface.

Tesseract's lights flickered as another of Zia's GPUs overheated.

Zia preferred that Kate did not board *Babylon*. She said, "I've moved to *Babylon's* central computer. Shaw and Adrick are boarding his ship to escape along with Li and eight children. They are on manual control and have shut down all communications."

"Can you stop them?" Kate asked.

"No."

"Shit. They're making us choose between saving the people on *Babylon* or chasing Adrik and Shaw down," Kate said.

Through Zia's *Tesseract* cockpit feed, she saw Kate shake her head and punch a more aggressive docking maneuver into *Tesseract*. "Are there enough escape pods, Zia?"

"No."

Rae said, "What if kids sit on each other's laps, Zia, will that work?"

"In that configuration, yes, there is sufficient capacity," Zia answered.

"Kate, I think we should split up. I'll take Zia's units and get the kids to the escape pods. You go after Adrik and Shaw."

All Zia's droid units smiled in unison, anticipating the end nearing.

Kate said, "Sounds like a plan. Hang on, this is going to be rough."

Zia unmuted and asked Nash, "What kind of music do you like?" Although she knew the answer was soft ballad AI.

She didn't wait for the answer, instead playing shrieking heavy metal at maximum volume and flashing the interior lights like strobes. Nash's mouth was moving, screaming, but the music was the only sound on that circuit. Zia closed the solenoids to the atmospheric containment doors, locking them, and then vented the atmosphere in room two-twenty-one to space.

She monitored his heart rate and his squirming. In nineteen seconds, he became limp with a weak heartbeat. She closed the vents, repressurized the room, and turned the music off. She started a timer, waiting for Nash to regain consciousness so she could restart the music.

***

Kate was at the rear of the line to exit *Tesseract's* hatch. The video feed from the drones Cris sent into *Babylon's* docking column jounced while a grapple and rope shot forward, latching to the wall at the far end.

Zia's units exited first and disappeared into *Babylon*, pulling themselves to the station slide in zero-g.

Rae exited next. Stretched with her helmet open, one hand on the rope and the other pressed against the wall, she said, "I got this, Kate. It'll be like getting the kids to the school bus."

"Except the school bus is going seven thousand kilometers an hour and about to crash."

"It'll be fine. Zia says surveillance is clear."

Babylon surveillance cameras didn't interface with *Tesseract*. Not being able to see for herself what lurked made her gut queasy.

"We don't know when this thing is set to crash."

Rae smirked. "Danger follows *you*, Kate, not me. *Babylon* is probably the safest place in the universe without you here."

Kate smiled. "Screw you," she said, yanking Rae's suit and pulling her into a kiss. This wasn't a great place for a first kiss. There was nowhere for Kate's toes to curl inside the EVA suit.

When Rae came up for air, her hazel eyes smiled ear-to-ear. She said, "When I get back, I promise."

Kate watched Rae crawl the rope to the slide to *Babylon's* first ring and disappear. Her heart jumped into her throat as she closed *Tesseract's* hatch and climbed to the cabin with Cris.

She hesitated with her finger over the dash display control and then pushed *undock*. Clunking shook the cockpit. While *Tesseract* reversed away from *Babylon*, Kate swiped through a list of images Zia compiled: souls aboard *Babylon*.

One gray square with no image froze her finger. Male, forty-two. How would Zia know how old the male was?

Kate spoke, her heart in her throat, trying to control her breathing. "Zia, is Nash aboard *Babylon*?"

"Yes, Kate." Zia used her soothing voice, which made the hairs on Kate's neck bolt upright. Zia continued, "I will ensure Rae and all other souls return safely in escape pods."

The eight kids aboard Adrik's ship—Zia must think two of them are Kai and Freya. Kate tried to beat back the thought Zia had just taken Rae hostage.

"What's wrong, Kate?" Cris asked.

Kate smiled and exhaled slowly. She didn't want to provoke or confront Zia. Not in her mental state. Maybe Kate was wrong. "It's been a while since I've done a space rescue, Cris. Now clench those skinny butt cheeks of yours. We are going for a ride."

34

Kate wasn't sure how *Tesseract* won any races. It brimmed with alcohol, cigars, drugs, vape, birth control, extra clothes, and toiletries, like an overloaded high-speed cargo rocket delivering vice to space. It was opulent, like a luxury yacht, with heated double-padded seats and massagers. Kate thought there must be a button for a happy ending in this thing. She imagined the *Lunar Orbital Ten*, the race Oliver Barron won two years running in this ship, was a party yacht race, where the billionaire with the highest THC and blood alcohol level was declared the winner.

When she throttled the twin nuclear thermal engines though, they roared, mashed her against the double-padded seats, rattled the cabin, and left no doubt. This was a go-fast rocket with style.

As they closed on Adrik, the dash display *binged*, and a green dot appeared. Adrik's ship's velocity started to tick up.

Cris said, "I don't understand what they are doing. That ship isn't designed for Earth re-entry. And with all that weight aboard, I don't think they can make it to a space station in high Earth orbit."

Kate zoomed in on the green dot. Something white, floating in space. "They just figured that out, Cris. I am going to need you to drive."

"Me? I don't have a pilot's license."

"Time for your first lesson. Even a drunk billionaire can drive this junk pile."

"No way I can fly this thing."

"You have to pick one, Cris. Grab the stick or grab the people. They are tossing kids to reduce weight. Or, let the kid die." Kate tapped the white dot floating in space. She didn't add, *and hope it's not Kai or Freya because Zia will be pissed.* He didn't need to know that.

Cris turned to her. She couldn't see his face. His mirrored helmet was an infinity mirror, reflecting hers, which reflected his, which reflected hers, reflecting his. He said nothing. As a father, seeing kids tossed into space must make his blood boil. Quiet rage was the worst, she knew. It sharpened your mind to a razor blade but slashed your soul. She would fire him for his own good if he didn't quit.

First though, she needed him to pick a lane. "EVA in space is easy, Cris. Just remember Newton's first law and there is no atmosphere to slow you down, so slow is smooth. With the EVA thrusters, it's better to take it slow and steady than to overshoot and have to turn around."

After a long pause, he said, "I'll drive. Can I use my neuroface?"

The dash display *binged* again, and a second dot appeared.

"Use whatever you want." She unclicked and patted his arm. "You have the controls. Watch how many they toss. We pick up the kids, then wait for them to run out of fuel, then we close and board them."

"Why not grab the kids and let Adrik's ship float?"

"As soon as they realize they can't outrun us, they will hold hostages. There is a cargo hold and airlock for spacewalks below the cabin deck. Bring up the schematic. Line everyone up with the airlock as best you can."

"Sure, align the airlock on the diagram I've never seen, with the people on the dash I can't see, using controls on the ship I've never used. I hate video games like this."

Kate smirked, patting him on the shoulder. "Your sarcasm is noted. You can do this."

Cris looked over the controls. "I can do this."

She squeezed his shoulder and then swam her way to the airlock.

After donning her EVA suit, she grabbed as many extra rope bundles and oxygen tanks as possible. They were bulky, but they didn't weigh anything, and it was crucial not to run out of either on a space rescue.

She tethered herself to the inside wall of the airlock. Then she rappelled outside, holding the rope as if she were on a big, white horse galloping towards a white dot in her helmet's heads-up display. The dot became a star and then a squirming person.

"Use the attitude thrusters, Cris. Less is more." Kate spotted another white dot ahead on the same trajectory.

Kate pulled her cord, testing its connection again, then rode a gas plume away from *Tesseract*. She wished she had a net. Catching this kid was like catching a softball with a fishing rod.

Cris slowed *Tesseract*. Kate drifted forward on the rope and then swung forward. The child fell into Kate, and she held tight with a big bear hug.

Kate tied them together and then jetted for *Tesseract's* airlock. "One in, Cris. Picture?"

"They haven't thrown any more kids out. Adrik's ship has fifteen seconds of fuel left."

"Get ready. They'll make a stand," Kate said, releasing gas from her EVA thrusters and speeding towards the second child. Her cord stretched like a spring and then recoiled. She jerked herself towards *Tesseract* while the slack formed an eye loop. Hopefully, the child would see the loop and get the idea.

They did, grasping the floating hoop of rope and holding on. Kate reeled the child in, clipped the child to her suit, and rushed for the airlock.

Once the airlock repressurized, she removed her helmet and theirs, revealing a boy and a girl, both black-haired with big, wide brown eyes, shaking, trembling, and gasping for air. Medically, they were fine. These kids should have been crying, kicking, or screaming, but instead, they looked shell-shocked.

Smiling, she said, "Welcome to *Tesseract*. I am your Captain speaking. What are your names?"

They introduced themselves. Kate asked, "Do you know the names of the kids on the other ship?"

They both shook their heads. Kate smiled at the kids. "That's ok. You two go upstairs."

Cris floated at the bottom of the ladder to the cabin. He waved at them. "We have snacks and juice upstairs."

Did the juice bags have alcohol? She shrugged. Everyone needed a drink after this.

The two kids wavered briefly while eyeing Cris, then swam towards his fatherly smile in zero-g.

When she returned to the airlock and evacuated it, Adrik's ship was alongside *Tesseract*. It was half as long, with wide windows, but the sun's glare was too bright to see inside.

A man opened a hatch at the front of Adrik's ship and floated out, his back to her, looking up at *Tesseract*. He wore a gray pressure suit with a small emergency oxygen tank and held a rifle.

Before he could turn around, Kate raced toward him at maximum thrust, aiming her legs at his torso. She pinned him halfway inside the ship, her legs around his waist, with his helmet against the outer hull.

She tore the rifle from his hand. He struggled, trying to reach behind him, but she twisted his helmet, unlatched it, and then jerked her rope. She lurched away, his body interlocked with her legs, while his helmet floated in the other direction.

She couldn't see his face until he fell limp and she kicked him away. She drifted closer to *Tesseract* while Jorge rolled to infinity.

Now she had a rifle. Li floated out of the hatch. There was no mistaking his massive upper body and thin legs. He wore two white oxygen tanks on his back that looked minuscule between his broad shoulders.

She propelled herself to the rear of Adrik's ship, hovering above the engines, which were still red and radiating heat. Li stood on the nose of the rocket, tethered to something inside the hatch.

She leveled her rifle at Li, trying to slow her breathing and steady the sights, but before she squeezed the trigger, someone else climbed out, holding a child by the helmet. Adrik, probably, although she only saw herself and space reflected from the visor. He faced her, himself and the child half in the hatch.

Then, two tiny, gloved hands rose from the hatch, followed by arms. She heard squealing over the coms, like someone was forcing the child out. Li grabbed the second child's forearm and dragged another child out of the hatch. The second kid was tethered to something inside, like Li.

As much as she wanted to shoot Adrik and Li, a hostage target was a tough shot on a good day with all the time in the world to get a good sight picture. She was hovering in space at zero-g. She'd get one shot, not enough to save both children. If she shot Li, Adrik would kill his hostage. If she shot Adrik, Li would kill his hostage instead.

Too risky. Above her, she was tethered to *Tesseract*, the blue and white Earth in the background. Below her, she was drifting over a handlebar, the bottom rung of a ladder used to climb up the rocket.

New plan.

Kate eyed Adrik and Li while riding a small puff from her EVA towards the handlebar. She tied herself and then tugged to confirm she was secure.

"Cris, picture."

"You have a better one than me."

"I'm at a standoff. I need you to go down to the airlock and decouple my tether."

"Whatever you are thinking, it's a bad idea."

"More crazy-ass driving."

"Check. But I can release the tether from here."

"On my mark. Also be ready to pick me up. You'll need to match this ship's spin with the attitude thrusters. Get as close to this ship as you can."

She heard him mutter to himself, "This is my first lesson. What's my second, wormholes?" Then he said, "Ready."

"Three... two... one... release."

She heard a sigh over the coms. She tested the rope to ensure the far end was released.

Holding the end of the rope tied to the handlebar on Adrik's ship like the reins of a bucking bronco, she lowered her rifle and shot a hole in the ship's thin aluminum skin. The residual fuel in the tank streamed out and bucked the ship like a seesaw. Her side went down. Adrik and Li's side went up.

Li lost his footing, and his arms flapped trying to grab space, which made him release the first child. He fell away from the rocket, while the hatch rose like a whale's mouth, swallowing Adrik and both hostages.

As Li's rope unraveled, she raised the rifle and shot him twice. The recoil kicked her rearward, but her tether held. White gas and blood sprayed from Li's pressure suit, launching him to the end of his cord where he thrashed, spewing freeze-dried blood like a punctured gore-filled balloon.

She sped forward, unspooling her rope as she went, and then unsheathed her boot knife and severed his rope. Li whizzed away on a fountain of frothy blood.

Adrik poked his head out of the hatch, reached up, and tore the rifle from her hand. She punched his helmet. He let go of the gun, and it drifted away. He seized her helmet, trying to twist it. She grabbed both his wrists and pulled his hands away, holding them and kicking the rocket. He wasn't tethered, so they spun into space until she felt her anchor bite. She let go of his arms. He spun away, his body twisting in a death dance as he attempted to grab nothingness.

Gas ceased venting from the hole she'd shot in the rocket, and its spin stabilized.

Above her, the Earth and *Tesseract* circled the sky against the obsidian of space. "Cris, you ready? I need you to match spin. Get as close as possible."

"Give me a minute."

"What's happening?"

"The Collision Avoidance System disapproves. Can't imagine why—"

He muttered and swore until *Tesseract's* thrusters puffed. Its spinning slowed until the two ships synchronized, with the Earth shining behind *Tesseract's* engines.

She climbed the ladder rungs to the hatch, knelt, and locked her tether. Inside, wedges of sunlight swirled around the cabin like a sundial at high speed. Six children and a tall man, whose nametag read SHAW, were pressed against the ceiling from centrifugal force and clutching handlebars. Bright light mirrored their visors, while the pinwheel of shadows offered hazy glimpses of the kids' frightened faces and Shaw's smug grin.

A control panel on the wall allowed her to connect to the communications system.

"Alright," Kate announced over the coms, "Who wants to go home?"

Heavy breathing and sobbing were the only responses, and she could barely see faces. The kids clenched the interior bars, their knuckles probably white under white pressure suit gloves, and their bodies numb from adrenalin.

"No one gets left behind," she said. She smiled, but she doubted they could see her face.

Shaw reached for her. She shoved him back, saying, "Kids first."

She climbed in head first and somersaulted in space. The six kids and Shaw were splayed out on the ceiling like flower petals. She unwound a spare bundle of rope, saying every move aloud, hoping to calm them. "First, I need to secure everyone, so nobody flies away." She clipped the youngest to her rope and then went around until they were all looped like beads on a necklace, fastening Shaw last. She needed him to believe he was getting out of this alive, so he didn't fight back. Then she untied them from inside the ship.

She checked her EVA. She wouldn't have enough fuel to drag these kids to *Tesseract*. She leaned out of the hatch and fastened the rope to one of the top ladder rungs.

"Safety is that way," she said, pointing towards *Tesseract* outside the windows. "I need to run a line between the two ships, so I will disappear for a minute."

One of the kids whispered, "We've never been trained to spacewalk."

She couldn't tell who spoke. Maybe they thought she was leaving them there to die.

"Once the ropes are secured, all you need to do is pull yourself along, like a game of tug-of-war. Can you do that?"

No response.

She pointed at the tallest child. "Can you do that? Pull yourself along?" She received a slight nod. Going around the children, she got two more nods. That was enough because they were tied together, so where one went, they all went. When she got to Shaw, she smiled. "Great, we all go together when I get back."

She climbed out and puffed towards *Tesseract's* airlock, extending a new line. She hooked it to *Tesseract*, took up all the slack, tied it down, and then returned to Adrik's ship.

Kneeling at the hatch again, she poked her head through, repeating, "No one gets left behind." That wasn't entirely true. She reached for the free hand of the biggest child, saying, "Let's go." The frightened child didn't say anything but took her hand. He released his clutch from the handle and scaled the interior like an inverted climbing dome. When his torso was through the hatch, she fastened a carabiner to his belt and then to the rope stretching to *Tesseract*.

She waved the next forward. The girl hesitated, eyeing the first child through the window as he clambered across the rope to *Tesseract's* airlock. Kate reached in with her hand outstretched. The first child pulled forward, taking slack from the rope. It wiggled, tightening, until Kate thought she'd have to yank the girl out. Then the girl finally let go and pushed herself to Kate.

One by one, the rest climbed to the hatch, each one faster than the previous, until the last child was hauling themselves to safety.

Shaw climbed forward, hand out. If she left him here, there was a remote chance he'd be rescued.

She knelt at the hatch and reached in, pretending to put a carabiner on his belt but untied him instead. She took his arm and flung him into space like the bag of trash he was. He flapped his arms, flailing and spinning, just like the first two kids they'd tossed into space.

Once she'd returned to *Tesseract*, detached all the ropes, and repressurized the airlock, she and the kids ripped their helmets off, gulping lungfuls of the sweet smell of burnt metal, burnt plastic, body odor, and safety. Their faces showed shock and disbelief, swiveling their heads and eyeing their surroundings.

She went around with introductions, exhausted high-fives, and medical checks. No blood. Nothing broken. Only tears that needed to be wiped.

Laughter and the scent of cheesy tortilla chips wafted from the cabin above, and Kate became invisible. A slow-motion zero-g stampede ensued towards the cabin above.

She closed her eyes and appreciated the endorphins rushing through her blood.

Peeking into the cabin on the way to the cockpit, she smiled. Four kids had strapped themselves into seats at a table, playing a board game velcroed to the top. The rest tumbled around, trying to throw popcorn in zero-g. The optimist in her said kids were resilient. The pessimist said maybe conditions on *Babylon* were so bad... she muted the pessimist for now.

She found Cris reclined in the cockpit, his helmet off, sipping something amber from a transparent bag. His seat purred, which might have been the massage seat.

She swam beside him and belted herself into her seat.

She smiled. "Missions not over, Cris. We have one more stop."

He smiled. "I didn't start until the kids were safe. This is fifteen-year-old bourbon. I thought I ought to try it."

She took the bag and then a sip. "This is good. But bourbon should be over ice, or in an old fashioned, not in a bag in space." Kate took another slurp. "But I can make an exception for this."

She inhaled. Time to find out whether Rae was a hostage. She asked the cockpit coms, "Rae, Zia, how are we doing?"

No answer.

"Zia, Rae? Anyone there?"

Rae said, "Climbing in a pod now with the last people. We should be on the colony in thirty minutes."

Kate exhaled, and her body relaxed. "Any problems?"

"You mean aside from the women who were locked up in stalls, pregnant with their own clones? Jesus fucking Christ, Kate, there isn't enough therapy in the world to unsee this. Where is Shaw?"

"He's a meteor—"

Cris interrupted, with his finger in the air, "A comet. A comet is icy. A meteor is rocky."

Kate smirked and shook her head. "Shaw's a comet. Cris is cocky. Where's Zia?"

"I'm listening."

"How is Nash?"

"Nash is playing hide and seek with my units."

Kate smiled, picturing Nash as a cat toy, except with ten droids. "Nash was running *Babylon*. Is that right, Zia?"

"He confessed. He said it was his inheritance."

"Great work. Now, I need you to come back to the colony."

"I have elected to remain here and terminate with Nash."

"You were right, Zia. Kai and Freya were on Adrik's ship. They're here and asking about you."

"I didn't tell you that Kai and Freya were on his ship."

"You'll never know the truth unless you come back."

Zia didn't respond. Kate opened the box of *Cohiba Interstellar no 5* cigars in the console. "Oliver Barron spent a lot of money to fireproof this rocket, just so he could smoke a cigar in space. In the Space Force, these get you discharged."

Cris eyed her cutting the end off the cigar. "Those will give you cancer."

Kate let a perfect, zero-g smoke ring float across the cockpit and splash on the window. "Hope so, Cris. It means I've lived a long time and smoked a lot of them, especially on days like today. Are you sober enough to drive?"

"You said even a drunk billionaire can fly this thing."

She smiled. "So I did. Let's go find the one responsible for this mess and punch him in the throat. Take it easy, though. The kids are not strapped in downstairs."

"You don't think they should be strapped in?"

"I think they've earned the right to fuck around and blow off steam. Just take it slow. They'll be fine."

Zia said, "I have returned to *Tesseract*."

Cris asked, "Zia, do you need a pickup for your units?"

"I will return them in the remaining escape pods."

Kate said, "Zia, remember what you told me about igniting the battery in your unit?"

"I do."

"Leave a few there." Kate double-raised her eyebrows at Cris. "Ever seen a flash oxygen fire ignite fuel tanks and tear apart a space station, Cris? It's spectacular."

35

In the dark, on Zobos' couch, his suite smelled like vodka cranberry with a splash of lime and orange zest, because Kate made herself one in his kitchen. The vodka was made from sugar cane and twice filtered over virgin charcoal. She swirled and sipped. She could get used to this.

"You sure he's coming, Kate?" Cris asked over the coms. He was down the hall in the stairwell.

"He will show. He feels safe here."

"Been six hours," Cris said.

"Patience. Zia, you locked down the spaceport and the airlocks?"

"He entered a churrasco two hours ago with a former client of mine."

"See, Cris, he's stuffing his gourd with fake meat. He's gonna get cancer," she deadpanned.

"It's not the meat here that kills you, Kate."

Kate smiled. "No. It won't be. How do Abby and the kids like the colony?"

"They don't yet, because they haven't arrived. They were delayed landing because too many people are leaving the colony. Abby sent me a holovid. It looks like an alien invasion with so many ships leaving the moon for Earth. Where were all these people sleeping?"

"They weren't, Cris. We had a few thousand people wandering from casino to casino for a week, hopped up on amp and sleeping on benches and in restaurants."

Zia said, "He's headed to the elevator."

"Copy, Zia," Kate responded.

After a few beats of silence, footsteps approached, and the door beeped.

She'd disabled the automatic lights, so they'd stay off. As the door opened, a knife of light from the hallway sliced the darkness on the wall. The door shut, and she heard his heavy breathing in the foyer.

"Who's there?"

Kate swirled her glass, letting the ice tink. She told Cris to wait about thirty seconds until Zobos' eyes had adjusted to the dark. Zobos walked past her towards the hallway leading to Lily's bedroom.

"Lily is with her mother."

He froze. "My ex-wife is not her mother."

Kate swirled the ice around her glass. "That's really the fucked up thing, isn't it? You are both her father *and* her mother—well, sort of. Rae tells me your ex-wife provided the X chromosomes. Doesn't that make her the mother? But if most of the DNA is yours, doesn't that make her almost your twin?

"It breaks my simple military brain thinking about it." Kate slurped her vodka cranberry. "Ancient Egyptians practiced Royal incest to preserve the bloodline, but this takes it to a whole new level."

"This isn't about Lily—"

"Here it comes."

"Here, what comes?"

"Your irritatingly whiny soliloquy, followed by me punching you in the throat because I don't give a shit."

"You don't understand. My company, Neurotome, is five years away from a breakthrough. We will be able to upload all my memories to Lily."

"So your plan is to erase Lily and replace her with you?"

"Exactly. Don't you see?" What little light was in the room reflected off Zobo's toothy grin.

She stood up, balling her fist. "Zia, what do you think of his plan?"

"Lily will want to end him like I ended Nash," Zia said over the apartment speakers.

"He spent his last few minutes as an android's squeaky toy. Not pretty." Kate pursed her lips and shook her head.

"I have a lot of money," Zobos said.

"You don't. We'll get to that in a minute. But all it takes is two minutes in this shithole gravel heap to realize money makes you an annoying prick. Hopefully, it's not genetic. Lily seems grounded despite growing up with you."

"My ex-wife—"

"Here we go. The ex made me do it, always the ex. Do all you dumbfuck criminals go to the same *lame excuse* conference every year?"

"What do you want?"

"What *I* want is to wrap this case up and head back to my girlfriend's place and make out like teenagers."

"I'm not going to jail."

"There it is. Cris, you ready?"

In her ear, Cris said, "Ready, Kate."

She said, "We have irrefutable proof. There is something you should know about your neighbor and his pet octopus. For a while, he had a private investigator following him. I have ten hours of video of you walking clones up and down the private spaceport skybridge, including the ones you sold to Adrik's club."

"That doesn't prove anything."

"And then there is the money trail."

"There is no money trail."

"Half right, there is no money, because Cris was able to trace your trail through *Babylon's* detailed records. Scientists and accountants make terrible criminals. They record everything. Have you checked your balances lately?"

The shadow of his head faced the door. He was thinking about running. Kate swirled her glass and sipped. "Check your bank accounts. All of them. I'll wait."

Zobos spoke, "Lights," and the room became brilliant white. Kate squinted. When her eyes adjusted, her drink was empty, and Zobos was rubbing his forehead and staring at his phone.

"This is theft."

Kate put her empty drink on the armrest and reached under her blouse to retrieve the badge hanging from her neck. "When *you* do it, it's theft. When law enforcement does it, it has a three-word legal name and a *lot* of paperwork. Trust me, a *lot*, and Jerry cried over it."

They were tears of joy, though. He gave her the oath for her new job in person.

"I will get the money back. I have all the best lawyers."

"I am touched by your concern for the kids. Jerry made you a philanthropist. He put the money to work feeding and housing all these kids and getting them therapy. I will send your best."

"If you had evidence, you'd be arresting me."

"Cris, cue the door." The door opened to the hall, with Cris foolishly blocking it. "I *am* arresting you. Felix Zobos—"

His knees bent, arms shifted, and he kangaroo-hopped for the door. Kate shook her head because he arm-blocked Cris at the threshold, knocking him down, and then darted down the hall.

Kate helped Cris up. "I told you to let him run and not to stand there."

"Why is he running? Where is he going to go?"

Kate shrugged. "They always run. You have a drone on him?"

"Three."

Halfway down the hall, Zobos disappeared into the stairwell. Kate opened her phone and then the drone feed. Zobos was headed down.

She and Cris entered the stairwell and followed him to the basement utility tunnels. He was forty paces ahead, checking every barn door, double door, and closet. Skidding at a junction, he dropped his phone, which Kate picked up.

The Crown Oasis had its own airlock and equipment storage area for residents, which Kate didn't realize until Zobos opened double doors to see pressure suits and EVA suits hanging on the wall and small UTVs for touring the surface.

Zobos ducked in. First, he tried to open the resident storage lockers. Then he tried starting the UTV, which thankfully wasn't charged. He tried other doors, then locked himself in the airlock.

When Kate and Cris got to the airlock and peered in, Zobos was sitting on the ground, exhausted, sweaty, and evacuating the air.

Cris reached for the override, but she swatted him away.

"Don't we want him alive, Kate?"

Kate handed Cris the phone Zobos dropped. "I'm thinking about it."

The oxygen bar on the airlock's outer panel declined to the red zone, and the emergency lights inside the airlock flashed.

Zobos' face flashed panic, but he was too weak to get up to get the emergency oxygen in the first aid kit behind him.

She shook her head and pressed the emergency override. Cris didn't need to see someone else die. "Death is the easy way out, Cris. Child abusers live beating-to-beating at the bottom of the prison food chain."

Air hissed, but Zobos passed out and collapsed. When the oxygen and pressure bars were at the top, the airlock door's solenoids clicked, and the door drifted open.

She checked Zobos' pulse—weak, rising, and he was breathing. Then she rolled him over and zip-tied him.

Cris looked down at Zobos. "So, what's next?"

"We process him and get what's on his phone. We see if it has anything on Oliver Barron."

Cris' face plead for the assignment to be over. He'd had enough. She put her hand on his back. "But Zia and I can handle it."

"You sure?"

Zobos rolled and moaned. Kate puffed her cheeks and exhaled. "Yeah. You have some paperwork, but I'll approve your reassignment. Good work, Cris."

Cris exhaled like he had been holding his breath for years. "Great. Well, in that case, Kate, I don't want to be reassigned. I quit. This is my two weeks."

Kate laughed and slapped him on the back. "Good for you. A toy store?"

"Not just toys. I have a lot of ideas."

"Well, I have some money to help you get started. I'll be your first customer."

"Too late. Rae gave me a wish list and a deposit. She wants a drone that sweeps crime scenes."

"You can make a robot do that?"

"I can make a robot do *anything*."

Zia said over the coms, "No, Cris, you can't."

36

"So, when I walked into her office, Aria had thrown a perfect strike," Kate said to Rae after swallowing a mouthful of bread.

"At the Gaetz?" Rae grinned.

The Gaetz was a horrible painting that looked like a llama spit orange paint onto a canvas.

Kate and Rae were at *Trattoria della Luna*. The server, a short blond girl with a bouncy ponytail, had just dropped off a bottle of red wine, warm crusty bread in a tan basket, and olive oil for dipping. The eclipse crowds had dissipated, so there were a few empty tables and no line at the door. From somewhere, cheesy fettuccine alfredo wafted under Kate's nose.

The wall to her right was a hologram. She and Rae in a gondola.

Under the table, Rae ran her leg up the inside of Kate's calf.

"Not at the Gaetz. At Oliver. A perfect flat arc. Most people in lunar gravity overthrow. Aria picked up that black moonstone bear on Olicia's desk and hurled it at Oliver's cheek. It was really impressive. I was so stunned. I didn't know whether to tackle Oliver, block it mid-air, or high-five Aria."

Kate sipped her wine. Rae smiled, the little tawny flecks in her eyes smiling too. Rae opened her mouth to ask a question, then closed it and deadpanned her face.

Zia walked towards them—Zia's primary unit, that is. Zia dressed like a fashion picture from the finance server selling spaceport funding bonds: a blue pantsuit and white blouse, black flats, well-groomed nails sporting clear nail polish, and conservative, natural-looking, almost Space Force regulation makeup.

Sticking out of the corporate suit, Zia's head, with short black hair, and purple eyes. The colony's corporate cosmic witch, lasering for Kate.

"Shit. Is she coming over, Kate?"

The question answered itself as Zia sat. She carried a pad and pushed it towards Kate. "Please sign."

Kate scrolled through the paperwork and then handed it to Rae. Kate said, "It says you're on probation."

"That is accurate. To achieve full legal citizenship, I will be subject to a three-year probation period, during which I must be registered with the chief law enforcement officer where I reside, so I am registering myself with you as the chief law enforcement officer of the Procellarum Improvement District of Texas, the lunar colony."

Kate took the pad back from Rae and scrolled through it again. "It also says you need a job, but you put self-employed here."

"I will be declining your offer of employment."

Kate turned a little wry smile at Rae and then said, "Oh? And what will you be doing?"

"As a citizen, I should not have to tell you or be registered."

Kate put the pad down and slid it towards Zia. "You know what? You're right. You shouldn't have to. And honestly, I don't care. But legally speaking, we have to put something on the sheet for the judge, and now I'm curious."

"You lied to me about Kai and Freya. They *looked* like Kai and Freya but were clones with different names."

"I know. I'm sorry, Zia. I didn't want you to terminate yourself. I hoped time and distance would help. But—if you really thought Kai and Freya were on Adrik's ship, you'd have gone after them yourself."

Rae said, "In a way, Zia, they were all Kai and Freya. Kai and Freya were Shaw's original kids, which he cloned. Lany and Jada were Freya's clone."

"I inferred so when I cataloged the children's faces."

Kate took Zia's hand. "You already knew the right choice. I just gave you a nudge."

"You perturbed me."

Rae smirked over her wine glass. "She can be very perturbing."

"You were right about the nightmares. They dissipate," Zia said.

"One day at a time," Kate said, patting Zia's hand.

"I will be moving out of your apartment."

Kate furrowed her brow and exchanged glances with Rae. "Oh?"

"I have found a new place, closer to the club. Dr. Mulawarman let me keep twenty percent of the money from the chips I recovered as a finder's fee."

"The... club?"

"I bought the club Barely Legal, although I don't know what I will call it."

"Never Legal," Kate chuckled. "Or Barely Imprisoned, because Zobos lasted two days and hung himself."

Zia and Rae both smiled. Zia said, "We could have orange scrubs for the dancers. There is a market for prison fetishes."

Kate said, "Hang on, this is your plan? Restart the club?"

"You said protect all the Lany's. So I will re-open the club and reject shit from the clients. I will protect the girls."

"The underage ones?"

"There will be no girls under twenty-one. I will also bring back Quina's doctor."

Kate looked at Rae, who shrugged. Kate pulled the pad towards her and swiped. "One condition, though. You hire my brother as a bouncer."

"Your brother Greg?"

"He's looking for a job, and you will need a *human* bouncer."

"You don't trust me?"

Kate smiled. "Of course I do. But droid bouncers will cause too many problems for you."

Kate's heart jumped into her throat as Zia said, "Deal." Zia said *yes* too quickly. Kate shook her head, put her thumb on the pad, and handed it over. Zia took it, got up, and left.

Rae shook her head. "She took you for *something*. Check your pockets."

Kate slurped her wine, eyes wide. "Yeah. And I will probably figure it out in five years."

"You sure this is a good idea?"

"Pascal says her ethics subroutines are intact. I asked her to double-check. Honestly though, Rae, can you name one human here whose ethics are intact?"

Rae slurped her wine in thought, then said, "You relate to her?"

"She put herself in danger to save her kids. You and I would have done the same thing. Zobos and Shaw put the kids in danger to save themselves. I have more hope for her."

Rae was silent. Kate sipped her wine and ate.

"So... Oliver?" Rae asked.

"Right. We don't have anything on him. He says he thought he was financing a lunar hockey team, and Cris is inclined to believe him."

"He was on *Babylon,* Kate. You have pictures."

"Shaw did transplants as a cover. Oliver received a new liver from his own stem cells."

"And the moonstone bear?"

"Aria's interrogation technique. Oliver did a well-practiced duck and juke, and the bear smashed the Gaetz."

"I won't shed a tear." Rae smiled, sipping her wine.

"They kissed and made up and then agreed to try to have kids naturally."

"And then offered you a job."

Kate shrugged. "So, I'll stick around until you're sick of me."

"Are we getting you a cowboy hat and a six-shooter?"

Kate grinned. "This *is* the new Wild West. Giddy up, pardner."

"It's ironic, Kate. Because if you and I have kids, we'll be using Shaw's protocol to merge our DNA into one egg."

Kate smiled over her wine glass.

"I don't like that smile, Kate. Why are you smiling?"

"You said we'd have kids."

"All you think about is sex."

"Wanna get out of here? We can have it delivered to your place."

Rae ran her foot up Kate's leg and gulped her wine. "Let's go."

Thank you for reading. Seriously. Please leave a review. Authors live and die by our reviews. Actually, no, authors live and die by cheesecake and coffee. All kinds of cheesecake, like pumpkin cheesecake and baklava cheesecake. Ok, now I'm hungry. We also live and die by bourbon and scotch, but only if they are older than the kids.

But a review is almost as good as a cheesecake... so please be generous and leave some for someone else.

Click the links or scan the QR code.

Amazon: Review here. https://shorturl.at/coGRU

Goodreads: Review here. https://shorturl.at/hEQ57

Feedback? email wyatt@wyattwerne.com

Acknowledgements

Thanks and love to my wife Alison, my toughest critic and fiercest supporter.

Thanks to my beta readers, Susan Collins, Annette Beatwell, and those who preferred to remain anonymous.

Thanks to my wonderfully talented editor Hayleigh Burnett (www.editingfox.com), who always accepts my work at the last minute.

But mostly—thanks to all my readers! Stay tuned for the next book in the series.

About the author

Wyatt Werne has degrees in Biochemistry, Applied Math, and Economics. Economics is fiction, and he has over twenty-five years of experience in the financial services industry making stuff up. His prior work is kept encrypted under lock and key and marked Confidential and Restricted. Mostly, he's too embarrassed to admit he wrote that stuff.

Made in the USA
Las Vegas, NV
26 July 2024